W0010454

The Year Without A Summer

A Novel

ARLENE MARK

Published by SparkPress, a BookSparks imprint,
A division of SparkPoint Studio, LLC
Phoenix, Arizona, USA, 85007
www.gosparkpress.com

Published 2022
Printed in the United States of America
Print ISBN: 978-1-68463-147-6
E-ISBN: 978-1-68463-148-3 (e-bk)

Library of Congress Control Number: 2022902416

Interior design by Tabitha Lahr

The Year Without a Summer
is dedicated to:

My family

Lisa and John
Carter, Harley, and Jolie

Peter and Elizabeth
Kathryn and Ethan

Steve and Anna
Axel, Elsa, and Hugo

Who had always counted on living and loving
in a safe world on a healthy planet

And now trust that they can contribute in
their own way to help restore their earth

And especially to Reuben, husband, father,
and the grandchildren's Papa-Papa,
our trusty weathervane always
pointing out fair weather ahead

Contents

Chapter One

In the zone or cold blast?

*J*amie shifted his weight on his snowboard at the top of the mountain and set his sights down the slope. If only winter break were longer. He'd be even more equipped for team competition this year—and the rest of his life. He sighed and then pushed off, ready to face the unforgiving beasts waiting for him on the run. The moguls sat up like whack-a-moles, to be conquered one by one as he carved his way down the mountain. The crisp scent of pine reminded him to keep alert as he hurtled between mighty trees on both sides.

As he faced the first bump, he inhaled the frosty air, trusted his Capital Outsider board, and let the exhilarating freedom carry him along. He'd started timing himself the first day they'd arrived at Killington. Today he was going for six minutes, a whole ten seconds faster than yesterday. His mind raced along with his body. Setting a goal made him even more primed to compete. His school team still had two competitions. If he trained while he was here, he'd win for the team. With a great record, he'd make the high school team next year. Then, who knows? Maybe states, then national.

The only thing that could boost the loads of fun he was having was if Lucas were snowboarding with him. Jamie laughed. Speedy Lucas would be at the bottom already. When Lucas got back home, they'd go boarding again. Soon, Jamie hoped, but his brother couldn't just up and leave the war in Afghanistan when he wanted to.

At the bottom of the hill, he lifted his goggles and slid to the side to make way for others swooshing in. He checked his time. Close. He couldn't wait to ride the lift to the top and speed down again. He'd make six minutes by the end of the day. After that, he'd work on other moves—maybe do a few corkscrews and alley-oops to test his balance and control. He had enough time for at least three more runs today and all day tomorrow to get his speed up.

He squinted in the bright sunlight. Was that his dad under the WELCOME sign at the snack bar? As Jamie looked closer, his mood plummeted. His father stood with his arms folded across his chest, his mouth set in a hard line. Jamie unbuckled his bindings, picked up his board, and headed for the snack bar. His stomach knotted up. It usually did these days any time he had to deal with Dad. All they ever seemed to do was fight. Now here was trouble again. He braced for it and forced his legs ahead.

"Dad. Hi. Never saw you up here before. The view's great, right?" He forced a smile, hoping it might soften whatever was coming.

His father frowned. "Get your gear. We're leaving."

Jamie winced. So much for softening the situation. "No way. We still have two days—"

His father's jaw clenched harder. "We're going now." He turned and stalked off toward the parking lot.

Jamie's breath caught in his throat as he watched him go, then followed. "Dad, what happened? Did I do something wrong? Is Mom okay?"

Dad didn't answer. He reached their SUV and swiped the snowflakes off the windshield. Jamie fumbled his board onto the roof rack and locked up, then glanced back at the mountain and the lifts. A couple of kids he had snowboarded with the last few days were rocketing down the runs, laughing and probably planning where they'd get together later. He moved to grab his snowboard and run back. Let Dad go home if he wanted to. But Dad was double-checking the locks.

"They're secure," Jamie said, giving up hope of staying. "I'm not stupid."

Dad grabbed his arm and gave him a shove. "Just get in the car. We've got a long ride."

Jamie pulled away. "Okay, okay. Don't push me." His jaw tightened as he slid onto the back seat. It wasn't fair of his father to yank him off the slopes without telling him why. So much for his goal of speeding up by ten seconds and winning for his team. He forced a breath to carry his disappointment out the window and buckled his seat belt.

Dad got in the car but didn't start the engine. Instead, he announced, "I got a call from your science teacher."

Jamie swallowed hard. "What did he want?" But he knew. He hadn't even looked at his science notes before the test he'd taken last week.

"Why didn't you tell us you failed the exam?"

The word *failed* hit him like a snowplow. "I didn't know I failed. It was hard. But I got some of the answers." Jamie couldn't believe Mr. J had called Dad over winter break when they weren't even in school.

Dad started in on him again. Jamie tuned him out. He remembered hearing the word *remorse* on a TV series he liked. That's what was running through his head right now, regret and sorrow. Why hadn't he studied?

"Your teacher said you'll have to do a lot of extra work to pass the class. You have a greater chance of being left behind and repeating the year." His father shook his head. His disappointed expression said it all. Big surprise. Dad started the engine. "Buckle up. Mom's waiting at the condo."

Jamie did as he was told. Maybe the worst was over. But the silence that hung in the air between them as they drove to pick up Mom told him otherwise. How could he speed fearlessly down the steepest runs, flying over bumps and dodging other obstacles, and then be sitting with his dad, scared of his words?

Mom was waiting with their gear out front as they pulled up to the condo. Jamie hustled from the car to help load their bags. He yanked one up with both hands and flung it into the trunk.

Dad clapped a hand down hard on his shoulder. "Don't throw your anger around. You know why we're leaving early. You agreed to try harder in school, and you didn't follow through. You don't know how to focus."

Jamie fought down his anger. No use saying that his dad didn't understand anything about how all the pressure felt— pressure to be a good student, like his older brother, Lucas, hadn't been—as if he could make up for his brother's choices somehow. He couldn't have stopped Lucas from enlisting in the Marines and being sent to Afghanistan. Jamie's days got used up worrying about him. He missed his big brother so much. He also missed his dad, how he had been before all this. He used to make up games and play with them. Jamie remembered how he'd wait for Dad near the door to surprise him when he came home from work. Those days were gone. Now when Dad came home, he seemed worn out, his face always set in a frown. He was never in the mood to play.

Jamie slipped from his father's grasp and turned to his mother. "Anything else inside, Mom?"

"We're all set," she said and slid onto the front seat. "Thanks, Jamie." As she turned to face him, her forehead wrinkled. "You could have tried a little harder. You know that Dad and I are always available to help you with schoolwork."

Jamie nodded. He wanted to say, "Sorry, Mom. Don't be upset. I'll try harder," but this wasn't the time. He imagined a cartoon bubble over her head, describing him: *Dork*. Or maybe *Loser*. No. That's how *he'd* describe himself. Mom wouldn't. He squinted and pictured what she might imagine—him struggling to hold off an avalanche of empty homework sheets about to cover him. That was more likely how she saw him. In his imagination, the avalanche wasn't soft and fluffy and fun to play in like snow. Instead, hard-edged sheets of paper cut into him.

As Dad put the car into drive, Jamie cracked open his window. He watched the KILLINGTON SKI RESORT sign get smaller until it disappeared as they turned the corner.

Down. Up. Down. Up. Cold air blasted him from the window he opened and shut with the electronic button. Controlling other things in his life with a button would be great. Like school. And Dad. And all that pressure.

"You okay back there?" Mom called as they turned onto the highway.

Jamie, lost in his made-up game Escape Out the Window, nodded absentmindedly.

"Answer your mother!" His father's command jolted him back to attention. "And stop fiddling with the window."

Jamie banged his head on the back of the seat. "Yeah, I'm okay." Then he added, "Mom."

Jamie knew his dad only wanted to hear that he was okay doing what his dad had said: "Get your grades up," and "Apply yourself in school," whatever that meant. He might do what he had to in school if Dad would only stop bugging him. No matter how badly he wanted to, Jamie couldn't argue back or tell Dad that he could probably do the work but that Dad's hounding always stopped him. Nothing he did seemed to please his father, so why even try with grades? But if he said any of this, Dad wouldn't really listen. He'd just start lecturing him again about focusing, how Jamie had lost his way in school, and that everything he did now would impact his future. Forget about telling Dad that maybe college wasn't for him. His father would go ballistic, just like he had with Lucas whenever Lucas did something Dad didn't like.

Mom changed the subject, and Jamie hunched down in his seat. Maybe if Dad couldn't see him in the rearview mirror, he'd forget Jamie was back there for the next two hours as they drove home to Albany. He let out a sigh of disappointment as reality set in. The perfect temperature and powdery snow here almost guaranteed to advance his speed and moves on the slopes. No longer. Two whole days when he was supposed to be boarding, wasted because of a stupid science test. No one to blame but himself. Dad was right. He'd made an agreement with his parents that he'd work hard this semester. In exchange, they'd agreed to take him snowboarding for February mid-winter break. He should have studied for the test, but he'd been so keyed up about the trip that he couldn't concentrate on stupid science and memorizing chemical formulas. Who cared about chemicals? Now he'd have to bust his butt the rest of the year.

Another day on the slopes would have helped his racing time. But Jiminy Peak wasn't far from home. He could always take the bus there on Saturdays to get in some last-minute practice. Maybe he'd go tomorrow or Sunday, if he could talk Dad into letting him.

He reached over and pressed the window up-down button again. Air blasted in. His mom glanced back. Her eyebrows shot up.

"Sorry. Guess I was on automatic." Jamie shook his head at his lack of control. Maybe Dad was right. He had to pull it together.

He was 99 percent ready for the last two school snowboarding competitions. High school could be a new start. He had tried to be interested in school this year, but schoolwork bored him. Nothing he was expected to learn had anything to do with his life or his future. He didn't have a clue what he wanted to do, except for following the snow. That could take him out West someday, where he could get a job at a ski resort and be out on the mountain as much as he wanted.

"You know, Jamie," his father called out, interrupting his daydream, "if your brother had applied himself, college could have—"

Jamie bolted up in his seat. "Geez, Dad! Leave Lucas out of this. It has nothing to do with him. He didn't want to go to college. And don't worry about me graduating. It's only eighth grade, and I still have four months till the end of the year."

"Jim, please. Let him relax a bit." His mother intervened at the right time, but his dad went on.

"No, Grace. He has to hear this." His father adjusted the rearview mirror locking onto Jamie's eyes. "You can't expect to get on in life by waiting till the last minute to get down to business," his father scolded. "The world doesn't reward procrastinators. You have to focus."

Mom reached over and patted Dad's arm. "Jim, that's enough for now."

Jamie balled his fists, irritated that he had upset Mom, who usually took his side when Dad was being unreasonable. "I don't expect the world to reward me, Dad." If he had to say what hurt him most about his dad's opinions and predictions it would be the way he said them, like a drill sergeant to a dumb soldier. If he had a dollar for every time his dad told him to focus, he'd be snowboarding on a three-thousand-dollar Channel Sports CC.

"Well, you'll have more time for schoolwork now that snowboarding competition's over," his father shot back. "That's a start."

Jamie did a double take. "It's not over. I still have—"

Dad took his eyes off the road and met Jamie's gaze in the rearview mirror. "For you, young man, the season is over."

Chapter Two

Temperature steady

*I*f only winter break weren't so long. Clara was tired of being at home. She was more than ready to graduate eighth grade and move on to high school—and the rest of her life. She closed her social studies book. The last of her homework was finished and ready to hand in, two whole days before winter vacation ended.

She was following through on what she had promised Papi— to be strong while he was gone, help Mami at home, and take good care of Diego, who was, Papi reminded her, even at eight years old, a lot like him, strong and steady. This was her responsibility now, all because of María. The hurricane with such a gentle name had destroyed their home, their island, their life in Puerto Rico. María had taken away cool breezes, evenings walking on the beachfront with her family, lemon ices, Mami and Papi holding hands.

Clara stopped imagining. Those parts of her life had disappeared, as well as Papi, who was back in Puerto Rico, helping to repair the damage from María. He had called them all to the kitchen table after they'd only been here a short while and told them it was his responsibility to help their friends rebuild their homes. His construction work at Built-Rite had ended for the winter, so he had time to go back home before more jobs came along in the spring.

Clara wished he hadn't called the island *home*. She was trying her best to make Albany their home now. They had spent their whole life in Puerto Rico until María forced them to start all over again here almost two years ago.

———

She glanced at her little brother, sitting in front of the TV. Super-heroes, giant mechanical figures thrashed on the screen, shrieking and roaring, tossing cars into the air. Clara covered her ears and shut her eyes to stop the terror stirring inside her. Loud crashing sounds tossed up memories of the hurricane they'd survived. The word *hurricane* came from the Spanish word, Huracán, the Carib Indian god of evil. Clara shivered. The storm they had lived through was definitely evil and never far from her thoughts. How could it be, when it had changed everything? She rubbed her temples; then she forced a big smile and plopped down next to Diego. "Hey, can you get back to those big guys later?"

He scrunched his face but shut the TV off and slapped his arms across his chest. "Okay, now what?"

She knew that posture but let him have his moment. She pulled a sheet of paper from behind her, placed it on a table in front of them, and drew a happy face in the top corner. "Good job with your multiplication. Now you're all ready for school on Monday."

Diego slumped. "School's boring."

Clara thought of Jamie, a boy in her class who spent a lot of time doodling in his notebooks. He didn't like school, either. Clara reached for Diego's hand and gently squeezed it. He had worked on his math facts every day of the February break, with little nudges from her, and had filled in all the answers, most of them correctly. "It gets better as you get older. You'll see. I'm so proud of you. You know your times tables now."

Diego made a face and shook his head. "Not all of them. They're hard to remember."

"I know. I felt just like you when we got here. I had to learn things that were hard to remember, like dates of battles that didn't seem important to me. You could probably remember them because you like your superhero battles. But if you learn just one new times fact every day, soon you'll know them all. And multiplication is important."

Clara wondered if Diego actually understood what multiplication meant. To a lot of kids, numbers equaled points in video games; whoever had the most won. But to Clara multiplication had other meanings. Like, "one wish" times "nine" equaled nine wishes for her future. Or "one Clara" times "two places—Puerto Rico and New York"—equaled two. But two *what*? Two different Claras? Did other Latino kids living in the States feel this way— like they weren't sure who they were? Math didn't always give you the answers you needed.

What she needed right now was to help Diego and Mami and herself settle into their new life. It sounded so simple, but she wasn't quite certain how to make that happen.

"I miss Papi," Diego said. His hands twisted the edge of his shirt.

"I know." Clara raised her chin, blinked back tears welling up, and put on a cheery face for him. "I do too, but he'll come home soon, and guess what? He'll take us to the stock car races again, and we'll buy those foot-long hot dogs and rainbow ice cones like we used to get on the beach in Puerto Rico."

"When?" Diego asked.

Clara moved her hands slowly back and forth in front of her. "I'm looking into a crystal ball and . . . the answer is . . ." She crawled her fingers over to tickle him. "*Soon!*"

Diego giggled and squirmed out of her reach. He picked up two of his superhero action figures and set them to battle.

She regretted mentioning the beach and Puerto Rico. Or

reminding him of the howling beastly hurricane they'd lived through two years ago. He was just going on six back then, but she could tell he remembered by all the questions he asked her. She hoped he would forget that he was so scared he had hidden between Mami and Papi.

Over the five weeks since her father had left, Clara had taken on more and more responsibilities at home. She waited with Diego until his bus arrived almost every morning and then played Go Fish and checkers with him for hours after school, but she also made sure he did his homework after making a snack for him. She took him to the park for sledding when it snowed and to the library.

She sorted through a pile of bills to make sure they were correct before Mami paid them. She placed rent and utilities like electricity and heat on the top and stuck Post-it notes on the envelopes that said "Pay." She couldn't bear to think about any expenses she might generate if she got into the Academy, a private school, next year, even on scholarship. She'd study drawing and drafting, maybe paving her way to becoming a builder like Papi or even an architect. But all that was still a dream.

Finally, she sent her good thoughts to Papi because they didn't talk to him very often. The mail wasn't back to normal on the island. They'd sent letters every week but had only received two. The cell towers weren't reliable so phone calls had mostly stopped. The next time Papi called, she would stretch the truth a little and tell him they were doing fine and not cause him any extra worries. But that wouldn't stop her from worrying about *him*.

She glanced at her watch. Ten o'clock. Five whole hours until Mami got home. Clara couldn't wait. It would only take her ten minutes to run to the Thurbers'. Little Gus would be waiting at the big front window, waving and jumping up and down when he saw her. Watching him didn't seem like work, even though she was earning money by babysitting. He had a room full of toys, but he always pulled out the bag of blocks. He loved building as much as she did.

What a perfect life he had, and what a perfect mom too. She was pretty and young and did interesting things like yoga and taking art classes and volunteering at a museum. Mrs. Thurber had luncheons for her friends. Clara babysat Gus one Saturday when eight women came for lunch. Mrs. Thurber said they were all tennis friends when she came into the playroom with some tiny sandwiches for her and Gus. The party was a lot more formal than her mother's gatherings in their home in Puerto Rico. Those were almost always family—aunts and cousins and one or two of Mami's friends whom Clara called "Auntie" too.

Mrs. Thurber ran a beautiful home. Any time Clara was there, her worries disappeared. Soft music played throughout the house, and silver-framed photographs of Gus, his mom, and probably his dad covered the top of a piano and tables in all the downstairs rooms. The cozy, comfortable, warm, tasteful Thurber home spelled a loving and happy family.

As Diego inched toward the TV, probably thinking she wouldn't notice, she called out, "Hey! Why don't you make a calendar? Then you can check off the days with colored markers until Papi's on his way home. You're so good at drawing, I know you can make a really funny calendar."

He turned. "Can I draw superheroes instead of check marks?"

"Great idea," Clara said. "Why didn't I think of that? There's a sketchpad and some markers in my top drawer."

"I'm on a mission," he reported and marched off.

She had no problem motivating her brother—most of the time. Or motivating herself. Schoolwork wasn't an issue. But fitting in there proved harder. She never knew where she stood with the girls in her class, especially Molly, who had been her first new friend. Well, maybe the second. Her first had been Jamie, who had welcomed her to school the first day there. Then Molly started waiting for her before first period class and saved seats next to her in other classes. Clara was thrilled when Molly invited her to a sleepover with two of Molly's good friends. Molly had really helped her feel included, until she didn't—after the math test. She still wondered if that's why Molly had invited her—to get math test answers from her. But she hadn't let Molly see her answers, and that was the end of being friends.

Now Molly didn't seem to have time for Clara. She hung around with other girls who were more like Molly than like her. Maybe Molly considered Clara too different because she wasn't white like most of the kids in their school. Maybe Molly didn't like Clara's strong opinions. She didn't always agree with Molly. Clara didn't always agree with Valeria or other friends in Puerto Rico, but they had remained close. Clara had texted and talked to them on the phone every few weeks, but lately she couldn't get through. She missed all the things they had done together, like hanging out at the beach, listening to music, dancing, and sharing favorite street foods. She missed going to Old San Juan, racing Valeria and Regina to the top of Castillo San Felipe del Morro, and then looking out from the top at the ocean below and talking about their futures.

She didn't want to think about another reason Molly might have dropped her—Jamie. Clara pictured him the first day she'd arrived at school. He'd smiled, walked right up to her in the classroom, and said, "Um, uh, I'm Jamie. You're new." Those few words and his friendliness took some of her stress away and made her feel almost okay. He'd pointed to a seat next to him, and she took it. Molly must have gotten the idea that Jamie liked her just because he had been kind to her. Molly had probably kept her feelings hidden until she got what she'd wanted from their brief friendship.

Her dizzying thoughts stopped as Diego returned with the sketchpad and moved his facts sheets out of the way. Clara leaned over and gave him a hug. "For good measure. 'Good measure' means extra, so you have extra love all around you now."

Diego slipped out of the hug, but his small grin told Clara he liked it. He opened the pad just as Mami walked in from work. "Mami," he yelled, leaving his materials and running to her. "When can we get Xbox One? All the kids at school have it."

"*Mi amor*, Xbox *cuesta mucho dinero*," Mami answered. She set her purse on the table and put a quart of milk and a carton of eggs in the refrigerator.

Diego's hands dove into the brown grocery bag, knowing they'd find a treat. He pulled out a lollipop and tore the wrapper off. "I love grape."

How a sweet lollipop the size of a marble thrilled her brother. Clara wished a lollipop—or something—could make her feel that way. Maybe someday.

Diego hugged Mami and begged to watch his last super-heroes programs for the day. Mami said okay. Mothers were so easy to bribe with a hug. Clara remembered doing the same thing when she wanted lacy socks in third grade. Now the family had expenses, and she never asked for anything extra. Mami's part-time job and Papi's savings barely covered their bills and rent. Clara silently thanked Mami every day for taking charge after Papi left, but she still wished that Mami hadn't encouraged him to go. That was Mami, though, supportive and brave. But nothing was the same without her father.

Everything costs a lot of money, Clara mused as she glanced around the small living room of the furnished house her parents had rented. The sofa's hard cushions poked her in the back, and the chairs around the kitchen table didn't match. Someday they would own their own house and furniture *they* had chosen.

Still, the house they would buy here wouldn't be anything like the one they had loved on their tropical island. She was reminded how everyone in Puerto Rico affectionately called the island *Nuestra Isla*, Our Island. She missed the big windows in all the rooms and their patio that went the whole way around the house with a special place for eating. She missed their lemon and orange trees and the bananas she could pick and peel fresh to top her and Diego's cereal. She missed her bedroom, too, on the second floor, with its own tiny patio, her favorite place to sit and read in the cool breeze that floated off the salty sea. She missed having friends over and laughing themselves silly out there.

Diego used to pull her into his room to watch the spiky fronds of the palm trees dance and make shadows on his wall. Now they looked out at gray shingles on the house next door. Diego's room was even smaller than hers, but he didn't complain.

When Papi got back and they went house hunting, maybe they would find one with a big backyard like the Thurbers'. Maybe then she would start to feel at home here.

Diego switched channels, looking for more superhero programs. Clara wished she could buy him the Xbox, so he'd feel the same as the other kids at school. He probably didn't even know the console cost five hundred dollars.

Sweet and spicy aromas floated from the kitchen. Clara followed her nose. "Mmmmm."

"*Sopa de pollo, mi amor*," Mami said, stirring the pot of chicken soup. "And *pan* in the oven."

Clara nodded. "Great. I can smell the bread." Mami had taught her how to make these favorites, but Clara would never tell anyone at school. They might make fun of Puerto Rican food. Clara couldn't tell Mami this, either. Why should she hurt her feelings? So Clara kept her thoughts to herself. Maybe she'd store them in the journal she'd started on their family computer. She'd ask Jamie if there was a code for privacy. Unlike their homework, he knew everything about computers.

"And I made *dulce de leche* for *postre*," Mami said, proud of another Montalvo family favorite.

"Mami, don't mix—" Clara slapped her hand over her mouth and willed away her criticism. That could go in her journal too. She wished Mami and Diego wouldn't mix Spanish and English like some Latino kids did in school because they thought they sounded cool speaking Spanglish. Clara didn't agree. She never let on that Spanish was her first language. Her English teacher in Puerto Rico who was from the US mainland had told her she spoke English perfectly. She would keep it that way. At least she could remind Diego when he mixed. He'd had a teacher from the mainland too, and his English was really good.

Clara opened the computer at the kitchen table to keep Mami company. Every time she turned on the device, she thought about Mami saving a little of her salary each week for it so that their family could be *moderna*.

Clara clicked onto the journal page where she typed her hopes and dreams and sometimes, like now, her complaints and worries. Tears welled up, but she flicked them away and made sure Diego wasn't nearby before she asked, "When will Papi be home?" She dragged *home* on forever, sounding exactly like Diego.

Mami came over and smoothed Clara's hair. "Soon. Remember what Papi said. It was his *responsibilidad* to help Tío Andrés and our *familia*." Then she added, "And other families who lost everything."

"Why is it his responsibility, Mami? We need him too. Why didn't they just move to the States like we did? They didn't have to stay when they didn't have houses or lights or water."

"Clara, your papi went because he is a generous man. You don't have to worry. He is careful. And he is healthy and strong. We were *afortunados* and had *amigos*, friends that told Papi about a job here. We had *oportunidades* to leave after the hurricane and we should be *agradecidos* every day. We must do our part here. Papi wants you and Diego to do your best in school so you can have *buenos futuros*."

But Clara did worry. Still, she agreed with Mami, even if she *was* mixing languages again. They were fortunate that friends had helped Papi find a job here.

"I am thankful, Mami. Diego and I are doing our best." She stopped talking, willing Mami's explanations to make all the worries in the room disappear. But they hung in the air.

"*Acuérdate*, Clarita?" Mami said. "When Papi's boss said the company would pay for some of his expenses in Puerto Rico, Papi said it brought tears to his eyes. He brought Coco Rico and ginger ale and *bizcocho de piña* for us to celebrate."

"I remember," Clara said. She liked the nickname Mami called her when Mami worried and wanted to mother her. She needed the affection right then. "That cake makes my mouth water right now. It tasted fruity fresh just like the ones from Tío Andrés's bakery in San Juan. Maybe we can buy it again when Papi gets home."

Clara stored that hope in her mind. Maybe it could speed up his getting home. She couldn't face the possibility that he might not get back to them. Repairing the damage done by a monster hurricane was major work. He might be injured. Another storm could hit. Anything was possible.

—

As Clara walked up the Thurbers' smooth stone walk, Gus waved from his spot near the window. She danced with funny moves to make him laugh before making her way to the front door.

"Come in, Clara." Mrs. Thurber was in black leggings and a pink fleece jacket. Gus ran to Clara and hugged her legs.

"Hi, big Gus," Clara said to the four-year-old. "Let's go. Are we building today?"

"Yes!" His eyes shone with excitement. "Big towers! Can we see who can build the highest?"

"You have a gift with Gus, and probably every child, Clara." Mrs. Thurber said, smiling. "All morning he's been asking, 'When's Clara coming?' Every time I'd say, 'Three fifteen,' he would moan, 'That's too long.' So that's what we've been up to. Waiting for you. Anyhow, I'll be back by five fifteen. Have fun." Mrs. Thurber picked up her yoga mat and left.

In the playroom, Gus started to stack. Clara handed him blocks, and together they built their tower so high that it wobbled, then crashed to the floor. Gus clapped his hands and started building again. She did too, caught up in the little boy's excitement.

By the time they had finished working at their construction site and had snacked on vanilla-iced cookies, Mrs. Thurber was walking into the playroom. Clara wished she could stay longer. Was this the kind of life she wanted? She thought about Mami and Diego at home, and Papi, far away, all of them doing their best for a good future.

Clara stared out the window for a few moments. A big sigh escaped her. "I love your backyard. Maybe when it's warm out, Gus and I can play there. It reminds me of our yard in Puerto Rico."

Mrs. Thurber smiled. "Super idea, Clara. By springtime I may need you for a few extra hours if you have time. Gus will be in preschool all morning and ready to play in the afternoon."

"That would be great." More babysitting meant more money. Maybe she could give some of it to Mami for the family house fund. "I'll check with my mother. I can get my homework done early."

Mrs. Thurber handed Gus two toy trucks from the kitchen table, and he ran off to race them. "It must have been hard to leave your country for a new one and for your family to start over with everything here unfamiliar to you."

"It was, but the hurricane destroyed everything we had there." Clara didn't bother telling Mrs. Thurber that Puerto Rico had become a US territory in 1898, and that everyone in her family was a US citizen. "It's not the same there anymore. We'll build our lives here, just as soon as my father returns. He went back to San Juan to help build houses."

Mrs. Thurber placed her hand on Clara's shoulder. "How brave of him. And how brave of you to help your family here. You can always talk to me about things that come up. If you need help with anything, anything at all, please ask."

Clara nodded. She couldn't tell Mrs. Thurber how much more secure the offer to help made her feel, even though this smart, interesting woman didn't know anything about Puerto Rico or that she and her family were American citizens. Hadn't she learned that in school or by reading the newspapers? The kids in school probably didn't know either. Maybe she would tell them someday.

"Thanks." She looked at her watch. "I have to go. I can't be late for dinner." She walked down the pretty street but wanted to run. Away from the Thurbers'? Or home to Mami and Diego? She wasn't sure. She needed to be understood and accepted as Clara Montalvo, a Puerto Rican American. And to fit into her new life.

As she walked the rest of the way, her insides felt a little shaky as she thought about going back to school for the remainder of eighth grade. Maybe she'd try to be friends again with Molly who, she wanted to believe, had been kind to her when she had needed it most.

Even though the year was almost over, a few months remained. She hoped she could accomplish all her goals. She wasn't sure where she had picked up this idea, but she felt she was supposed to have life figured out by eighth grade. So far, she hadn't discovered how to keep her opinions to herself or how girls here could be friends with somebody one day and not the next. She wasn't sure what she could do about missing Papi except miss him. She would help Mami and Diego to feel at home here and hope to get her family all together again.

Some days she questioned if it were possible for her to do any of this. Surely there had to be a way. If anyone could find it, she could. It helped to think of herself as someone like Mrs. Thurber, with a perfect life, even if that perfect life was a long way off.

Chapter Three

Sudden storm

For once, Jamie couldn't wait to get to school. He had to talk to Coach. Jamie hoped Mr. J hadn't called Coach over the break too. Maybe he'd get a hint from Coach whether he was still in good standing on the team. He had to participate in the two competitions left in the season to keep up his good record.

He hurried out the door, then remembered he'd forgotten something. He ran back up to his room, slid the social studies and science books that he hadn't even opened during break into his backpack, and hurtled back down the stairs.

"Leaving already, Jamie?" Mom called to him from the upstairs hallway.

"Yeah, Mom. Have to get in early."

"Glad you're making a new start," she said. "Remember that Dad and I are with you all the way, okay? See you later. We love you." A few seconds later she added, "Enjoy your day."

"Thanks, Mom." Jamie glanced back and shot her a smile he hoped signaled that she'd just made his morning better. "You too. Later."

Dad had left for the bank already, but his words still rang in Jamie's ears: "For you, young man, the season is over." The finality

20

of them stung but as Jamie ran to school, he repeated out loud, "It's not over. It's not over." As he got closer, he rehearsed what he'd say to Coach. Something like, "Hi, Coach. How're things? Have a good break?" He might even add, "Great to be back." Then for sure he'd say, "Can't wait for the next competition." He'd do whatever it took to stay on the team.

At school he raced downstairs to the athletic office. The air smelled full of excitement—uniforms, sports equipment, and sweat. Darkness filled the office. Bummer. His deep sigh sucked all the spirit out of him. The wall clock ticked toward eight thirty and the first bell. Still early. It would only take him thirty seconds max to get upstairs to class. He'd wait a little longer, hope he could dodge getting a late slip. He glanced up and down the corridor, hoping to see Coach heading his way.

The bell rang. Two minutes till class started. But he waited. This was important. He had to find out if Coach knew he'd failed the test, and if Coach did know the worst, whether the season was over for him. Any minute now, Coach would show up. Jamie's heart raced against the seconds ticking away. Wait or be late?

A few seconds could make the difference between enjoying the day like Mom had said or messing it up by upsetting Mr. J on the first day back. He couldn't afford to do that. He didn't want to think about what his dad would say if he got another phone call from Mr. J. Dad's criticism felt like a rock strapped on his back. If he wanted to keep snowboarding, he'd have to get his science grade up, and fast.

Taking the steps two at a time he bounded up to the first floor, where the school smell he hated—glue, maybe ink, floor cleaner, and cafeteria—hit his nostrils. The odor reminded him he was trapped for the next five days straight.

Hoping to sneak into science class unseen, he tiptoed in fast and slid into his seat.

"Mr. Fulton." Mr. J called out without looking up from his desk. "I assume you have a late slip for me."

Jamie winced. "Um, sorry. I was downstairs waiting for Coach. See, I have to talk to him and—"

"You're late for class," Mr. J barked. Kids glanced at Jamie. "If you have sports business to handle, you'll have to do it on your own time. This is science time."

"Yes, sir." Jamie hoped his respectful tone would prove he got the message. Mr. J wasn't mean or strict, but everyone knew he meant business. His dress slacks and striped shirts definitely marked him as a serious teacher, but he acted pretty low-key. Most teachers didn't let kids call them by a nickname—Mr. J for Mr. Jennings—like he did.

His teacher went back to his PowerPoint on classifying elementary substances using chemical formulas. Jamie glanced at the screen up front. He calmed down but couldn't help resenting being forced to sit through this lecture. When would he ever need chemical formulas in real life?

Three-quarters of the way through class, Jamie slumped in his chair, daydreaming about being back on the mountain. Mr. Jennings tapped him on the shoulder. "And so, as I was saying about disastrous happenings in our world today, which you may have missed, Mr. Fulton, this month's topic is historical natural disasters."

Jamie startled and peeked at Mr. J, towering over him now, even though Mr. J was on the short side. His longish hair wasn't cool by Jamie's standards, but he figured Mr. J had been "hip" in his day.

Jamie swallowed a yawn and tried faking it. "Natural disasters. Great topic."

Mr. Jennings raised an eyebrow as he stared down at him. "Yes? Go on."

Jamie's mind crashed. *Think. Think.* Mr. J was most kids' favorite teacher. If you asked them why, they'd say he was always fair, funny sometimes, and he treated kids with respect. He wasn't a preachy know-it-all. Jamie agreed with all that, but here he sat, in a bad situation with his favorite teacher. Maybe funny and fair Mr. J would let him off the hook.

"Natural disasters . . ." He scrambled to come up with something. ". . . Kind of like sitting in school during snowboarding season."

A few laughs broke out but died down fast as Mr. J frowned. Jamie smiled up at him sheepishly. "Just kidding." *Uh-oh.* He probably shouldn't joke after failing his science exam. Clara, who sat across from him, shook her head, which he took as a warning to cut it out. One of the best students in the class, she would never make a wisecrack to a teacher.

"*What?*" he said to her out loud.

"Don't you have any idea?" Clara answered. "You obviously didn't hear Mr. J talking about the disastrous weather happening everywhere and—"

Mr. J turned to Clara and said, "No private conversations, please."

Jamie sat up and regretted getting her in trouble.

Clara quickly turned the situation around. "Mr. J, can we do our report on a recent disaster? I'd like to do hurricanes. Specifically, María."

Jamie smiled at Clara's cleverness. Of course, she already knew what she wanted to write about. Clara, always on time for class with her books neatly stacked and her hands folded, waited for kids like him to get it together too. She was still cool and moderately funny when she wasn't on his case for not working. And she was kind to everyone.

"A perfect choice, Clara," Mr. J said.

Jamie thought Mr. J emphasized the word perfect, but Clara could only be called a perfect student.

"Hurricanes have been occurring more often in this part of the world lately." Mr. J turned and addressed the class. "The rest of you, please choose a natural disaster that you want to understand better. Find out where they happen most often and what contributes to their occurrences. Report the consequences and anything else that intrigues you about your natural disaster. You may work independently or in pairs, present your findings orally, in a printed report, or create a PowerPoint. Lots of possibilities. But please let me know your plan. Any questions?"

Jamie's head buzzed with a lot of questions, but no way would he ask them. The only thing he truly cared about was whether the project could help him pass science.

"No questions?" Mr. J said. "All right, then. Be prepared tomorrow to tell me what you've chosen for your project and—"

"Tomorrow?" Jamie blurted. His hopeful mood plummeted. No way could he have a topic in twenty-four hours. He'd never done an assignment overnight.

Mr. J shot Jamie a warning glance for interrupting, then continued, "—a paragraph on your reason for choosing that particular natural disaster."

Jamie grimaced. How could he even start this homework? He had real work to do—finding out whether he was still on the team.

———

As soon as the bell rang, Jamie ran downstairs. He had five minutes before his next class. The athletic office was open, and he hurried in. Dan, one of the assistant coaches, glanced up from his clipboard. "Jamie. How are you?"

"Terrific. Great snowboarding in Vermont. Coach in?"

"No. He's at a training conference. He'll be in tomorrow." Dan went back to his paperwork.

Jamie stood there for a few seconds, disappointed, but hoping for a few encouraging words from Dan. His eye caught the competition schedule on the bulletin board. Two names were circled in red pencil, one of them his. He quickly gave up on any encouragement and left the office before Dan could see his panic. He rushed down the hallway toward math class, mentally erasing that red circle around his name with each step. He had to make it into the room before the bell. The last thing he needed was trouble in another class. The small red circle that he'd just seen said a lot. He had gotten what he'd gone to the office for: a hint about his standing on the team. Mentally erasing didn't do much good. His name, circled in red, couldn't be anything but bad news.

Chapter Four

Low barometric pressure

J amie got through the rest of the school day somehow, but that red circle haunted him. Whatever it meant couldn't be good. Another stress. Plus, he had the assignment due tomorrow for Mr. J. He left school as soon as the bell rang. No hanging out with his boarding buddies today. He would have talked to Chuck, the other guy whose name was circled, but Chuck was out that day. He'd been absent a lot before break too. Jamie hardly ever missed school, so that couldn't be the reason for his red circle. He tried to come up with other possible explanations but finally gave up pretending. There was only one: failing science. He knew the requirement for competing on a school team: good grades.

As he walked home, he tried to focus on a plan. He pulled his jacket closed. Cold today. Maybe snow. Good. *Focus.* He had to do the assignment, give it all he had. He'd sit at the computer until he found a topic. That didn't sound too complicated. But the paragraph on his reason for choosing was impossible. He didn't want to do the project, so how could he say why he chose it?

Starting the assignment might convince Dad that he was trying, though. He had kind of tried in school. He'd opened his books, but he had to admit he hadn't read too far when the material was on stuff he didn't care about. If it bored him, and it usually did, he'd shut the book, open his notebook and doodle snowboarding moves Lucas had taught him. Then he'd remember Dad saying, "You have to focus." Even if he found something mildly interesting, Dad's words would travel from his head to his hands, and they would slam the book shut.

He passed the town library and gave a nod. He wondered if Lucas had used the library and how he had gotten through school. He'd ask him in his next letter. Writing to Lucas was the only time he could sit down and focus. He could tell his brother about school and the team and ask him questions about what it was like in Afghanistan.

So far, he'd only gotten two letters back from Afghanistan in the five months his brother had been there. Lucas had written Jamie lots of news about his eight months of basic training and the kind of maneuvers they had to master at Paris Island, South Carolina. That sounded pretty cool, but in his latest letter Lucas hadn't said much, just that he was okay and learning a lot about the Afghan people. Lucas wrote about the courage the people had, facing so many obstacles, like the Taliban, not having enough food to eat, worrying about their children's education, and a lot more.

Jamie always choked up when he read the letters. His problems were so small and insignificant compared to his brother's. Jamie had read the letters so many times, trying to find the brother he knew in the words, but he could sense a change in Lucas. Jamie memorized the letters anyhow. Reading them brought his brother, far off in Afghanistan, a little closer to home.

Lucas always ended his letters with, "Bite the bullet." Jamie googled those three words so he'd know for sure what Lucas was telling him to do. The best definition he came up with was, *to endure something that's hard to do—something unavoidable.* Like school. He thought about the words. Lucas had to bite the bullet every second.

Halfway home, he mentally wrote a letter to Lucas and admitted that he felt left out of his brother's life. He wasn't fighting a war with guns and explosives like Lucas, but inside it felt that way. He wasn't sure who the enemy was, though. That's what Lucas had said once, and Jamie couldn't get it. He figured the guys across the field from Lucas were the enemy. But Lucas had written back that the most difficult challenge he and his fellow Marines faced was recognizing the enemy. Jamie stopped and reminded himself he wouldn't say all this in a real letter. It might pressure Lucas, and Jamie didn't want to do that. He'd wait and tell his brother all these thoughts someday, once Lucas was done with the war.

He turned when footsteps sounded behind him. Clara, out of breath, caught up to him.

She smiled and her face lit up like sunshine on a gloomy day. "Hi. Did you have a good time over break?"

"Yeah, for sure. Vermont snow was perfect. How about you?"

Clara shrugged. "It was okay. I stayed home. Watched my brother, helped my mom, babysat."

Jamie nodded. It didn't sound like much of a vacation. At least he'd gotten away, even if his trip had been cut short. "Cool, but sounds like you need another break." He figured that was okay to say.

"Yeah," she said. "But it's good to be back at school. About our assignment. It must be hard to know what to write about when you haven't done much research or many reports. I guess when you do homework every night, you get in the routine of schoolwork. You might try it sometime."

"Sure," he agreed without meaning it. "Homework. Every night." She sounded a little snarky, and he wasn't in the mood for it. "Listen, Clara, school's not really my thing. But I've got to do this assignment. My grade depends on it. So do a lot of other things."

"Just google natural disasters," Clara said. "You'll find a topic."

"Easy for you to say," he shot back. He didn't know why anger ran through him just then. Probably the red circle and Lucas in danger, and now, natural disasters. What could possibly interest him enough to want to write a whole report on it? He thought about satisfying his dad and figured he had no choice. "You're a straight A student, Clara. I'm not."

Clara shrugged and walked off without answering. Jamie immediately regretted his comment. It had sounded snotty, but the words shot out of his mouth before he could stop them. Feelings that he'd never identified before usually held him back. But now anger and resentment, frustration and disappointment all spilled out. He looked to the sky for relief. A few snowflakes would do it. How could he turn it all around, start all over with Clara?

He called out, "I actually know how to google, Clara. Thanks." He wasn't sure if he was genuinely thanking her or trying to get back at her. She kept walking until she joined up with some kids from their class, Rodrigo and Juan, and a few others Jamie didn't recognize. The Latino kids at school kept mostly to themselves, so Jamie hung back.

"See you later," he mumbled, hoping Clara would turn and invite him to walk with the group. He wouldn't fit in with her Latino friends, but he wanted to be part of the fun. Rodrigo and Juan were dancing backwards, rapping reggaetón in Spanish. The girls following the boys were all huggy and giggly. Clara clapped her hands to the rhythm and danced as she walked. He hardly recognized her around these kids. She was lively, so different from her usual quiet presence in school.

He remembered the eighth grade dance at the beginning of the year. His teammates dared him to ask Clara to dance. She danced with lots of cool moves. He tried to follow but couldn't get the rhythm. Being that close to her gave him goose bumps. Then he and Clara bumped foreheads three times and almost accidentally kissed. He could have easily faked bumping again and kissed her. Instead, he chickened out. "Sorry," he'd mumbled, and she'd answered, "Me too." He wouldn't miss the next chance *if* he ever got one. That was for sure. Maybe. He didn't want to scare her off or embarrass her.

He glanced back at the kids having fun. Looks didn't matter, he'd always thought, but maybe they did. He didn't look anything like Rodrigo or Juan or Clara. He had light skin and reddish hair. Clara's skin looked like sun-kissed sand. Her dark hair fell like a waterfall down her back, almost to her waist. Jamie's fingers twitched. He wanted to run his hands through it. He huffed. No chance of that happening. A lot more than different skin and hair color separated him from Clara and the others. They all shared so much in common, including a language he didn't know, which the Latino kids took advantage of any time they wanted to talk about something without the other kids understanding.

Jamie wondered how it felt to live in two different worlds like Clara did. Would she clap and dance for him if he danced like these dudes? That would be cool, but he didn't have the slightest idea how to do those moves. Or how to understand Clara's intentions.

A few snowflakes landed on Jamie's face. He licked one off his lips, recalling the powdery Vermont mountains. It was easy to read a ski slope but not Clara. Why was he still thinking about her? Sometimes she treated him really nice, almost like she treated her girlfriends. Other times she was so busy with her schoolwork and her Latino friends that she ignored him, like now.

He walked ahead, daydreaming again. He'd liked Clara from the day they'd met in seventh grade when she'd looked a little lost. He'd imagined how he'd feel in a new school where all the kids already knew each other. He'd always been pretty shy around her. They were friends in class but had never hung out after school or on weekends or anything. He smiled as he imagined taking Clara skiing or snowboarding. She would try her best to get down a slope perfectly on a snowboard. But she'd be sliding all over the place because snowboarding isn't easy. He could see it clearly and almost laughed at the image. He could teach her how to get up on the board and balance. He'd stay with her as she made her way down the slope, an easy one for starters. That would be really fun. Too bad it would never happen. Some of the kids in their class were dating, but everybody gossiped about them. If he invited Clara snowboarding, Molly and her nosy friends would surely find out about it and spread rumors. He was certain Clara wouldn't like that.

He shook himself out of the fantasy and thought about the pages and pages of the boring stuff that he'd soon be facing, and of Lucas's sign-off, "Bite the bullet." He looked up at the snow falling and let the flakes land and melt his worries for a few seconds. Maybe he could get a start on his work before his parents got home so he'd have something to show them that night. Maybe that would give them a reason to talk to Coach about that circle around his name. They could tell Coach that he was focusing, doing better in science. Maybe that would be enough for Coach to keep him on the team for the two remaining competitions. It had to be.

He ran the rest of the way home, popped two waffles in the toaster, drowned them in maple syrup, scarfed them down, and marched upstairs, Dad's words echoing. *"No more procrastinating."* Snowboarding posters covered every inch of his walls. *Don't look at them—focus.* He googled *natural dis*, and *asters* popped right up like the computer knew he needed help fast. A page of links filled the screen—avalanches, blizzards, earthquakes, sinkholes. None of them interested him, not even avalanches, which were the biggest dangers for snowboarders and skiers. He closed the page and focused on a poster of a snowboarder twisting in the air above him. Lucas had showed him that move. He'd worked really hard to master it. His body had been sore for weeks. Lucas was a great teacher. He was good at a lot of things. Except writing letters home. Jamie opened his email. Was he procrastinating? Maybe, but he still started a letter.

Lucas, hi. I'd really like to know how you are. We haven't heard from you in a while. When will you be home? I need to tell you so many things about . . . everything. I was going to say school, but now it's home too. I don't think I'd enlist to get away from Dad and how hard he comes down on me for my grades, but I'd sure like to get out from under all the pressure. Maybe you can give me some hints.

And girls. I have a lot of questions on that topic—but later. Right now I have to find a natural disaster to report on for school so I'll sign off and, as you like to say, bite the bullet. J.

They were both biting the bullet now. He hoped that Lucas could get some strength from knowing that.

He relaxed into his desk chair after writing all his worries out to Lucas. He could choose war as his topic for science, but war wasn't natural; it was man-made. Plus he might find too many terrible things that could happen to Lucas. It was bad enough that they didn't have any recent news about him.

He rubbed his eyes and determined to get back to disasters. *Focus*, he told himself, but it seemed impossible. The screen saver that he'd made grabbed his attention. Red, white, and blue fireworks exploded, lights circled, and rockets burst in midair. This scene always reminded him of the best times of his life—Lucas and fireworks on the Fourth of July. Lucas always made him stand back. Then his brother would light the fuse, run over, scoop him up, and race around the yard, holding him under one arm. Lucas only stopped when Mom yelled at them for scaring the neighbors' dogs—and the neighbors too.

Lucas always opened the sparklers and lit one for each of them. They marched around the backyard twirling sparkling figure eights and circles for Mom and Dad, who watched from the porch, clapping and shouting, "Happy Fourth of July!" Dad beat one of Lucas's drums as Jamie and Lucas marched, and Mom cheered. Jamie wished it could still be like that—Dad acting funny and having fun and Mom laughing—and that they'd never run out of sparklers.

Home wasn't the same without Lucas. What would it be like when his brother returned? Would Dad be glad to see him, or keep reminding Lucas he shouldn't have gone?

"Get over it," Jamie said to himself. "You have work to do." He let himself feel sorry for himself for a few more minutes, then, scrolled back to the natural disasters page. At the bottom the words "volcanic eruptions" stood out. He knew about volcanoes. He still had the baking soda and vinegar model volcano he'd made in fifth grade. Mom made him put it in the basement because it was crumbling and looked like a big avalanche spilling all over his shelf. He could still bring back the amazing sound it made as it erupted: *Whoosh!*

Jamie clicked on "volcanoes" and skipped over unfamiliar words till he got to ". . . and caused the historic Year Without a Summer."

No summer? Incredible. And unbelievable. He read on.

"Tambora, in 1815, one of the most powerful volcanic eruptions ever recorded, shot twenty-seven miles of ash into the atmosphere with four hundred million tons of cloud gas, causing global climate anomalies . . ."

Whatever that meant. He tried to picture the ash and gas but all he could imagine was black clouds.

"European and North American temperatures dropped to below freezing, and it snowed in June."

Snowboarding in summertime. Yes! Jamie skimmed for more good stuff.

"Tambora even caused warm temperatures in some parts of the world, as a reaction to the heat. This warm air moved into the Arctic, making it melt faster than usual. Explorers began mapping out the area and started hunting for what would become the Northwest Passage. They didn't find it because the water froze again. The crazy weather Tambora caused lasted for about three years. Other men would eventually find a passage, though."

How cool to be an explorer. He sat back and imagined the thrill of trekking through the Arctic and discovering something that nobody had ever seen. Why couldn't they teach things like this in school? That reminded him: he had an assignment and a paragraph to write. He opened a new page and started typing.

My topic is Tambora, the volcanic eruption that happened in Indonesia in 1815. It shot ashes into the sky, and the clouds they made moved so far that the eruption caused the Year Without a Summer in the United States and right here in Albany. So I want to know what else happened because it was winter in June with snow when it should have been summer. Can't wait to know more and do my report on Tambora.

Jamie, surprised and satisfied that he'd finished his homework, closed the laptop. This was a topic he could get excited about. And if he did well on the project, he'd definitely be out on the slopes again soon.

———

Before dinner that evening, he watched the news with his parents. He thought it would show Dad he was motivated to learn about important things. Dad sank lower onto the couch and Mom tried to hide her crying as the TV screen filled with footage of coffins being unloaded from planes. Jamie winced. Mom hardly ever cried. She handled everything without complaining, but she couldn't handle Lucas being in danger. Jamie wished she hadn't seen the coffins. He wished *he* hadn't seen them either. He couldn't imagine Lucas coming home in a box to Mom, Dad, and him or waiting on the airport strip like these families. The three of them would never be the same if that happened.

Jamie pushed away the thought and the awful dread it brought up. Sometimes he used to ask something about his brother, like how Lucas had acted as a kid or in high school, and Dad would shoot him a look like he didn't want to talk about Lucas. So Jamie had stopped asking. Dad's head hung so low now that Jamie wondered if he would ever look up again.

The way Dad appeared now and how he refused to talk about Lucas confused Jamie. He couldn't tell if Dad missed Lucas or if he were still angry with him for enlisting without talking about it with him first. When Lucas had told Dad he was enlisting, Dad grabbed Lucas, shook him, and yelled, "You can't do that. I forbid it. You don't know what you're doing."

Lucas had pulled away and walked out of the house.

Even though Lucas was gone and Dad wasn't yelling anymore, Jamie felt as if he stood in the middle of their battlefield. Lucas going off to war was as bad as a natural disaster for their family.

At the dinner table he fidgeted with his meatloaf while Mom tried to make small talk about work. She'd almost sold a house that day but had high hopes. He could always tell when Mom was talking for the good of the family. She did that a lot these days. Jamie sat between her and Dad, his brother's absence across from him as real as a person—or maybe a ghost. Jamie knew Mom and Dad felt it too. He wanted to say something to lighten the mood, but fear rose in him, his heart pounding just like when he'd first faced a mountain of moguls. He'd gotten over that fear, but this was different. This one, even though he was just sitting at the dinner table, didn't go away. Worry and sadness twisted his stomach into knots. There was no room for food.

When he couldn't stand the heavy silence any longer, he blurted, "Remember how we heard that Taliban attacks were up nineteen percent?"

"Yes, Jamie," Mom said in a soft voice. "What about that?"

Dad glanced up as he slid a forkful of potatoes into his mouth.

"Well, Lucas wrote us that he's on security duty right in the American compound, so I figure he's definitely safe. He's not out in the action where the Taliban are attacking. Besides, we're there with him in spirit. That helps to protect him."

His parents stared at him like he was from another planet. Mom finally nodded. Dad stabbed a chunk of meatloaf with his fork.

He'd hoped pointing out that Lucas was inside the compound would make his parents feel a little better, but mentioning the Taliban seemed to upset them more. How could he have done that? He wouldn't bring the increased attacks up again, that was for sure. He felt especially guilty over adding to Mom and Dad's worries with ordinary school stuff like his science test. He'd do anything to give Mom something to smile about and Dad a reason to raise his head high. He had to try.

Maybe hearing about his science assignment would cheer them up. "Dad! You won't believe what I read today. Natural disasters can affect credit and stuff, like what you do at the bank." He heard false enthusiasm in his voice but couldn't control it. He had to make everyone ease up.

Dad put his fork down. "You were reading? About credit?"

"Yeah, Dad. It was amazing stuff. I couldn't stop reading. I didn't quite get some of the information, but for science, everyone has to report on a natural disaster. I found one, a humongous volcano called Tam-something, over in Indonesia."

Jamie told them everything he remembered. Excitement erupted in him as he rushed to get the story out. "The most incredible thing is that the volcanic eruption impacted places as far away as here in Albany. It turned winter in the summertime, with six inches of snow in June. Can you believe that?"

Dad shook his head. "It's hard to believe, but stranger things have happened. Interesting. I've never heard about it before."

Jamie beamed with pride at telling Dad something he didn't already know. And that he found it interesting.

"But what does that have to do with credit?"

"Um . . ." Jamie tried to remember the explanation. "Something about us selling grain to Europe because it was too cold for crops to grow there, and how American farmers needed to borrow money to buy more seeds and stuff. I didn't understand it all."

Dad nodded. "I'll read the article. Maybe you can get it for me. I would have thought that snow in June in the northeast would be more widely known."

"Me too. How could a volcano thousands of miles away make it freezing cold here? Kids probably got to ski all summer." Jamie bit his lip. Skiing wasn't where he wanted the conversation to go after their Vermont blowout.

Mom turned to Jamie. "You sound so involved, honey. That's great. I didn't know anything about that volcano, either. I'll bet a lot of people never heard of it. I'm proud of you for sticking with all that reading."

Jamie's chest swelled. He glanced at Dad and waited. Maybe Dad would say something about his research too.

"Now, now," Dad said, pushing the last mound of meatloaf and mashed potatoes onto his fork, "let's hold off on the *proud* until Jamie gets those grades up."

Jamie pushed down his disappointment. Dad had been a staff sergeant in the army. He was used to giving orders, not compliments like Mom. Jamie couldn't blame him, but he'd still love to hear a little praise once in a while. He had his topic and had written his paragraph. That was progress. He grinned. He could already see his science grade going up. Soon he'd be off the hook with Dad. He'd be snowboarding again, competing and all. He wouldn't need Dad's compliments. He'd take his brother's advice and bite the bullet.

Chapter Five

Clear blue sky

*C*lara left her friends at the corner and hurried the rest of the way home. She pulled the mail out of the mailbox and rifled through it—all junk, except for a thick envelope addressed to her. It was here! She ripped it open. Lots of forms. She found the first sheet and read, "Miss Montalvo, we are happy to consider your scholarship application for ninth grade at the Academy."

Clara jumped and turned and danced. Yes! She read on about the information they needed—a complete record stating she had fulfilled the eighth grade academic and extracurricular requirements (service projects), financial need data, and letters of recommendation from school personnel and other community professionals who knew her well. She read over them again, stopping at service projects in parentheses. She'd have to work on this one but silently thanked Ms. Dunne, her counselor at school, who was helping her to apply. She pressed the forms to her heart. She was being considered. Should she tell Mami?

Mami didn't even know she'd applied to the Academy. Clara hadn't wanted to tell her until she was sure of having a chance for the scholarship. Then Mami could sign the forms giving permission. It was no use trying to figure out how they could afford fees or extras if she didn't get in. But they were considering her for next year! She'd do anything to be able to go there. She couldn't get the art and design studies the Academy offered in a regular public school. Her mind started working overtime, coming up with ways to earn the extra money she'd need to enroll. She could babysit more often, maybe find some other families who needed help evenings and weekends. Papi didn't know about her applying either. She wondered why she felt guilty for holding onto this secret but rationalized it by thinking she was saving them extra worry.

She remembered Saturdays, going to work with Papi in San Juan when he had some time to show her what they were building. He'd let her hold some of his tools, maybe pound in a nail or tighten a screw. After María tore buildings and homes apart, she understood the importance of Papi's work. The idea had flashed in her mind then: *That's what I want to do—build homes and schools and other kinds of buildings like Papi, maybe even study architecture, and create structures that will withstand hurricanes.*

If she went to the Academy, she would miss Jamie. Even after today's argument, she knew she would feel drawn to him again tomorrow. Her heart melted when he needed help with schoolwork and looked at her like a sad puppy, as he had today. But she had to be true to herself. She hoped they would stay friends if she transferred. And there was still the rest of the school year. Maybe they'd be able to spend more time together. Maybe, Clara dared to muse, he'd even ask her to go for a soda after school or to the movies one Saturday.

Several of the boys in her class were asking girls like Molly and Katy to do stuff outside of school. For now, though, she wouldn't be spending any after-school time with Jamie. Besides having to be home every day after school for Diego, she had her babysitting the one day a week Mami was home.

Clara opened the front door. "Diego?"

She waited for the "Hi, Clarita, we won!" but there was no answer. She plopped her backpack on the kitchen counter next to the computer and opened the cupboard. She couldn't wait to surprise her brother with a treat—and to surprise herself, too, by creating something from mostly nothing. She took a few items down from the shelf.

A few minutes later, Diego stormed into the kitchen. "You beat me." He dropped his backpack to the floor. "The first day back to school too."

Clara playfully pulled his woolen hat over his eyes. "You would have beaten me by ten minutes any other day, but we got out a little early. Guess what I'm making."

Diego took his hat off. "S'mores?"

"You guessed." She offered her hand for a high five. "That's better than beating me home. How did you know, little brother?" Diego was her love. Only a foot shorter than her five feet, five inches, he was sturdy and strong, like Papi had said. Papi would love seeing Diego starring as goalie on the fourth grade soccer team, where he was always ready and steady for a ball from any direction. Clara always applauded his saves. Mami did, too, on the rare days when she could make his matches.

"'Cause you always make things I love," he said. "Remember how we used to make s'mores on the beach in San Juan? Maybe someday we can go there again. To live."

Clara winced but nodded at Diego's dreams. They were the same as hers, but she was too superstitious to voice them. If she didn't stick with her goal to create a new life for them here in Albany, it might not work out, and she would have failed herself and Papi.

"Do you think Papi's going to die?" Diego stared as if he needed her answer.

"Of course not," she snapped, maybe a little too quickly. She hoped he couldn't tell that her heart was thumping. She pretended not to notice that Diego was waiting for more. Should she tell him she believed that anything was possible? She had no idea what the situation was in Puerto Rico or how dangerous it was. Were electricity lines still down? Did Papi have fresh water to drink? Was it safe where he was putting homes back together? How could she truthfully answer Diego? She'd think about it later. "Let's make your favorite treat." She took the crackers, marshmallows and some chocolate from the cupboard. "Come help me."

"Can I break the chocolate?"

"Wash your hands first."

They layered the marshmallows and chocolate. Then she peeled a banana and piled on slices. Diego said, "Wait," and brought the peanut butter over. He smeared on spoonfuls. "This makes them our own special recipe," he said. Clara nodded. They topped their "creations" with graham crackers, pressed all the insides down, and Clara slid the baking sheet into the oven.

Her mouth watered while they waited for the treats to melt together. She imagined biting into their concoctions, a word she liked saying because it sounded witchy but magical. She hoped for anything magical these days, even if magic happened only in fairy tales. And almost as good as that, Diego had added the special ingredient to concoct their own unique s'mores. She liked that idea—a special ingredient to be unique.

Diego shot wadded paper balls around the table yelling, "Score!" every few seconds. "Are they done yet?"

Clara couldn't wait any longer either. Melted marshmallow and chocolate bubbled as she pulled the baking sheet out of the oven.

Diego's eyes lit up as he reached for the closest treat.

"Careful. They're hot," Clara cautioned just like her parents would have done.

Diego licked his fingers and Clara was finishing her last bite when Mami walked in.

"Mami, we made s'mores," Diego yelled. He held up two hands, still marked with chocolate.

Clara held out a s'more to her mother, grateful that she didn't have to tell Diego any more about Papi right then. It didn't seem the right time to tell Mami about the Academy. She wouldn't want to deal with something new and maybe troubling after a tiring day.

"*Gracias, mi amor.*" Mami accepted it like a gift. She sat with Diego and Clara and bit in. "*Muy delicioso.*"

"You sit, Mami. I'll clean up. Then I have to start on a project. If you need any help with your homework, Diego, call me."

"I only have reading. One page. Can I watch some TV, Mami?"

Mami nodded. "Half an hour, then to work."

Diego wandered off, and Clara sat at the computer while Mami unpacked groceries. A few minutes later Diego ran back to the kitchen and tugged at Mami. "Come. *Rápido.* The man on TV said a hurricane was heading for Puerto Rico. Hurry, Mami."

Clara ran ahead of them. "It's probably about María. They still talk about it on the news," she reassured her little brother, though she wasn't so certain. She couldn't pass on her fear to him. "There couldn't be another hurricane. It's not the season." Their island couldn't survive another hurricane after María.

The screen was a blur. Roofs and boats and furniture flew like monsters. Where was this? It couldn't be Puerto Rico. Could it? Cars, bent out of shape like deformed birds, hit the screen. She jumped back and pulled Diego with her. She hoped Diego saw the destruction like his superheroes crushing the bad guys. Then it wouldn't be real—just a TV show. Where was this happening? Mami pulled them both back to her, but Clara tugged away. She was feeling it again—scared, nauseous, dry mouth. María wouldn't leave her alone. The memories were so real they attacked her. She fell to her knees and covered her ears. She fought back but María always roared louder.

A lump formed in her throat as she recalled two years ago, waking in the early morning, hearing the wind howling and snarling like a beast. Crashing sounds filled her ears. Loud wailing, shaking floors. She heard herself screaming as her bookshelves collapsed, just missing her. Papi rushed into her room, grabbed her, and pulled her along to get Diego.

Papi pushed them into the storage room with thick concrete walls. Mami rushed in carrying food and water. Frijoles. Clara's stomach growled. But she couldn't eat. How long would they be there? Screeching, crashing, cracking, and louder howling shook the walls. Would they fall in on them? Diego's eyes were saucers. He didn't cry, but his watery eyes said he wanted to. His lips were pressed tight, and he held onto Papi's arm. Chills went through Clara even in the sweaty heat. Hot tears welled, ran down her cheeks, dripped on her lap.

Papi's eyes kept checking the walls. Hers did too. Clara imagined the monster wind blowing them down. They could all blow away—and never find each other.

With each boom, Clara squeezed her eyes shut and waited for the walls to fall on them. Was her house still there? Her school? Her friends! *Please let them be safe.* The winds groaned and growled louder. When would they stop? She reached for Diego's hand and didn't let go.

Papi kept saying, "It will be okay. María will die down soon." But María's angry winds weren't dying down. Nothing could ever be okay again. Papi kept saying it, though. Clara had snuggled closer to Mami and Papi and Diego, all she had left in her life.

Clara fought these memories and tried to stand up, get back to now in their living room in Albany. When would María stop haunting her? They were just memories that couldn't hurt her now. She pinched herself, then glanced up. The TV was still roaring.

Diego peeked out from behind Mami every few seconds. He was shaking and rubbing his leg as if it hurt. Clara knew why. During María they'd had to run after the door crashed in on their little shelter. María blew them, but Clara couldn't tell where to. The wind had swept Diego away in one roaring blast. Mami screamed for her little boy, her shrieks swallowed by the winds as she and Clara crawled into the kitchen that was just an open shell.

They waited and waited. Finally, Papi fell onto the floor, carrying Diego. They dripped with water and Diego's leg was bleeding, but they were alive. The four of them hugged—together again.

Clara shook herself back to the present again. This wasn't María. Hurricane Ariel didn't even care that this wasn't hurricane season and was driving down on the Bahamas, destroying everything in its path with furious wrath. She'd read that word in a novel. Anger. Revenge. Cars upside down, boats flying in the air, signs blowing and bending so you couldn't read them, broken trees everywhere, homes that Hurricane Ariel, the first of the year, had stamped into pieces as if they were dollhouses. Then, chunks of . . . what? Flying through the air. One looked like a swing set, another a sandbox. Clara covered her eyes. Yes. This hurricane destroyed just like María.

"Hurricanes are unusual for February in this part of the world, but this one, Ariel, may be heading for Puerto Rico," the newscaster announced.

"No!" Clara gasped. *Is Papi going to die?* flashed through her mind. "No!" she shouted and stared at the screen, sickened by what she saw. "It can't be. Does Papi know Ariel is coming? We have to warn him. Mami, call him. No!" She reached for the phone. "Let me. I can do it faster."

Mami turned the volume down, but Diego stuck to his spot in front of the TV.

Clara's fingers trembled as she punched in a number. She shook her head. "No answer. An electronic message."

She took deep breaths while she waited for the beep. "Papi, please call us. A hurricane is coming to Puerto Rico. Find a safe place. Please." She imagined metal signs and parts of houses flying through the air, injuring people, maybe even killing them. They hadn't been safe in their storage room with the strong walls. Her voice trembled and tears ran down her cheeks. "We love you."

Clara gave the phone to Mami and hurried back to the TV screen. She and Diego held onto each other as they watched the

Bahamas blow apart. She shielded Diego's eyes when more roofs blew off and more cars tumbled like toys.

Mami tried Papi's number again. "*Ocupado*," she said and collapsed on a chair.

"Mami, keep trying. If it's busy, it means Papi is using his phone." Clara bit her nails and stared at Mami, willing Papi to answer. Diego watched the TV as swirling debris flew through the air. He kept covering his eyes, then peeked through his fingers at the screen again as if he had to see.

Clara's fingers were tired of punching in numbers on her phone. She hadn't given up, but after three hours, she couldn't keep her eyes open. Her head kept dropping to her chest. She finally rested her head on the kitchen table. When she opened her eyes, Mami sat across from her, her face flushed from wiping her eyes so Clara and Diego wouldn't notice she'd been crying. But Clara did.

Diego was on the sofa asleep. At least he'd found relief.

"They think the hurricane moved out to sea," Mami said. "Not to Puerto Rico, thank goodness. Maybe we can get some rest now."

Clara turned on the TV for proof. She couldn't find news anywhere. Maybe Mami heard correctly. Clara allowed herself some relief, too, by assuming Ariel was no longer a danger. She moved over to her computer and stared at the screen. Her hands shook as she considered trying to research María. She told herself that María was old news even though it roared back with every letter she typed. Was she paralyzed forever? The thrashing memories might never go away. Mr. J had said hurricanes were occurring more often in this part of the world, but he didn't know hers swirled inside her most of the time. She'd told him she would do her report on María. She would do what she'd said, but after that she hoped she could forget about hurricanes forever.

She googled *hurricanes*. Page after page of links covered her screen. But she couldn't concentrate. Her mind went to her walk home from school that day. It seemed like weeks ago that she and Jamie had argued. He probably hadn't even heard about Ariel. Why did she even care? The only thing she cared about was reaching her father. But she couldn't forget what she and Jamie had said to each other. He'd tried to show her he wasn't so bad at schoolwork when he'd said, "I actually know how to google, Clara." Maybe she shouldn't have walked off. She could have said something like, "I could help you get started." But she hadn't. Had her pride gotten in the way? She tried to think of other reasons.

They did things so differently, and she wasn't about to change. She had noticed with new friends here that once they saw the differences, even small ones, they kind of ignored you. Sometimes she thought it would be better to act more like the Latino kids, who only made friends with other Latinos. But she wanted to know her other classmates, and she wanted to fit in with all of them, not just the ones who spoke Spanish or knew about *empanadas* or *tostones*. Surely, she had more in common with the mainland American kids than the differences that always ended up mattering the most.

Something inside of her ached, but she told herself to get over it. She didn't have time to waste trying so hard to get along with these kids. She had work to do. And she had to keep Mami's and Diego's spirits up.

Mami had turned the TV volume down. The screen and the quiet created an eerie atmosphere in their living room. Scenes she had already watched reappeared. Had the hurricane really moved out to sea? Every few minutes, another roof or fisherman's boat went flying through the air. Hurricanes swirled in unpredictable patterns, so she couldn't trust that Ariel no longer posed a danger. She turned away for now, though, and steeled herself to do what she had to do.

As she opened one link and then another, she promised not to let herself become overwhelmed with what people reported about Hurricane María. She took a deep breath and told herself to fight the memories or she couldn't do her report. She wouldn't be able to do anything. She rubbed her aching neck, sat up straight in her chair, and concentrated on the facts, not her emotions.

Three thousand homes destroyed.

She stopped there as sadness and fear rose. Emotions, of course. People with their homes gone. "We left, Mami. Why didn't other people leave too?"

Mami didn't answer for a few minutes. Clara watched her forming her thoughts to try to make sense of something so painful. "They wanted to live where they belonged." Clara wanted it all bundled together fast in an answer that made sense to her, but Mami took her time. "After the hurricane, your grandparents didn't have power or clean water. But the island was their home. They didn't want to start over in a new place at their age. *Gracias a Dios* that people who could help took the injured to hospitals."

Clara nodded and listened to Mami's version but had to add her part. "We had to grab our stuff and leave so fast. Diego and I were so scared, Mami." She glanced at Diego, still sleep, looking so little curled up on the sofa, as vulnerable as he had been when María had swept him up. She hoped he wasn't having bad dreams.

"I wish we could have saved you and Diego from María," Mami said as if she had read Clara's thoughts. "I know you think about it and it still scares you."

Clara got up and stepped into her mother's embrace. "Mami," she asked, "How many people were killed? I never wanted to know before, but I need to know now. It doesn't say for sure on the Internet."

Mami bowed her head. "That's not easy to answer. People in hospitals didn't get what they needed. Many people died. Your poor grandfather didn't get his heart medicine . . ." She turned away for a few seconds. "He almost died. The government first said only sixty-five people were killed. Then fourteen hundred people. Finally, the number was three thousand. Nobody wanted to give the real count."

"Can't they just count the dead bodies?" Diego asked, rubbing his eyes as he wobbled over to them.

Mami hugged him and ran her fingers through his hair. "Diego, a lot of older people died of other things. There was so much confusion. Hospitals were not ready for so many patients. The government didn't count people who died in hospitals. It's very *complicado*."

Clara's mouth opened wide. "How could the government tell those lies? Didn't they have food and supplies to help the people?"

"*Mi amor*, most people in the government were trying, I think. But Puerto Rico didn't have enough of anything. They had sent our emergency supplies to another island that had been hit by a different hurricane. So Puerto Ricans, always ready to help, were left without what we needed when María came."

Clara punched in Papi's number again. She waited, then hung up. No service. Would there ever be service? Would they ever talk to Papi again? If they didn't, did it matter that she worked so hard in school, or that she earned a scholarship and took care of Diego and Mami? Did any of it matter if Papi wasn't in their lives? She had so much to think about. How could making sweet s'mores for Diego earlier end with another horrid hurricane and no news from Papi? Diego's earlier question about Papi dying gave her cold shivers again.

Chapter Six

Break through

When the first bell rang in homeroom, Jamie's heart beat even faster than when he stood at the top of a steep slope, ready to push off. Kids opened notebooks and turned on their laptops. Girls were laughing and passing their phones back and forth, probably sharing selfies. Molly started over toward him with her phone. He wished she would leave him alone. A lot of guys thought she was cute, but she was a pain—always talking about someone or tearing them down. He bluffed interest in the book on his desk. The bell rang. Great. It didn't matter that his book was upside down.

He raised his hand and waved it, hoping to get called on, as the class quieted down. He remembered doing this back in third and fourth grades when something the teacher said excited him. That was long ago. But now, he couldn't hold his new excitement in any longer, and science class hadn't even started.

"Mr. J. I have it! My natural disaster. Volcanoes. I have the title too. 'The Year Without a Summer.' This humongous volcano erupted way back in 1815 and lots of really cool things happened. It's all on the computer. It snowed here in Albany in June. Can you believe—?"

Mr. J stood right next to him. "That's very interesting, Jamie. Can you keep track of all your information until science class starts in a few minutes? I'm still checking students in."

Jamie pressed his lips together to trap his enthusiasm. It was almost impossible, like trying to stop after pushing off down a mountain.

Finally, science class started. Mr. J went row by row, and the kids told him their topics. Tornadoes were the hot disaster. Landslides, sinkholes, avalanches, and floods were chosen too.

When Jamie's turn came, he blurted his last words, "Yeah. Can you believe it? The Internet says the cold weather made it a great year for maple syrup in Vermont. And there's more. Some English writers went to Switzerland to go hiking. It was too cold and muddy because the volcanic ash blotted out the sun's rays. Anyhow, they stayed inside and had a contest to see who could write the best horror story. That's pretty cool."

Kids laughed. Some shook their heads. He didn't care.

"And this too. The bicycle was invented around then. Horses didn't have hay to eat because of the cold weather, and they probably couldn't work and someone—I forgot his name—invented the bike to get around. Best of all—it didn't say this actually—but kids probably skied all summer."

Clara raised her hand and Mr. J called on her. "Bad things happen in a disaster." She stared at Jamie. Her blotchy face scared him. Had he stressed her out? "Disasters aren't cool. Look at how Hurricane María destroyed Puerto Rico. People lost their homes and—"

"Did your family lose yours?" Nick, one of Jamie's friends, asked.

Clara nodded. "That's why we came here. When María hit, we thought we would blow away—our house and everything." She shuddered. "We hid in a little room for hours. Every blast of wind shook the walls. I thought they'd fall in. We had to stay there, but we were kind of trapped. We didn't know when we could ever come out."

Clara covered her ears as if she had suddenly creeped out. Jamie winced. He knew that feeling. Then she must have realized she was in class because she quickly dropped her hands to her sides again. He hoped no one in class would laugh.

"When we did come out, everything in our house was gone, and most of the house too. So many services on the island are still not working. We don't know when we'll see my—"

Clara's voice wavered, and she looked down at her desk. Jamie wished he could help her, but he didn't even know what she was talking about because she never finished the sentence.

When she raised her head again, she turned toward him. "Did you see the destruction that Hurricane Ariel caused in the Bahamas yesterday?"

He shook his head, tried not to meet her eyes.

"Don't you watch the news? Or go on your phone? All you have to do is google current disasters. You're clueless about the world and what's going on. It's not all fun and games like you think it is. People are in danger in so many places because of disasters. Just because you've never worried about anyone . . ."

She stopped. Jamie's face grew hot. She sounded furious with him.

Mr. J picked up where she left off. "You're right, Clara." He waited for a few seconds until the whispering in class quieted down. "Thank you both for your contributions. Jamie, your project choice sounds promising. I'm glad you found the computer so helpful." Mr. J turned to the entire class. "But the computer doesn't represent primary sources. You're all going to have to do further library research on your topics."

Jamie sighed. He never knew where to find anything in the library, so he hardly ever went. He turned to Clara. "Sorry I didn't hear about that hurricane. You're right. I should watch the news." He didn't mention that he had to watch it every night with his parents, but that his father switched channels, looking for coverage on Afghanistan. "But I still think snowboarding in the summer would be the coolest."

Clara frowned, but her anger seemed to have died down. "What actually did happen to the summer?" She narrowed her eyes like she suspected him of causing Tambora.

Jamie ignored that and leaned toward her, eager to tell her. "What actually happened? That's what everyone wanted to know. All the ash blocked the sun's rays. If it happened now, I could be snowboarding all year long. I'll bet kids back then were stoked. Maybe it'll happen again."

Clara was stabbing her pencil into her notebook. He'd never seen her do that before and almost said, "Better your notebook than me," but he didn't get the chance.

"Do you know what you're saying?" Clara asked. He saw her anger coming again, like an avalanche. "You think a volcano erupting and blocking the sun's rays is good news. Do you even know what a natural disaster is, Jamie?"

"Yeah. I know. It's when . . ." Suddenly his mind blanked out. The rest of the class around them seemed to disappear. Clara's questions stabbed and made him feel like a child. Of course, he knew what a natural disaster was. "It's like a tornado with that cool tunnel swirling in the air, or a flash flood that surprises people and they have to use boats to get around, or a bad car crash. Something that happens really fast. Without warning." He stopped before saying, "Or when your brother goes to war. Fast. Just like that."

Clara's eyes opened really wide. "Yes, without warning. So how can you call a tornado cool when it destroys homes and—?"

"Maybe it misses the homes." He tried to lighten the mood with another joke.

"Don't you get it?" Clara said. "Natural disasters mean just that—*disasters*." Her voice rose, enough that all the other kids were watching them. "Have you ever experienced a disaster?"

He thought about that for a second but couldn't win this argument. "What's up with you, Clara?" he shot back. "Stop messing with my topic."

"I'm not. How can you be so—?"

Clara stopped, probably because Mr. J was walking toward them. He didn't look happy. Jamie turned back to his notes.

"Look, you two," Mr. J said. "We've had enough of your outbursts. What's so compelling that you're arguing during class?"

"Jamie's being juvenile. He thinks that disasters—"

"I'm not. She's saying I think it's a—"

"You two have to stop." Mr. J frowned. "You cannot disrupt class any longer."

Jamie glanced at Clara—her head was lowered. She didn't look up until Mr. J walked to the front of the room and continued explaining about the reports.

"So in terms of your projects, class, you have two weeks to complete them."

Jamie had lots more to tell Mr. J, but he'd have to wait. Clara was typing something on her laptop. When Mr. J asked if there were any questions, she stopped, stared at her screen for a few seconds, and raised her hand.

"Yes, Clara?"

"This is upsetting." She pointed at the computer screen. "Under Volcanic Eruptions. 1815, Tambora, the one Jamie thinks is so great. 'In the Northern Hemisphere, winter temperatures killed crops, livestock starved in the worst famine of the century, and eighty-eight thousand people were killed.' Jamie thinks that this volcanic eruption is good news because it snowed here in New York State in June. It's definitely bad news, but he's obsessed with snow and snowboarding."

"Skiing too," Jamie added.

Kids laughed. He did too. Nick told him to cool it.

"It's not funny, Jamie," Clara insisted.

Jamie turned to her. "Don't be mad. It's just an assignment."

Clara stared a hole in him. "It's more than an assignment, Jamie. Don't you see that?"

Mr. J appeared next to them again, his arms folded, his forehead crinkled. He reminded Jamie of Dad. "Did I hear you say, 'Just an assignment,' Jamie?"

Jamie sat up and faced Mr. J. He'd better think fast. "What I mean is, um, uh . . . Clara can have her opinion, but I can have mine too. All these things wouldn't have happened if the volcano hadn't erupted and spread ash all over the world. But I didn't cause the volcano. I was just telling her about it. That's what I meant. It's our assignment."

Clara raised her hand. "But doesn't he see that it was a disaster, which means—"

The entire class started talking at once. People seemed pretty upset.

"Why don't they stop arguing and both do volcanoes?" Burly shouted. "They could argue in their reports."

Jamie scowled at his friend. The last thing he wanted to do was compete with Clara on a report. No way could he do that.

"Yeah," Molly chimed in. "They could debate. Take sides. We could judge, but I already know Jamie would win."

"Ooohs!" came from the class.

Jamie smacked his forehead and waited for the noise to stop. Cool of Molly to think so, but Jamie knew better. Being more popular than Clara didn't matter. He had no doubt she would write a better report. Plus, he wanted Clara to like him. Beating her in class would probably make her hate him instead. He wished Molly would just shut up.

Other kids jumped in. "Have them debate."

"What's a debate?" A few kids were asking questions and chanting, "Debate, debate!" Mr. J clapped, trying to restore order. Clara's head was practically buried in her book.

Jamie wanted to disappear too. He let out a big, frustrated puff of air. "No fair. I'm not doing a debate. I found this topic first. It's my project." He felt like a little kid saying he wasn't playing anymore and was going to take his toys and go home. But he had to stick up for himself. His grade depended on it. His snowboarding future did too.

Kids were still talking, almost arguing now. Mr. J clicked the lights off and on, a first. He frowned. "Class! This is unacceptable. Jamie. Clara. You've disrupted the class enough with your bickering." Mr. J paced for a few minutes around the silent room, then suddenly stopped. "But . . ." He waited. Jamie couldn't. What was Mr. J thinking? ". . . you students have a very good idea. Thank you. So, Jamie and Clara, you can thank your classmates for turning your argument into something productive."

The class began to stir. Kids shuffled their feet, moving around like they couldn't wait to hear what would come next. Jamie stayed low in his seat. He definitely didn't want to hear any more, but Clara was sitting upright again.

Mr. J started pacing again. "I see your point, Clara, about the seriousness of that volcanic eruption. And I also hear Jamie's excitement about what he discovered."

Jamie clasped his hands above his head. "Victory!"

Clara's face signaled surprise at what he was doing. Kids snickered.

Mr. J quieted the class with one raised hand. "Not so fast, Jamie." He cupped his chin and nodded like he'd made his decision. "I like the volcanic eruption debate idea for you and Clara."

"What?" Jamie blurted.

Clara shook her head. "I already have my topic. Hurricanes."

Mr. J put up his hand again. "Just a minute, Clara. I understand that you want to report on hurricanes, but there might be some major lessons for all of us right now if you two tell us what you were talking about earlier. We don't know a thing about the Year Without a Summer, and I'd sure like to know what happened back then—the beneficial things Jamie mentioned and your findings, Clara. I want to know all about the hardships. We could learn why you two argued so strongly about this natural disaster. And the class could learn how to debate by hearing you do it. Clara, it's up to you to decide if you're willing to put aside hurricanes for the time being."

Jamie peeked sideways at her. Clara stared straight ahead, as if she had stopped listening and nothing could change her mind. Great. That would let him off the hook and it wouldn't be his fault.

Mr. J kept going. "You could debate Jamie on the consequences of that volcanic eruption. You two have a good start."

Jamie slumped deeper in his seat. Never.

Mr. J had made his way over to them and now stood between him and Clara. "I'm willing to forget about your outbursts in class, but only if I see you working together on this topic and defending the points you were making to each other. There will be extra credit for good work too." He glanced down at Jamie. "I think someone in this room could use all the extra credit he might get." Mr. J turned to Clara. "Clara?"

She didn't budge, as if she didn't hear Mr. J talking to her.

"Very well then." Mr. J seemed to take her silence for agreement, but Jamie didn't. "A debate it is. See you all tomorrow."

When most of the class had gone, Jamie hurried up to Mr. J. "Can I talk to you?"

"Go on, Jamie."

Jamie explained how excited he was that he had found his topic and that for the first time ever he was psyched to start his research for the report. But he couldn't do a debate. He told Mr. J how he got all anxious and shaky and sick to his stomach when he had to talk in front of people about stuff he didn't know much about, and that he had a hard time trying to get words out when he was nervous. He tried his best right then to stumble over them. "Like if I did tor-tor-tornadoes or ty-typhoons." He sounded silly. He tried words that started with F. "Or fl-floods or for-for-forest fires." He tried again, in case Mr. J didn't get it. "Or even vol-vol-canoes."

Mr. J's eyebrows shot way up and then his face turned into one big frown. He put his hand on Jamie's shoulder. "I know you love to joke. But stuttering isn't a joking matter, Jamie. Mimicking someone's problem is unkind. I've never heard you at a loss for words." Mr. J smiled just a little. "Or seen you shaking. You're definitely fidgety in class, but you're running yourself down as far as your abilities." He let out a big breath. "Now, let's get back to what we were talking about because you have a lot of catching up to do."

Catching up? He could only do that on a ski slope. But what he thought would catch him up in school wasn't happening. His shoulders slumped. Mr. J was right. He hadn't worked much all year and had proved it by failing his test. He heard his dad's words somewhere in the back of his head: *Your actions have consequences.* Man, did they ever.

Mr. J kept talking. "Do you believe all that you've said, or is it another joke? Sounds like you've convinced yourself you can't do the debate. That's very clear, and I understand."

"Really? That's great, Mr. J!" Jamie's spirits lifted. "I knew you'd understand. Thanks." Jamie wiped his forehead. "Boy, what a weight off my back now that I don't have to do this debate thing."

Mr. J held up his hand. "Hold on a second. I said it sounds as if you convinced *yourself* you can't do it. You didn't convince *me*. You're more capable than you think you are."

"But—"

"That's the assignment, Jamie. I don't give out punishments, but this is as close to it as I've ever come for your continual interruptions in my class."

Jamie winced. What about Clara? She had been disruptive too. He didn't dare ask.

"And we won't use this time to talk about your exam." Mr. J's eyebrows shot up. "But at this point you need to do some serious work if you want to pass science."

Jamie had his answer.

"Why not challenge yourself?" Mr. J said. "Consider the research and debate practice for next year in high school, where the workload will be a lot heavier. You're a fearless snowboarder. You take on steep slopes. Go for it."

Jamie couldn't face Mr. J. He spoke with his head lowered. "I don't think—"

"As a rule, I don't contact parents unless there's a good chance of a student failing and—"

Jamie straightened. "No! Don't call them."

Mr. J glanced at the clock. "I've got a meeting now, Jamie. I hope we've settled this matter."

Jamie had no way out. Sure, he'd found his topic, and he'd learned some unusual new things. Reading about a cold summer had surprised him, but how could he talk about it in a stupid debate? Debates were for smart kids on debate teams. He'd seen a debate in *Rocket Science*. But this wasn't a movie. This was real life. His. Could Mr. J be right about him being better than he thought? He didn't believe that for a second, but he was amazed that Mr. J did. He had to admit it felt good.

Even if he could bring himself to find information for the debate, he would be working against Clara, whom he'd hoped would be more than a friend sometime soon. She was the smartest person in class. Debating her would be an even bigger obstacle than the giant moguls on the black diamond run he had yet to conquer at Jiminy Peak. He had no idea how he'd ever do it. But if he wanted to pass science, he'd have to find a way.

Chapter Seven

Gathering clouds

*A*s Jamie left the classroom, Mr. J's final words, "I hope we've settled this matter," followed him down the hallway. He really needed Clara's help. No way would he pass science without it. He'd never been trapped in a hurricane, but he felt just like Clara had described it, as if the walls were closing in on him. Mr. J had made it perfectly clear that he had to do the debate. Clara had made him seem like the worst person in the world to think that the eruption could have brought about good things. He had to tell her he understood that bad things happened. Lucas flashed in his mind, but Jamie forced away thoughts of his brother at war. He didn't have time for them now. He had to find Clara.

Everything would be a lot worse at home if he didn't take Mr. J's advice and do the debate. He couldn't give Mom and Dad any more worries about him and school. He'd never thought about what anger felt like before. It hurt, because it was stuck in his body and couldn't find a way out. He didn't even know who or what he was angry with. Mostly with himself for getting into this situation, but he was angry about other things too: Lucas in danger, and not knowing how his brother was from day to day.

Jamie kept a list of the towns Lucas had traveled through and tracked attacks and explosions. Whenever he saw a threat, he'd dash off a text to Lucas to warn him, even though he knew his brother probably wouldn't get the message or respond. But at least it helped him feel like he was doing something to keep his brother safe over there.

Right now, he had to do something to help himself—convince Clara to do the debate. He checked the art room and the computer lab. She usually worked on extra projects in one of these places at lunchtime, but no luck now.

On his way to the cafeteria, he took out his phone and fast-clicked a photo Lucas had sent—a shot of him with other soldiers, all smiling and dressed in camouflage. Probably new friends. Lucas looked different than before, kind of built up. He probably worked out a lot now. The last time the two of them had horsed around in the backyard, Lucas was thinner.

The memory brought instant thoughts to mind—all the things he wished he'd said to Lucas before his brother had left, like thanks for teaching him to ski and snowboard and for showing him winning basketball moves. Jamie wished he'd told Lucas that he was the coolest person he knew and how he tried to live by his sayings. Like, "Honesty is your friend."

To be honest, Jamie had to think hard about that one. He figured he was mostly honest, but when he thought about all the times when he didn't tell people what was really in his head, he began to wonder. Or when he joked around. He wasn't sure if that had anything to do with being honest.

He liked another one of Lucas's sayings and could almost hear Lucas telling him, "Believe in who you are." It sounded so positive. Lucas believed in who he was. Jamie thought he believed in who he was, but right now, he was juggling so many balls he wasn't sure of anything. Or what he believed in. Or who.

He thought of Dad's words in the car: *"If you don't start focusing on your schoolwork, you're never going to amount to anything."* He didn't want to believe that. And he didn't like recalling the rest of Dad's message about doing something worthwhile and then saying Jamie's days on the team were over. They wouldn't be over if he did a good job on the debate. Now if only Clara would cooperate.

She wasn't in the cafeteria, so he peeked into some classrooms. Finally, he ducked into the library, which was empty except for Miss Britten at her desk. She smiled, probably to make him feel welcome, but he didn't. He hardly ever went in there. He checked all around the room until he spotted Clara at a table piled high with papers and books.

"Clara. Hey!"

Clara glanced at Miss Britten, then made a face at him. She whispered, "What do you want? I can't believe you got us into all that trouble."

"Me?" he said, loudly. "You must be joking."

"Shhhh," she whispered again. "You're not supposed to talk out loud here."

Jamie laughed. "Like we're not supposed to in class?" She didn't show even a hint of a smile at his joke. "So what are we going to do?"

Clara gave him a questioning look, as if she didn't know what he was talking about. "We?" She closed the book she was reading, placed the ones she'd been using on a library cart, and gathered her papers. "I have to be somewhere in five minutes." She walked off, and Jamie followed her out to the hallway that was filled with kids going back to class after lunch.

Clara walked fast, and Jamie hurried to keep up with her, trying to get his words out. "Look, Clara, I don't want to do the dumb debate either," he began. "But we—I—have to or I'll . . ." He didn't want to say "fail" but he could tell Clara knew that's what would happen. Dad's words, *"You'll never amount to anything,"* echoed as he walked.

He summoned a bit of courage and blurted, "I need to pull up my science grade, Clara. You could make that happen by doing the debate."

Clara stopped for a few seconds but didn't say a word. Her face was scrunched up, like she was figuring out how to say something he didn't want to hear. Then she moved to the side to let kids pass. Her hands went to her hips. Yep. Time for a lecture.

"Jamie, listen to me. You can't expect me to make that happen—pull up *your* science grade just because you let your work slide all year. I'm counting on a good grade in science, and I've worked hard for it. It could make all the difference in my future too. I know about hurricanes from personal experience, and my project is settled, or it *was* before Mr. J yelled at us because you said all those ridiculous things about Tambora."

"They're not ridiculous." Jamie scratched his head as if that would clear his thinking. She had a point about her topic. Hurricanes were important to her, but he couldn't give in. "Look, I can't help it if you don't agree with me. You said things back to me too, but you don't even think you're in trouble like I am. Maybe you aren't. I don't think Mr. J specifically told you that your grade might be lower if you didn't debate me. He sure told me. I *have* to do the debate, and with you, because we were the ones Mr. J yelled at. He said there would be extra credit for good work. That could make a big difference for me. Maybe for you too."

Clara's jaw tightened. He knew that look; it meant she'd had enough. He readied himself for another speech.

"I'm not arguing any more, Jamie, or changing my mind just because you only think about yourself and how you can have fun with your . . . your . . . childish obsession. And how you impulsively blurt out things that are ridiculous." She seemed out of breath, but that didn't stop her. "One project won't make up for a whole year of . . ." She stopped, then crinkled her brow like she'd just thought of something else. "Why do you wait till the last minute to do things?"

Jamie shrugged. "I try . . . a little." He smiled in another attempt to lighten the conversation. He couldn't help himself, and he thought it might work. Clara's mouth turned up a little, so he kept up the joking. "Then I get bored and think about something else that's fun."

"But that can't help your grade, and *I* can't help your grade either. I don't need extra credit, Jamie." Clara's hands covered her face. She rubbed her eyes. "The real reason I have to do hurricanes is because my dad is in Puerto Rico right now, helping to rebuild after all the damage from Hurricane María." She stopped and shook her head like she considered him hopeless. She lowered her voice. "You probably don't even know about that hurricane, either. Just like you didn't know about the one that just struck the Bahamas. These storms are a big deal, Jamie. People lose everything, even their lives."

Jamie stopped moving and looked straight into Clara's eyes. "Whoa. I didn't know your dad was down there." For a moment, he forgot about the debate. He wanted so much to reach out and take Clara's hand. He clasped his hands behind his back instead. "How cool that he's repairing people's houses. Lucky people. They must be really glad to have him there."

Clara nodded. "We have a lot of friends and relatives who stayed even though their houses were destroyed. María really was a disaster. She took everything we had. So we're starting over— here. But my mom, my little brother, and I worry about my father every moment."

Fear clouded her face, and Jamie regretted causing her worry.

"I mean it, Jamie. Anything could happen while he's down there. You can never tell when. Maybe we'll never see him again." Her voice shook, and she swiped at the tear that ran down her cheek.

He felt his own tears welling up at Clara's wobbly words, "never see him again." He cleared his throat to get a grip, but the tears brought on the stuff of his nightmares: Lucas crouching under dusty brush, bombs exploding around him, and tanks moving away, leaving him behind. "Hurry! They're leaving you. You have to get up. Go now!" Jamie always woke up screaming. Most nights he hated to fall asleep. He didn't want the nightmares.

He told himself over and over that Lucas wasn't out in combat. He was at the base. He was safe. But the nightmares still came.

He forced away the thought that he might never see his brother again and turned his attention back to Clara. He was surprised, almost shocked, that she had told him all that personal stuff about her family. He wished that he'd known before. Maybe he wouldn't have said what he had about disasters. But he had, and now they—or he—was in this mess. He wanted to tell her how alike they were, both scared they'd never see someone they loved again and both storing memories they wanted to forget. He had the urge to ask her if she ever got nightmares and was about to when she started talking again.

"So I have to do my hurricane project—for Papi." She shrugged. "It's probably superstitious to think this, but if I learn all about Hurricane María, maybe my dad will come home sooner."

Jamie nodded. He'd missed his chance to tell her something important, about Lucas being in danger every day too, but maybe another time. He had another important goal now. "I'd let you do hurricanes if I were Mr. Jennings." He quickly thought better of that and changed the subject. "Even though I really need your help with Tambora. I can't stop thinking about your dad down there. He sounds amazing, such a good person to go down there when it's dangerous and messed up."

"Yes. When we left, there were power lines down all over, houses with no roofs, and roofs with no houses. I couldn't recognize my neighborhood." Clara glanced at the big clock on the wall. "I'm late. I have to meet with a counselor."

Jamie followed her. "Clara—"

She kept walking. Probably didn't hear him over the noise as kids headed to class. Molly and two other girls from their class passed by staring at Clara and him. He'd noticed that Molly had been giving Clara the silent treatment for the past few months, but he wasn't sure why. He guessed Molly's remark in class that he would win the debate had been meant for Clara, who'd looked hurt. Maybe he should have said something to make her feel better, that Molly was just being stupid, which is what he thought.

He caught up to Clara and called out over the noise, "Mr. J told me that if I didn't do the debate, he'd call my dad and tell him I'd probably fail science."

Clara made a quick turn to him, her face a big frown. "Jamie, why are you telling me all this? I don't have time to talk now." She hurried along, but he kept up with her as she zigzagged through the crowd.

"Sorry, Clara. But I have to tell you." She was going to think him even more selfish, but he had to say it. "Mr. J called my dad over break. He actually called him while we were on vacation. Up in Vermont. That's pretty serious." Jamie shook his head as he recalled the scene on the mountain. "I failed the exam. My dad ended our vacation early. I was home all that weekend doing nothing. And now I'm the one in trouble for you and me talking in class."

Clara stopped again as if she was considering, then shook her head. "See you later." She walked off even faster.

Jamie stood in the middle of the hallway and watched her go, trying to imagine what she was thinking. When she glanced back, he gave a small wave. She rushed off without waving back.

Jamie wandered to the first empty classroom, stepped inside, and leaned against the wall to steady himself. His knotted-up guts made him double over. He'd tried, but Clara wouldn't help him. His efforts? Hopeless.

Lucas could tell him what to do if he were here. Jamie's heart raced faster than his future playing out in his mind. He would fail science. Maybe social studies too. Not math. Still, he'd have to repeat eighth grade. All his friends would be gone. Dad would be furious. Mom, sad. Lucas? Jamie didn't know what, maybe disappointed. His dry throat needed water. He staggered when he took a step, but he inhaled some air, then forced himself to stand up straight and rubbed his sweaty hands together. He'd made it this far.

He closed his eyes. If only he could take off down a slope, a really steep one, and forget about the debate, Dad's words, grades, and natural disasters. He could almost feel the crisp air on his face as he sped away from his problems. On the slopes he always managed just fine. At home and in school, he just couldn't seem to find his rhythm.

Chapter Eight

Passing clouds

*A*t home after school, Clara fought to erase the image of Jamie's little wave to her in the hallway as she rushed away from him. She tried Papi's phone again. Nothing. She tried Aunt Beatriz in San Juan. No service. She vowed not to give up. Recalling how Papi often took her to different places in Albany to get to know it, she decided to pretend they were still exploring. She put on her sweatpants, running shoes, and a light jacket. A whole hour before Diego got home was plenty of time. She grabbed her phone and took off. Jogging on nearby trails was an easy way to learn more about a popular outdoor space and get some exercise at the same time. She headed for Washington Park. In the springtime, she'd bring Mami and Diego for walks there. Papi would be happy to know they were getting used to lots of places in Albany too.

She thought about other ways she was helping her family. It was lucky that she'd found the babysitting job, even if she only worked once or twice a week. She loved buying little extras for Diego and Mami and even herself.

When she had more time, she'd spend it at the Thurbers'. Mrs. Thurber said she would teach her how to make those really good vanilla iced cookies and maybe show her some yoga poses. Clara knew a little about yoga because it was big in Puerto Rico, but she'd never imagined herself doing it. Now she pictured herself in a leotard like Mrs. Thurber, practicing the poses. She would see Gus and Mrs. Thurber on Saturday. Maybe she'd get to meet Mr. Thurber then. It was curious that Mrs. Thurber never mentioned him. Neither did Gus.

As she ran through the park, she noticed so many people out walking or sitting on benches. Even though it was still winter, it felt like summer. Jamie and his juvenile ideas about snow in June came to mind. The sun was shining brightly at three twenty, and there was no sign of snow anywhere. Only the bare tree branches hinted that it wasn't spring. It was all pretty strange, considering what she knew about New York weather.

Other joggers passed her. Some waved. How friendly. She waved back and remembered something else nice, running on the beach in her bare feet in Puerto Rico. Her mind quickly switched without warning to people running away from Hurricane Ariel and its roar on the TV. She ran faster to get away from that thought, but memories of María ran with her. She sped up to outrun them. She couldn't get stressed out again. It hurt too much.

She stopped running and, for the first time, allowed herself to see that her trauma had traveled with her all the way from Puerto Rico. María might never leave. She stretched and took in the fresh air. If only she could mentally send the memories back where they belonged. It would take time.

She jogged in place, trying to decide whether to use a few more minutes to keep going or head for home. A girl jogged toward her. Clara narrowed her eyes. Molly. Clara couldn't believe it. She froze. What would Molly say after seeing her with Jamie in the hallway today? Part of her wanted to take off but she forced herself to hold her ground.

"Clara. Hi." Molly sounded surprised to see her too. She came to a stop and caught her breath. "I didn't know you jogged."

"Um . . . yeah. When I can. I don't have a lot of free time."

"I can imagine, with your big debate coming up," Molly said. She leaned over, hands on her knees. "Poor Jamie seemed all stressed out. He really has no idea how to do one."

Clara wished she had taken off when she'd had the urge, but another impulse kept her sneakers in place. "You're right, Molly. Neither of us knows how to do a debate, but we'll figure it out. You heard the kids in class yelling, 'Debate, debate!' so we have no choice." She didn't remind Molly that she'd been one of the loudest yelling. And she didn't tell Molly that she hadn't even decided to do the debate.

She'd try to end this on a good note. She still wanted to be friends with Molly, who could be really kind, just not lately. "I still remember how nice you were to me when I just arrived. I never thanked you for including me in your friends' group. You made me feel like I fit in. I'd never moved schools before, so I didn't know what to expect. I hope other new kids get a first friend like you."

Molly smiled. "Yeah, we were good friends, weren't we?"

The lazy way Molly drew circles in the dirt with her foot hinted to Clara that Molly wished they were still like that, but she suddenly stopped drawing. Her smile turned into a smirk.

"But you didn't know how it was with Jamie and me before you came." She put two fingers together. "That close. I know why you like him. He was nice to you on your first day, and so now you think he still likes you. But that's how he is . . . friendly." She locked eyes with Clara. Molly's were steely. "You can't hold on to how he was that first day. He's nice to everybody. Especially me. Or he was before you got here."

Clara's hopes that they might become friends again disappeared. Molly could be kind, but she could also be awfully cruel. Obviously, she considered Clara her competition, not her friend.

"I have to go," Clara said. Before Molly could say anything more, Clara turned and ran toward the park exit. How foolish of her to try again for friendship with Molly.

Running feet sounded behind her as Molly caught up.

"You're just like her. You leave and never let me finish," Molly accused.

Clara stopped walking, "Who? Who am I like?"

Molly ignored her question at first, then blurted, "My mother! She grounded me for getting a C minus on my math test. You could have helped me get a better grade just by giving me a few answers."

Bewildered by Molly's breakdown, Clara said, "That was months ago. Cheating is wrong. I could have gotten into a lot of trouble. You too."

Molly's jaw tightened. She blew out a big breath. "Forget it. You wouldn't understand. She keeps saying she's leaving or we're leaving. To get a new start. I never know from one day to the next. I don't even care anymore."

Clara reached for Molly's hands and held them tightly even though Molly struggled to get free. Then her hands went limp. "I know. Parents are hard. They want the best for us, but it's impossible to see that sometimes because they have problems too. I'm sorry you have to go through all that."

For a brief moment Molly seemed to soften. Clara hoped that her words might have offered some support. But then Molly's eyes filled with a harsh meanness that made Clara shiver.

"Jamie was better before you came. You confuse him." Molly turned and ran off.

Shaken, Clara watched her disappear. She had tried to be Molly's friend and listen.

As she made her way out of the park, she couldn't wait to see Mami when she got home from work. She'd hug her extra tight and maybe even answer her in Spanish.

Diego got home five minutes after Clara did. His jacket poked out of his backpack. "It's so hot. Isn't it still winter here?"

"It is, but it feels more like February in Puerto Rico. Remember all our trips to the mountains for cool air?" Clara placed dishes of rice pudding on the table and tried to put Molly out of her mind while she was with her brother.

Diego nodded as he dug in. "And remember the *piraguas* we used to buy on the beach?" he asked after the first spoonful. "My favorite was grape."

With a mouthful too, Clara nodded. "I loved the piña and cherry." She remembered slurping the shaved ices they bought from the men pushing the colorful *piragueros* around El Morro, the old castle where her family liked to stroll together. "Maybe we'll find ices here in the summer. They might have other flavors."

She took their scraped clean dishes to the sink vowing to try new ones too, like black currant or blueberry, jams she'd tasted here for the first time. She'd be fulfilling her promise to Papi to adapt to new things now that they were in a new place.

"Come on," she said to Diego. "Adventure time."

They headed toward the animal shelter that she sometimes passed on the longer way home from school. A service project, never far from Clara's thoughts, might not be so difficult. The shingle or brick houses they passed looked kind of drab. In old San Juan, bright colored houses like Easter eggs lined the streets. She'd never decided on her favorite color, turquoise or pink. She wondered what Diego remembered about their sandy beige house that had been destroyed. It had always reminded her of the sunny beach nearby. She wasn't sure why she was remembering all these things from their old life right now. Maybe it had something to do with running into Molly and how hard and different things were here.

As she passed tall sticks with branches trying to be trees, she couldn't help comparing them to the majestic palm trees with breezy tops swaying. In Puerto Rico she could always smell the sea, no matter where they were. Everything was nearby: bodegas, restaurants, clothing stores, parks, friends' houses. The closest water to them here was probably the Hudson River she'd read about, but she couldn't smell it. One day she'd stand near that river and maybe even feel at home here.

Enough comparing. Nothing was the same anymore.

She glanced at Diego, who walked alongside her, probably carrying none of these memories. She missed that freedom but then thought about it. Of course, Diego had memories too. He'd loved their neighborhood in Ocean Park and walking on the beach slurping ices. He seemed okay with where he was today, though, not like her, wanting to bring back yesterday or worrying about tomorrow. She shook herself back to now and squeezed her wise little brother's hand tighter.

On Chambers Street they passed by business buildings and stores and then reached the pet shelter. A girl wearing a badge that said "Dora" welcomed them. Clara inquired about doing a service project with the animals.

"Oh, great. There'll be plenty to do here in the summer. That's when we can use extra hands."

Before Clara could ask about doing the service now, Diego spoke up. "What do extra hands do?"

Dora moved out from behind her desk and told them to follow her. "Dog pens need to be cleaned."

He made a face. "Ewww."

Dora laughed. "The animals love extra hands for petting and feeding them. And walking them."

"I'd walk the dogs," Diego said, and a bolt of excitement ran through Clara at her brother's independent spirit. Diego kneeled in front of each cage. "Awww." He couldn't bear to leave a kitten that meowed or cocked its head.

They could barely tear themselves away from the animals because they seemed like old friends now. Dora told Clara to come back in June and they could set up a schedule. Clara thanked her, knowing that would be too late.

On their way home, her phone pinged. She pulled it out of her pocket—a text from Mrs. Thurber. "Just checking on the chance you have any free time to babysit Gus. He misses you. Call when you can."

She closed her phone and glanced at Diego, kicking a balled-up newspaper in front of him soccer style. Diego was in the moment as usual, while she worried about Papi far away and Mami, working so hard, dealing with the debate issue, starting her Hurricane María report, and completing her requirements for the scholarship *if* she could find a service project in time. Homework and helping out at home didn't even count. She did these things naturally. Where could she find even one hour of free time to babysit Gus?

———

At home, she got Diego started on his homework, then sat in front of her computer without lifting a finger. Thoughts of arguing with Jamie came back. Papi would be disappointed if he knew her teacher had warned her about disrupting class. Her stomach knotted. Jamie was probably right. She had caused the trouble too. And of course, she'd heard Mr. J say, "It's up to you about the debate, Clara, to decide if you're willing to put hurricanes aside."

"It's up to you" stuck in her mind. Sure, she was trying to protect her grade, but was refusing to do the debate fair to Jamie? Molly's accusations kept coming to mind. But they weren't true. She had nothing to do with how Jamie was doing, before she arrived or after.

Clara's fingers rested on the keys. She stared at her screen-saver, two palm trees on a beach. She'd chosen it to remember what Papi had said before he left, that she and Diego were like the two tall palms in the front yard of their house in Puerto Rico. His two palm trees, Clara and Diego, would always stand strong together. Had one tree—Clara—fallen with this little incident in class? Even minimizing her part in it didn't help.

Clara had vowed to make Papi proud: to be strong, to set a good example for Diego, and to excel in school. She had stood up for her opinions in class but now wondered if that determination had landed her in this situation.

She couldn't bear to think of herself as a student who caused trouble. She pictured Jamie's face when he'd tried to convince her to work with him on the debate. He'd looked a little like Diego, desperately trying to hold tears back during the hurricane. Her throat burned at the thought. Jamie couldn't even say the word *fail* at first when he tried to joke her into doing the debate. And when he said all those kind things about Papi, she'd almost hugged him. Instead, she'd pushed those sentimental weaknesses aside. No time for them. But a nagging thought that she'd abandoned him in the hallway hung over her. She blew out a breath full of disappointment and sadness and maybe a tiny bit of determination that must have been waiting deep inside to break out.

Her fingers came to life on the keyboard. Her right forefinger rested next to the letter H but wouldn't move, wouldn't type the word *hurricanes.* That must mean that she couldn't take in any more information about them. The instant relief had to be a sign. When her left finger tapped the T, and the image of Jamie begging her to help him not fail crossed the page, she knew she was seeing things she was meant to see. Maybe she *could* help him.

She typed the word that they had fought over. Just seven little letters: Tambora.

> *In the spring and summer of 1816, a persistent "dry fog" in parts of the eastern United States reddened and dimmed the sunlight. Dramatic temperature swings were common with above normal temperatures as high as 95 F, dropping to near freezing within hours.*

Today in the park it was sixty degrees, and it was only the end of February. But Molly might have raised Clara's temperature a few degrees with her warning about Jamie. She kept reading but still couldn't imagine how the weather had changed simply because a volcano had erupted and spread ash. She could see why Jamie was so interested in the mystery. He could easily write up a report on Tambora and get a good grade. She wished she had kept her opinion to herself and hadn't told him what he'd said was ridiculous. She could have prevented this whole debate issue. Jamie had a right to express his opinion too, even though it wasn't very constructive to say good things had come from Tambora. Still, disrupting class made her as much to blame as Jamie. She sat with this thought for a few minutes.

She had to put aside hopes of turning in a hundred-percent perfect report on María. It might have earned her a good recommendation from Mr. J for the Academy scholarship and maybe even a chance of being class speaker at graduation. Molly was aiming for speaker too. She couldn't control what Molly did, though, or what Jamie did either. He would certainly put all his hopes into winning the debate. Thoughts rushed through her mind, crashing into each other like a hurricane: Jamie, Papi, Molly, María memories, her future.

She glanced back at Tambora. "Failed harvests in Britain and Ireland, begging for food, riots, arson, looting, the worst famine of nineteenth-century Europe."

She wondered what Jamie would say about these terrible things if he could concentrate on them for two seconds and not ramble about all the good that had come from Tambora. He had to convince the class that anything good could outweigh the bad and hold up his part of the debate so he wouldn't fail science. She could almost hear him trying to do this with his cool information and jokes.

Spicy Puerto Rican aromas filling the kitchen gave her strength. She knew exactly who she was in her little house with Mami and Diego. She breathed in the strong scents again for confidence to hold onto that strength.

As hard as she tried, she couldn't get the picture out of her mind—Jamie begging for her help, then following her like that puppy he reminded her of. She still told herself this whole thing wasn't *her* problem. Yes, it was. No. Yes. She hated to be confused, and she wouldn't be if Jamie weren't part of the confusion. It was his fault. She wasn't impulsive like he was. Well, maybe a little. She checked the time. Just after seven. She pushed aside the muddled thoughts clouding her mind. She knew a lot about herself and sat uneasily with that thought. Once she had decided something, her mind was set.

She picked up her phone. She wanted Jamie to really get what she was saying so she typed the words out instead of texting slang. "Hi, maybe you could ski or snowboard if you'd lived back in 1815, but you had better find more convincing facts about anything that actually benefited people after the Tambora disaster IF you want to stand a chance in our debate."

A few minutes passed. Then, *ping.*

"Wow! That's great. You're the best, Clara. I could tell you a lot of things about Tambora that actually did help people, but I'd better keep the facts to myself until I need them. See you tomorrow. Hey, thanks for texting. You're really amazing, but I hope you're ready for this!"

Clara stared at the text. She smiled at the word amazing. The rest was so Jamie, always ready for competition. She was too. And he was doing what he wanted—debating. But would she deprive him of the grade he needed by beating him?

Chapter Nine

Strong winds

*S*unday afternoon Jamie wasn't on a slope that he could master. He was in his bedroom, at his computer, digging out facts for the debate tomorrow, his only chance of passing science.

His phone pinged. "Dude TeamPzza Wedgs at 6."

Pizza at Wedges. Great. Seeing the guys on the team would take his mind off the debate. He stared at his screen, tapping his foot, weighing going out and having some fun versus going over his notes for the millionth time. Argh! He blew out a puffy breath. He had to focus. Rehearse. Have all his facts lined up. Be ready to speak up and persuade.

He'd done that all afternoon. He deserved a break. Who worked for two weeks straight on any assignment? He had. He grabbed the papers he'd printed out for Dad about credit. Dad would be so impressed that he'd dug out all this great information. Jamie couldn't wait to hand it to him and see his face light up.

He passed Mom at her desk. "Going out for pizza with some of the guys, okay?"

She looked up. "Sure. Ready for your debate?"

"Totally, Mom. Can't wait."

He must not have sounded convincing because Mom cocked her head the way she did when she wasn't sure of something. "I'm glad you can't wait." She went back to looking like good old Mom again. "Wish I could be there."

"Naw. You don't want to do that, Mom. You'd be bored by a bunch of eighth graders arguing, or I guess I should say debating. See you in a while." He glanced in the den for Dad. Not there. Credit could wait till later. He laid the papers aside.

As he passed the garage, the door was halfway up. He ducked under. Dad was bent over Lucas's motorcycle, polishing it. "Hey, Dad."

"Jamie." Dad stood and surveyed his work. "Yeah. Have to keep it in shape."

"Looks great," Jamie said, amazed that Dad would even touch the cycle. "Lucas will be glad you're taking care of it."

Dad huffed. "Well, I told him not to buy it, but he didn't listen. Now we're stuck with it. I hope he sells it when he gets home."

"Yeah, right." Jamie figured he shouldn't say anything else, like maybe Lucas would want to ride it again. "Be right back, Dad. I forgot something." He ran to the house, grabbed his credit printout and sprinted back to the garage. "Hey Dad, did you ever ride a motorcycle? Maybe in the army?"

"I did, Jamie. But it was just to get around short distances."

"Did you like riding it?"

"It was part of my job. Not joyriding." He gave another rub to the front fender.

Jamie tried to think fast before Dad got more critical. "Maybe when Lucas comes home, he'll take you for a ride. You can both—"

"Jamie. Enough. He's not home, and I don't want to talk about what we're going to do when he is." He gave Jamie the look that always ended the conversation.

"Um . . . yeah. Got it." Definitely time to change the subject.
"So, I'm just going out for some pizza. . . . Oh, yeah. I have my
information on credit if you want to—"

"You're going out now?" Dad's forehead wrinkled. "On a
school night?"

"I won't be long. I worked on my project all day and—"

Dad went back to gentle polishing, but he boomed, "One
hour. Hear?"

"Dad, I'll try. I don't know if—"

"You heard me," Dad repeated in a sharper tone. "One hour."

"Yes, sir," Jamie said, soldier answering his superior. All the
excitement over giving Dad the credit printout drained out of him.
He slid the papers under his jacket with a selfish bit of satisfaction
that he could withhold something from Dad. He considered that
for a second and recognized his childish response. He needed to
convince Dad he was trying in school, so he pulled the papers back
out. "I printed that article about credit for you. Want to see it?"

Dad stopped polishing and took the papers. "Sure. I'd like to
see what you read that got you so excited." Dad scanned the first
page right there in the garage, holding a greasy rag in his other
hand. "I'm glad to read this, Jamie, but don't spend so much time
on things"—he waved the papers—"that don't have to do with
your science grade."

"Dad. This *is* science. And it has everything to do with my
grade. I'm describing how credit worked during a natural disaster
tomorrow in my debate."

Dad nodded, laid the credit papers on the tool shelf, and got
back to polishing.

"I gotta go." Jamie moved away fast before Dad could have
second thoughts about his going out and before they got into
another argument. Why couldn't Dad be just a little like Mom—
on his side, even once?

When he got to Wedges, Nick, Pete, Max and Burly were piling into a booth. Jamie took an end seat and fist-bumped the guys. "Man, I so needed this break."

Burly asked Ricky, their regular waiter, for extra everything on two large pies, and they all pounced on the garlic knots as soon as the basket landed on the table.

Nick grabbed Burly's big hand as he reached out for a second one. "Hey. Slow down, Burl. We have two more Alpines. Gotta keep your weight down to race. And then state team tryouts. We need you, man."

Jamie laughed and almost choked on his mouthful. Making the state team was his goal too. Tryouts were a long shot for him, though, even though they were ten months away. He'd need lots of makeup practice if he didn't finish out the season. "So does Coach have the lineup for the next competition?"

"Guess we're all in," Nick said. "Except Chuck's history. He's moving, so that's one man down."

Jamie stopped chewing. "Whoa. I didn't know that. Where's he going?"

He hardly listened to Nick's answer. He was picturing the team list in Coach's office. Coach had probably circled Chuck's name because he'd be gone. And Jamie's name because he'd be gone too. Except *he* wasn't going anywhere.

The laughs, burps, and jokes went on around him, but his thoughts were somewhere else. Coach would need all the best racers, and he was one of them. Maybe he still had a chance. Maybe the debate would get things back to normal. All he had to do was be great tomorrow. He huffed. Was he kidding? All he had to do was not stress out, not throw up. That thought brought him back to the table. He wouldn't blow it. He'd prepared. Proof: he was here with the guys because he was ready, wasn't he? Yep. He knew his stuff. But could he get it out at the right time? Clara would, for sure. Suddenly the garlic knots he'd gobbled up felt like a big stone in his belly.

Someone touched his shoulder and interrupted the argument he was having in his head. "Hey, guys. Hi, Jamie." Molly stood next to him. Three other girls from class crowded around the booth and smiled down at the guys.

Jamie glanced up, gave a small wave. He was still breathing hard from all his thoughts about tomorrow. He'd put himself in a terrible mood. And now this.

The other guys mumbled hi and nodded.

"We ordered Cokes. We'll just squeeze in, okay?" Molly perched on the corner of the leather seat next to him. She pulled her phone out, held it in front of the two of them, and clicked.

Jamie reached for it. "Stop it, Molly. Delete that."

She stood up fast. "Nope." She glanced impatiently around the restaurant. "Where are our Cokes?"

Jamie slid out of the seat and glared at his classmate. "Hand it over, Molly. No fair taking pictures without asking first." He didn't want to be in a picture with her or be anywhere near her. Molly meant trouble. The guys would probably say she was hot in her tight jeans. She was okay looking, with long blond hair and eyes that switched between blue and gray-green, depending on her outfit. But he preferred girls with dark hair. Molly would be considered cool if she weren't so snarky mean. Like when she said he'd win the debate but didn't care if she hurt Clara's feelings. And she was supposed to be Clara's friend. Or she used to be. That was so messed up.

Molly was still laughing. "It's just a selfie. Everybody takes them." She held her phone behind her. "I was just trying to be friendly." She turned to her friends. "Let's get our own booth— more room. Come say bye before you leave, Jamie."

She flipped her hair with her hand, moved away fast, and bumped into Ricky, who swerved as he balanced two big pies. He slid them onto the table and the guys' hands landed. Cheese strings stretched like spider webs as they pulled apart the slices. Ricky returned with drinks and a ton of napkins.

Burly shook his head. "Girls. What a pain." The other guys laughed.

"Speaking of pain, I'm sure glad my project's done," Nick said. "I know more about avalanches than I ever wanted to. Never want to be caught in one of those whiteouts." He turned to Jamie. "You done with your debate thing? How does it work, anyhow?"

Jamie shrugged. "I'm not sure it *will* work. I just want to get it over with. The rest of the year too. What a bummer."

"Hey, man," Pete said, "how's your brother over there?" He waved his hand like "over there" was somewhere out in cyberspace. "Must be tough on your parents. You too."

"Yeah," Jamie mumbled. Nobody here could even have an idea of how tough it was. "We don't get much news. Got a couple of letters. I mostly follow what's going on over there online." He didn't want to answer any more questions. It was his fault though for coming. He should have stayed home, worked some more on his presentation.

"How long's he there for?" Pete asked.

Jamie shook his head. He had to answer. The guys leaned in to hear like they needed to know too. "No idea. It's a nightmare for all of us. He signed up one day and"—he snapped his fingers—"just like that, he was off to war." The words stuck in his throat, making him cough. He couldn't say any more about Lucas. "My dad was really bummed out. And that's all mixed up because he enlisted too. A long time ago, though. He was in Iraq. I guess when you're seventeen, you do things that don't make sense later."

The guys nodded and stopped eating for a few seconds. He felt their respect for Lucas and him too.

Nick shook his head. "Stupid war. We've been in Afghanistan since 9/11. Our whole lives fit into that space. Why are we still there?"

Jamie huffed. "That's what I'd like to know."

Max tossed his slice onto the pizza box like he didn't agree. "We're over there to wipe out the terrorists. That's why."

Burly snickered. "You wouldn't know a terrorist if you saw one. They wear regular clothes just like the other people there. I saw a special on TV. Really scary. Our soldiers are patrolling the streets loaded down with all their heavy gear and everybody around them looks like they're out shopping or just sitting around. And they all wear those long skirts and wrap their heads in big scarves. You can't tell a terrorist from anybody else."

"You'd know a terrorist if your chopper got shot down by a missile," Pete retorted. "Except you wouldn't be alive to see what the terrorists look like. If you survived, and you probably wouldn't, there'd be a terrorist with an AK-47 in your face."

Jamie winced and tossed his pizza crust down.

Pete kept talking, oblivious to his friend's sinking mood. "Even when our guys are in armored Humvees, they can get blown up by driving over a homemade bomb. They're all over the place. Boom!" He threw up his hands.

"Those are IEDs," Burly said. "Improvised explosive devices. You're right; they're deadly. And they're everywhere. I wouldn't enlist. No way am I getting blown up."

Jamie hit the table. "Hey, you guys. Shut up! Lucas isn't getting blown up."

Everybody got quiet. His stomach muscles tightened. Had he overreacted? Too late to worry.

He sat in the silence all around till he couldn't any longer. "Sorry." He pushed his plate away. "Lost my appetite."

Pete pointed to the empty pizza box. "Yeah, we all did."

They laughed a little too loudly, probably to rid the air of discomfort they couldn't handle.

They split the bill and headed for the door. Jamie looked for another way out but couldn't avoid passing by the girls' booth. He didn't want to give Molly a chance to snap another photo. So many signs that night said he definitely shouldn't have come. He didn't need all that talk about war and stupid trouble from Molly. He'd have nightmares for sure and be a wreck tomorrow.

As he passed by the girls' booth, Molly reached out to wave. Jamie veered around her hand and stopped in his tracks. Anger raged inside of him. Against Molly, against the war in Afghanistan, against his dad, and against himself.

"Don't be stupid, Molly," he snapped. "Why are you always causing trouble for people? You'd better stop it. You're doing a lot of damage." The word *disaster* came to mind, but he held back.

The guys were bunched up at the door, waiting for him. Katy and the other two girls in the booth were slumped down, probably trying to get out of his range, but he spoke to them directly.

"How can you be friends with this person who is so mean and destroys friendships by saying . . . saying . . . you know what I mean. She yells out who she's for in class, and it's not fair, and it makes people—Clara—feel like nobody." He grabbed his head with both hands to calm down. "Clara's new. She wants friends." He turned back to Molly. "You were her friend for like, for a week, then you dumped her. That's so mean and unfair, Molly. Clara's the smartest person in our class and is always ready to help someone. I'm glad she's here."

Molly's mouth was wide open. Jamie couldn't tell whether she was in shock or about to shout at him. He didn't wait to find out.

Outside, he and his friends fist-bumped. That always brought them back to normal even when things weren't. "That was cool, man," Nick said. The others probably hadn't expected that outburst from him. Jamie knew they thought of him as their always-joking snowboarding pal. Now he was explosive. They nodded to him in support, he figured, and then took off in different directions.

Jamie walked with Burly, who lived near him. The team spirit stayed with him all the way, as did his relief after telling Molly off. Calm felt so much better than anger. The cold air refreshed everything. Jamie blew warm breath on his fisted hands, pretending he was up on a slope where the cold never mattered.

Burly turned down his street. "See ya."

As Jamie waved, his phone pinged. Clara. He read the text. "Out partying? And selfie-ing? You must be super ready for tomorrow. If not, you can ask your friend Molly for help. I only agreed to do 'your' debate so you could pass science." There was a sad emoji at the end.

Jamie stared at the screen. He let out a yelp and smacked his palm with his fist. Stupid, stupid Molly. How could she do that? He raised his phone to crash it to the ground, then stopped in midair. Destroying his phone wouldn't help. Clara had the photo. She had to know that he'd never agree to a selfie with Molly. He glanced at the text again, said a few words Mom wouldn't like, then raised his phone again. He had to break something. Common sense kept interfering. Clara was right. She was helping him pass science, saving him. How could he have let this happen? He thought Clara knew that he liked her a lot, and he'd had a few hints that she liked him too. Now what was she thinking of him? He could call her and try to explain. But she had the selfie right in front of her—a fact like all the facts she was probably saving for their debate tomorrow.

He wouldn't get into an argument with her tonight. That would make it impossible to be steady during the debate. He'd have to wait until after class.

———

Clara stared at the selfie on her phone. Molly and Jamie. Molly was proving that what she'd said in the park about Jamie was true. So what? She flicked away a tear and swallowed a lump of what? Sadness? Her insides collapsed. She had thought she and Jamie were friends—and maybe could be more than friends. Like at the dance this year when he'd tried so hard to keep up with her. They'd ended up almost kissing. He made her laugh in class, made her want to understand his joking personality, and made her want to help him with small assignments. Sometimes, like now, he made her want to tell him off.

She studied the selfie again. Molly's pretty smile shone. Clara didn't think of herself as pretty, not enough to be Jamie's girl-friend, but until now she had felt a little like she was. Fair skin and blue eyes like Molly's made you popular. It probably didn't even matter if Molly said mean things in class.

The longer her thoughts raged, the more Clara berated herself. Molly had said it so clearly in the park: Jamie was nice to everyone. She should have known better than to think he liked her.

Chapter Ten

Sudden drop in temperature

C lara arrived in class early. Mr. J had already printed the schedule on the whiteboard. He waved her in.

9:15–9:45: Tambora Volcanic Eruption Debate
9:50–10:20: Avalanches

Kids piled in. Jamie slid into his seat seconds before the bell rang. A packet of papers fell and scattered on the floor around him. He shot a glance at Clara as he fumbled to pick them up. She turned away. She'd never tell him this, but she wished she could be as casual as he was about everything. He seemed to breeze through life having fun, not taking anything seriously. He probably considered her a brainiac, straight-A, boring student—more than ever now that they had to argue about a volcano.

Mr. J welcomed the class to Project Natural Disasters. "We'll begin with our first debate ever in this science class. Clara and Jamie will have thirty minutes today and thirty minutes for the next two Monday mornings. Other presenters will be scheduled each morning on the whiteboard." He said he hoped the projects had shown them the benefits of research and that he looked forward to learning what they had uncovered.

Then he turned to her and Jamie. "Clara and Jamie, please take your places in front of the room and begin."

Jamie watched Clara as if he needed instructions, but she gave him no help. She walked to one end of the long table at the front of the class and placed her note cards and laptop down. Jamie moved to the other end and, with shaky hands, set his stack of papers next to him.

Clara thought the way he mimicked her was irritating. They might have talked last night about how they would begin if she hadn't gotten Molly's selfie. As usual, goofball Jamie had to go fool around with his friends right before their big debate. Mr. J was right to call him out for always disrupting the class. He was going to screw this up too. Irritation pricked her. What had she been thinking when she'd agreed to do this stupid debate? It wasn't helping her at all; she'd done it only out of pity for him! She'd never make that mistake again.

Too late now to back out. Another thought occurred to her: just because she'd agreed to debate Jamie didn't mean she couldn't defeat him. He obviously didn't care how well he did since he'd chosen to go out the day before instead of preparing. Well, she'd show him. Determined anticipation swelled as she moved her open laptop to the center of the table. It was time to put Jamie in his place.

"This morning I'll try to convince you that natural disasters are no joke," she said somberly. "Especially the Tambora volcanic eruption that occurred in—"

The classroom door burst open and Molly rushed in, books spilling from her arms. She giggled as she sprawled at her desk, as if interrupting were funny. "I had kind of an emergency at home. Nothing serious."

Kids turned to watch as she unzipped a bag, emptied the contents, and put her things away. She kept giggling as she glanced around, like she expected the whole class to wait for her to get organized. "Okay. I'm all set."

Mr. J didn't look happy, but he didn't ask for a late slip or tell her to go to the school office. He turned to Clara and nodded. "Please go on."

Clara gave one last glance at Molly to make sure she was sitting still, then tried to get her opening thoughts back. She squeezed one fist, hidden behind her back, to try to slow down her thumping heartbeat. She couldn't help wondering if Molly had actually faced an emergency, maybe with her mother, or if she were lying. But she couldn't think about that now.

"As I was saying." She composed herself to go on. "The eruption happened in 1815, here in Indonesia."

She pointed to Indonesia on a world map on her computer that projected the map onto a large screen in front of the class. Kids were leaning forward. Maybe she wasn't talking loudly enough. She cleared her throat and kept going.

"The eruption shot gas and rocks thirty miles high into the atmosphere. The lava that flowed covered people"—she paused—"and they became statues. Remember Pompeii?" She heard some gasps from the class. Molly's hand covered her mouth. Clara nodded. "Yes. Statues. Over a hundred thousand deaths occurred directly because of Tambora, and thousands more on the other side of the world too." She took a breath and stood tall. She hoped she wasn't being too dramatic, but what she was reporting had affected her. And maybe even Molly, who might be getting the message about disasters.

The class's response encouraged her to go back to the map. "The gases spread thousands of miles from here"—she moved her hand from Indonesia across the map to their home state—"all the way to New York. The ash in the atmosphere prevented the sun's rays from reaching the earth, and Jamie's famous Year Without a Summer began." Clara stepped away from her laptop. "I give the floor to my opponent."

A few claps came from the back of the classroom.

Jamie stared at her. "Um, okay. Wow. Guess I'm the opponent," he said haltingly. He ran his fingers through his hair. "Yeah. I mean, not really. I thought we were friends. Um." A few laughs broke out. Jamie scratched his head and smiled at the class.

Clara burned with irritation. It was just like him to try to joke his way out and make her the bad guy.

"I'm going to wait a few seconds, maybe a couple of minutes till my heart slows down so I won't be so nervous."

More kids laughed. Mr. J gestured for Jamie to get on with it.

"Um, okay. Here goes. I agree with Clara. Tambora wasn't a joke. People *were* killed. It was a real disaster."

Clara couldn't help noticing when he locked eyes with Nick and Max. He'd probably told them to clap or give him thumbs up for being funny. She hadn't seen any thumbs so far, but she was determined not to feel sorry for Jamie and his weak start. She recalled the selfie with Molly and that steeled her resolve.

"This morning I'll try to convince you that . . ." He glanced at her, probably to see if it were okay that he used her exact opening words.

She glared back. She wouldn't give him any help.

His confident expression faltered; he seemed uncertain. "Um, see, after Tambora, a lot of amazing things happened. There was a lot more flat land for people to farm, and the land was really fertile because volcanic ash has tons of minerals. Well, not tons, but a lot, and that makes the soil really good for crops. And another thing: volcanic rock produces lots of cool things like diamonds and gold, silver, copper, zinc, and other metals that we use every day. Makes our lives easier, right?"

"You're so right, Jamie," Molly chirped. She applauded.

Clara swallowed tastes of envy and maybe disappointment in Molly as the class laughed at her sugary encouragement. Clara wondered what Jamie was thinking.

His eyes went down to his notes. He wiped his forehead

with his arm like he was sweating but it wasn't even hot in the room. "Sure, it was bad that bodies got covered with lava, but guess what? The bodies were completely preserved, like the ones in Pompeii."

She waited but he didn't seem to dare look at her after mentioning Pompeii as she had.

"Today scientists can study them and learn stuff about the people back then." He spoke directly to her, then, as if to prove he knew his facts by heart. "And all that land in Indonesia that you pointed out, Clara, is a great tourist attraction today. People love going there to hike. So it's good for people there to be able to make a living from tourism. And that's all because of Tambora." He turned toward Mr. J again.

Clara wondered if that was helping Jamie or hurting his performance. Did Mr. J think that making eye contact every few minutes was a good technique in a debate? Should she try it?

"And this is important to note," Jamie continued. "Nobody could send out warnings about the eruption and the gases spreading because there was no way. No phones."

For a split second, Clara thought of Papi and no phone service. But she couldn't dwell on that now. She had to pay attention.

"It wasn't until sixty-eight years later, in 1883, that the world got connected by undersea cables. So people just had to live through stuff that happened without knowing anything about disasters far off."

Clara interrupted. "Yes, 'stuff' like starvation. Crops failed everywhere in the Northern Hemisphere. There were no oats, no grain for horses. Farmers in China lost all their rice. They started planting opium to make a living." She paused to let that news sink in. "Yes. Opium. And that started the drug trade."

Jamie waved his papers, probably to get attention. "Yeah, the drug trade. That wasn't good. But guess what? Since people couldn't keep horses, they had to look for other ways to get around. Did you know that, Clara?"

She swallowed. Was he challenging her? Her heart beat faster.

"Yeah," he said. "A guy in Germany invented a bicycle. Well, it was kind of like *The Flintstones*, where Fred Flintstone had to run with this machine, but eventually somebody invented pedals."

Laughs broke out. "Do you have a picture of that Flintstone bike?" Nick called out. "That's so cool."

Jamie told Nick he'd try to find one in his pages and pages of research and the class laughed again.

Clara fumed. It wasn't fair. Jamie was winning just because he was being funny. And asking her questions, simply for effect. Was that allowed? She'd like to add some humor, but Tambora wasn't a laughing matter. She had to think of something, anything that might grab her classmates' attention.

"But Jamie," she said, "all those amazing things you talked about happened long after Tambora. So they weren't that amazing. They were predictable, right? People had to cope in one way or another with all the changes brought on by the disaster's weather."

He kept his eyes on her as if trying to get back on track. "Um, yeah, maybe, but about the crops failing . . ." He paused as if he wasn't sure where he was going with this point, then waved his hand as if the answer had magically appeared. "What happened, Clara and class, was that people started to rely on neighbors, and they shared whatever they had. That's good, right? They started eating other things, like the tops of potato plants and wild pigeons and hedgehogs and . . ." He looked pleased with what he'd just said as the class moaned "ewww" and "no way."

Clara stepped forward before he could continue. "Sure, people shared with neighbors, but who could they rely on when banks failed and a financial depression set in?" She decided to go for it. "Jamie, you might not know this about your Year Without a Summer, but Europe got colder faster than America, and Europe's crops failed. They had to buy grain from American farmers, who in turn had to borrow money so they could grow enough to send over." She glanced at him. "Are you following?"

"Totally," he said and broke out in a huge smile. "Continue."

That rattled her but she did. "When Europe's weather cleared up, America's grain wasn't needed any longer, and American farmers suffered. They couldn't pay back the banks what they had borrowed on credit and eventually, the banks failed."Jamie tried to break in, but she kept talking. "Even worse, in order to survive, the farmers had to move from the northeast to places that weren't going through the Year Without a Summer."

Jamie shifted from one foot to the other as if he couldn't wait for her to finish. She nodded for him to go, pleased at how much information she had just shared. Mr. J's approving nod from the back row told her she had done well.

"Thanks, Clara," Jamie said. "I'm so glad you brought up credit because I know a little about banks. My dad works in one, so I really studied this part." He glanced at the class, probably hoping his story about his dad working in a bank would get him extra points. "Sure, people lost money during that bad weather, but at least they learned how credit worked. Actually, you just told us." He looked at his watch. "It took pretty long though." He waited for some laughs and applause.

Clara couldn't believe his performance and the way he was calling attention to her style, but he wasn't going to stop. She could see he was having too much fun—at her expense.

Jamie said, "People learned a huge lesson about credit—that climate affects business and people's lives."

She opened her mouth to speak, but he held up his hand and kept going.

"And when people moved west to get away from the bad weather, it caused the biggest real estate boom ever. Lots of farmers settled in a place that got named Indiana. That was 1815." He moved closer to the class, probably for effect. "Did you know that?" He waited for their nos to stop. "And people moved even farther, and that place got named Illinois two years later. The Year Without a Summer actually helped shape our country."

Clara was about to begin her response when Mr. J stood up. "All very interesting but in the interest of time, do both of you have a closing point for Part One of the debate?"

Clara thought fast, then stepped forward. "Yes. In Upstate New York, on June Fourth, 1816, four students walked to school barefoot. A blizzard struck without warning. School closed, and the kids had to run for their lives because the snow was up to their knees." Her classmates' gasps pleased her. "This is from a book I read called *Tambora: The Eruption That Changed the World*." She stepped back.

Jamie moved up with a big smile. He shook his head, as if he were trying to convince the class that what he was about to say, she couldn't possibly understand. "Hey, Clara. Those kids loved getting out of school that day. It probably *was* cold to run home in the snow."

He hopped up and down like one of the kids with bare feet running in the snow. He got more laughs. He hopped around some more, as if they were in a foot of snow in their classroom. She couldn't believe it.

"But that doesn't sound like a disaster, Clara. Just a cool snow day, even in June." Jamie took his place and said, "Thank you all for listening."

Clara forced a smile but inside she fumed. How dare Jamie use the information she'd researched *against* her?

The students applauded, and Mr. J did too. "Thank you both," he said. "I must say this debate is different from typical debates. Normally the two parties present their findings, then go back at allocated times and argue. You did your share of arguing but not in the most traditional way. Well, we're not formal here, so we thank you for giving us a unique debate." He paused as if he were thinking about that. "I like it. We're learning many new facts. Keep up the good work. Okay! Up next—avalanches."

Clara was still fuming as she took her seat. Mr. J didn't say anything about Jamie breaking the rules of a real debate, not sticking to his points, and, instead, making the class laugh. If those were the rules, she would get even with Jamie next week with plenty of facts about Tambora's dark and depressing influence on writers and poets. He'd mentioned the contest about writing the best horror stories but that was probably all he'd found out. *I'll show him*, she thought as she stalked out of science class.

——

She stopped at the girls' bathroom to pull herself together after that performance. Laughs reached her before the group of girls burst in. Clara ducked into a stall just in time. She couldn't face any of them right now. She sat on the toilet lid and waited.

Molly's voice rang out over the rest who were comparing lipstick shades and selfies they'd taken. "So you've all filled in your ballots, right? I'll collect them after the last so-called debate. Or you can give them to me now. It won't matter."

"How'd you think of ballots?" someone asked.

"Simple. We want Jamie to win, right? So we tell kids to vote for him."

Clara bit her lip as she listened harder.

"But the debate's not over."

"So what?" Molly said.

"But Clara's so good. She has so much information."

Clara strained to hear, but she couldn't tell who thought she was good.

"But Jamie's funny," Molly said. "So cute. And Lucy, information isn't everything."

The classroom flashed into Clara's mind. Who was Lucy? Clara didn't know all the students in class and went row by row to find Lucy. No luck.

"What if Mr. J finds out?"

"He won't," Molly said. "I'm telling everyone I give a ballot to that this is totally secret. After the debate, I'll just tell Mr. J the whole class thinks Jamie won. If he asks how I know, I might show him the—" She stopped talking.

Clara panicked. Could Molly see her feet? She slowly lifted them ever so quietly.

"I might tell him we asked everyone who they thought did the best job. But I'll have to see how it goes. I don't want to get in trouble. I'm still hoping to be class speaker, and you can all vote for me, right?"

Clara couldn't hear them nodding but could picture it. She wondered if Lucy had.

"Jamie needs to win so he can pass science and eighth grade. We all want him at the high school next year, right?"

Clara pictured the girls agreeing with Molly.

"I mean, Mr. J never said not to do it."

Clara strained to hear, but the voices got fainter and mixed up. Molly must be desperate for Jamie's affections. She waited until the door slammed to come out of hiding. Of course, Molly would convince kids to vote for Jamie. But Mr. J wouldn't accept that kind of a vote. He'd determine who had done the best job. Clara wasn't worried about Mr. J's opinion. She was definitely better prepared than Jamie. What concerned her most was his being so unaware of what was going on and how Molly ruled.

Chapter Eleven

Tremors

At lunchtime, Clara made her way to her counselor's office to settle the service project. She counted to ten over and over to calm down after the bathroom hideout. No matter how badly she wanted to, she couldn't tell her counselor or Mr. J. Kids didn't do that. How clueless she had been, taking Molly's hands and offering to help. She winced as she recalled how Molly had pulled away, accusing her of things that weren't true.

As she walked, an image of Jamie surrounded by his snowboarding buddies, laughing and patting him on the back, flashed through her mind. Molly and her two friends had applauded him too. Molly would probably coach them on more applause for the next debate.

More Jamie points for Molly. Clara pushed that thought away. She had to keep her mind on her part of the debate. It wasn't a popularity contest. Mr. J would decide in a fair way which of them had done the best job. She made a mental note to notice next week if Mr. J laughed at Jamie's joking.

In her counselor's office, she waited as Ms. Dunne went through her scholarship folder.

"It doesn't count." Ms. Dunne looked up with a knowing smile after Clara attempted to pass the debate off as a service project. Clara couldn't resist adding another cynical line that Ms. Dunne didn't get—that she was helping a person in need, her classmate, Jamie Fulton. She wondered if she had been too impulsive, kidding around just like Jamie would have about a service project. But she wasn't able to hold in her comments with everything that was happening around her. Ms. Dunne couldn't help her with those things.

Clara glanced at the sheet the counselor handed her, then at Ms. Dunne. "I didn't really think the debate would count. It was a joke." Clara could count on Jamie to laugh at her joking. "I'll try to find a project this week." So much for telling Ms. Dunne about her already full schedule.

Her phone vibrated as she stood to leave. "May I take this? It's my mother."

"Of course, Clara."

"Mami, *hola*. What? Mami, talk louder."

Clara listened as Mami shouted in her ear. "*Un terremoto! . . . terremoto!*"

"Earthquake?" Clara shook her head. "Where, Mami?"

"Puerto Rico! *En el sur*," her mother said.

"No." Clara squeezed her eyes shut to rid her of the sight of buildings rising up and people falling into holes flashing through her mind. "Papi's not in the south, Mami. *El esta en* San Juan," she shouted, mixing languages. "He's safe, isn't he? But Tita and Tito live in Guánica. That's south. Mami, *digame!* Did Papi go there? Are my grands okay? Did you talk to Papi?" She tried to swallow the panic, not let Mami hear her terror.

Mami kept saying, "*No servicio. No servicio.*"

"We'll call someone, Mami. We'll find out." Clara's voice grew louder.

Ms. Dunne pointed to her computer screen. She had a news site pulled up.

"Mami, I'll call you right back." Clara clicked off and stared at the screen.

The announcer spoke fast. "An earthquake with a magnitude of 4.9 shook southwestern Puerto Rico this morning at 4:28 a.m. local time. Aftershocks continue to shake surrounding areas. No deaths are reported, but residents are flocking to shelters. Thousands of homes have collapsed. Hard times for people here after suffering the ravages of Hurricane María just a few years ago," he ended somberly.

Clara's hands went to her face. "My grandparents live in the south. My mother doesn't know anything. I know my father. He'd go straight down there to help his mother and father." She couldn't stop watching.

The announcer signed off, but he shook his head before the screen switched to a commercial. Things must be bad.

"No deaths are reported." Clara repeated the announcer's best news to Ms. Dunne, who nodded encouragingly. "A miracle." She had to keep her hope up. "He said southwestern Puerto Rico. Did you hear if San Juan was hit?"

Ms. Dunne's forehead crinkled. "He didn't say."

In her hurry to punch in a number, Clara dropped her phone. She picked it up with shaky hands. "I'm trying my father."

Ms. Dunne nodded.

"No service." Clara tried again. "I can't get through. We haven't heard from him for weeks." She couldn't hold in her terror any longer. She rubbed her temples. *Think. Think.* Where could Papi be right now? And Tita and Tito? Crushed under a house? Swallowed by the monster earthquake? Trapped somewhere? Crashing and rumbling filled her ears. Memories. No, she warned herself. That was María. This is something else. Her hands fumbled to hold onto her phone.

Ms. Dunne put her arm around Clara. "Let's get you excused from school. Get home to your mother. I can drive you."

Ms. Dunne's smile and clear blue eyes soothed Clara for a moment. She shook her head. "It's okay. I'll walk home. It's not far. Thank you for being so kind."

As they walked down the hallway, she had to push away images of Papi being swallowed by large cracks in the earth. How fast things changed! She'd been worried about finding a service project, Molly's ballots, Jamie's grade, their debate, and who was winning. Now none of these mattered. Her father and her grandparents were in danger.

Ms. Dunne waited while she got her books and coat in homeroom, then walked her to the school entrance. "Clara, is your mother home? I can't let you go if she's not there."

"She's on her way now. She'll be there."

The counselor hugged her. "I'll let the office and your teachers know you've gone for the day. I'm so sorry this happened, Clara, but we're here for you." She buttoned the top of Clara's coat, took off her own scarf and wrapped it around Clara's neck. It was warm and snuggly. *Please wrap some more*, Clara thought with longing as Ms. Dunne stopped and patted her shoulders and told her that things would work out. Ms. Dunne was a counselor. She had to be positive.

Ms. Dunne pushed open the door. Clara walked out a few steps and glanced back. Ms. Dunne was still there. She waved. Clara did too. If only she could hold onto this warm feeling a little longer. She turned and walked away from school, not ready to face the worst.

———

As she walked home, Clara called Mami at work. "Come home, Mami, as soon as you can. I told my counselor you would be there. Tell them it's an emergency."

She ran the rest of the way and turned on the TV. All she saw was destruction. She warned herself not to watch. The memories would come again. But she couldn't make herself turn off the TV. Chills ran through her as the ground buckled and houses tilted on the screen. It wasn't loud like a hurricane. There was no crashing and blowing. The land was throwing up and rumbling like a sick stomach. People wandered the streets in shock. Others ran in silence. Where were they going? Clara wrapped her arms around herself and rocked back and forth, too mesmerized to tear herself away from the awful images.

"All of Puerto Rico felt the tremors, and power is out over most of the island," the announcer said.

Clara tried phoning Papi again. No service. What if Puerto Rico never had service again? She pulled a magnet from the organization that had helped them settle in when they first arrived in Albany off the refrigerator door.

"Hello," she said to the woman who answered. "Is this Empire State Relief and Recovery? My name is Clara Montalvo." She dug deep inside for strength. "Your organization helped our family after María. I need your help again, please." She waited. "Yes, the earthquake. My father is in San Juan rebuilding homes after María but now the earthquake . . ." She took another breath to get out the rest. "I think he went to the south where it happened. We can't get in touch with him." She wiped tears away and listened.

The woman said that they couldn't reach people there either. Cell phone towers had been affected, and they had no information about service being restored.

"Is this something new?" Clara asked. "About cell towers? We haven't been able to get in touch with our father for weeks."

"The information we have is that all phone service is disrupted."

Clara thought hard. "Can you call someone else in the government? Maybe they know something."

"Miss Montalvo, I'm sorry, but I cannot help you with that. I can only provide the latest information that we've been given. The only thing we know for certain is that communication with the island is impossible right now."

Fearing the woman might hang up, Clara spoke as fast as she could. "Your organization gave us travel papers, got us on a plane, flew us here. Can I speak to the governor? He went to Puerto Rico many times after María to help. I saw him on TV. He'll know what to do. Can you tell me how to get in touch with him?" She pleaded. "I'm sorry. I'm not able to do that." The woman sounded sympathetic, but Clara needed more than sympathy. "I suggest you check the state website and follow it for further information."

Clara sank into the kitchen chair. Not what she'd wanted to hear. She thanked the woman and clicked off.

She typed in "State Capitol," and a website with lists of agencies and people's names and titles filled the screen. She punched in the first number on her phone. No answer. She tried the second. Same thing. Discouraged, she closed the laptop.

She thought of another call, one she didn't want to make, but her sense of responsibility took over. Time was running out. She punched in the number. Mrs. Thurber answered. "Hi, Mrs. Thurber. This is Clara."

She half-smiled at Mrs. Thurber's enthusiastic, "How are you, my dear?" She wished she could return her cheerfulness.

"I wish I didn't have to say this, but I can't keep babysitting." She tried to soften it by adding, "At least for now." She explained about the service project and how babysitting didn't count. It would take up all her free time. And she didn't even have one yet.

Mrs. Thurber's cheery voice changed to sadness. "Clara, I'll miss you terribly, and Gus will too. I don't know how to tell him you won't be here to play and build houses."

Clara smiled at the memory of the blocks houses and schools they'd built.

"Clara, please call me as soon as you have time again, and please stop by any time or call. You're always welcome in our home. You bring such joy." Mrs. Thurber didn't say anything for a few seconds. Then she said, "I hope your father's work in Puerto Rico is going well."

"Thank you. It's kind of you to say that." Clara fought to keep her voice level. She told Mrs. Thurber about the new earthquakes and trying to reach her father. "I'll definitely call you once I get organized with my project and I have extra time again." She almost choked on the word *extra*. There was nothing extra in her life. "Please tell Gus I'll come back soon, and we'll build again. Tell him to keep making his buildings stronger on all the sides so they don't fall down." She hoped he didn't forget her. "And thank you for saying that about my father."

"Of course. He's a lifesaver. And Clara, you know you can always call the American Red Cross. They go to disaster areas all around the world. Maybe they can help you locate your father."

The door opened and Mami came in as Clara listened intently. She swiped her tears and hurried her goodbye to Mrs. Thurber, perhaps cutting her off. She wasn't sure but wanted to be there for Mami. She reached out her hand. "Mami, *sabes algo mas?*"

Her mother didn't know anything more. Clara paced the kitchen, checked the time, and started to come up with a plan. She needed to be here when Diego got home from school to make sure he was okay when he found out about the earthquake, so she couldn't do anything else today. She went to the State Capitol website again and found the address of the State Capitol building, the bus number that went there, and the nearest stop.

Clara sat her mother down at the kitchen table and took her hand. Mami still looked nice and tidy in her light blue work uniform even after cleaning all day at the bank. Clara's heart filled with appreciation. Mami worked so hard for them and never complained. Surely, she could follow her mother's example and do her service project and help out without making a fuss.

"Mami, I have to do something to find out about Papi and Tita and Tito. Tomorrow I'm going to take the bus to the governor's office. It's only forty minutes from here and I know exactly how to get there."

Mami repeated, "No, no, no," but Clara kept talking, like Jamie had done in the debate.

"We're lucky we live close to people who can help us. I have to talk to someone there who can tell us what's happening at home." Clara winced at the last word. She'd promised herself she'd make every effort to turn Albany into their home, but this latest tragedy had proven that in her heart, it wasn't so easy to forget her beloved island. "We have to find out how our family is."

Mami grabbed Clara's hands. "*Mi amor, no puedes ir*," she said. Mami's dark brown eyes and strong hands held her captive. "*Tienes que obedecerme. Es peligroso. Eres una niña.*" Every word was Spanish now, just like other times when Mami was really upset.

"I always obey you, Mami, but I have to go. It's not far. It won't be dangerous. I'm not a child. Maybe they'll tell me something about the situation there."

Mami wept into her hands, then stopped and faced Clara. "You cannot go by yourself." Tears streaked her cheeks. "We all go. Diego, you, me."

"You'll lose your job if you don't show up for work, and Diego has to be in school. Please let me go. I'll come straight home afterward, and I'll tell you everything I find out."

"No, Clara! *No puedes ir. Soy tu madre y no puedo dejarte ir en el bus sola!*"

Her mother's growing stress filled her words. She was almost screaming. And Mami's Spanish words touched Clara more strongly than English.

Even so, Clara yelled back, "Of course you're my mother, but it's easy to go on a bus by myself!"

Mami shook her head. "No! We all go on the bus or nobody goes," she said just as Diego walked in the door. He dropped his backpack and looked at Clara and Mami, whose faces must have told him they were arguing.

"What happened?" he asked.

"Nothing," Clara said, emphasizing the word. She knew he was thinking something had happened to Papi. "We're trying to find out where Papi is, that's all." She rolled her eyes, trying to call on any bit of calm inside of her. She had upset her mother. Herself too. Now Diego. Papi wouldn't be happy.

Mami motioned Diego to the table and told him in a gentle way about the earthquake. She hugged him after every sentence. "Don't worry. We're still trying to get hold of Papi."

Diego had so many questions that Clara and Mami couldn't answer. They watched the news all evening but even the announcers didn't have answers.

As she saw more and more collapsed houses, cracked roads, and cars tumbled over, Clara knew she had to go tomorrow. The more she pondered the plan, the stronger her decision. She wouldn't tell Mami. She'd miss a day of school, her first absence all year. She might fall behind on one day's classwork, but this was more important.

She wished she had the patience to wait until Papi or a relative called to tell them what was happening. Would Papi ever come back? Was he even alive? Of course. Aunt Beatriz would have called if . . . But there was no service. Argh! She remembered Jamie talking about people not knowing what had caused the dark skies and all the bad things happening after Tambora because there was no communication. But this wasn't 1815. She should be able to talk with Papi.

Nothing was easy that evening. Diego kept trying to get Mami to make her move in a game of checkers that Clara knew she didn't want to play. Mami interrupted their game every few minutes and picked up her phone. She tried Papi, then Tía Blanca, then Tía Beatriz. No service. Eventually Diego made Mami's moves for her.

While Mami and Diego sat at the table, Clara went to her room and unzipped her backpack. She slid her social studies book in, along with a bottle of water and an extra sweater. She sneaked into Mami's room and found the Relief and Recovery papers in the nightstand drawer. She might need them to prove why she was there.

Back in her room, she cradled the white-and-bluish seashell she'd brought from Puerto Rico and held it to her ear, imagining the long swishing sounds were waves washing up on the beach in Ocean Park. She tucked the seashell in one of the pockets and pushed the backpack under her bed, hoping Mami wouldn't find it if she started cleaning every inch and corner of their little house in the middle of the night like she usually did when she worried.

———

After watching the latest news, which was a repeat of the earthquake scenes, Clara turned to Mami. "I'm glad Diego fell asleep. He's so sad even though he tries to be brave. It was nice of you to play checkers with him. I know you're tired. Let's go to sleep, Mami. You had a hard day."

Tomorrow, for the first time ever, she wouldn't go to school. Instead, she'd take a bus to the New York State Capitol and try to get information about Papi and her grandparents. She wouldn't leave without it. If she didn't do this, she would never forgive herself. As she closed her eyes she struggled with her decision. She hated lying to Mami, but she was convinced that the journey to the Capitol was one she had to make.

Chapter Twelve

Chance of sun

*C*lara stepped off the bus in front of the New York State Capitol. Her legs swayed a little after sitting so tensely on the bus. She stood in front of a long gray building with a turret on either end that reminded her of a castle. It went on and on as far as she could see both ways. Her confidence wavered. Maybe Mami had been right when she said they should all come. A pang of regret hit her for sneaking off against her mother's wishes. It had happened too easily; Mami hadn't seemed to suspect anything when she'd left for work this morning with Diego. Clara promised herself she'd be back before Diego got home from school, as usual. She had to be.

Right now, she had no idea where to enter the imposing building in front of her. People were walking up and down a wide stairway, so she headed for it. Her legs shook. She took a deep breath and pretended Mami was holding her hand. That helped.

A huge sign at the top said SECURITY. A guard in a uniform motioned her through a turnstile. She put her backpack on a conveyor belt as instructed and watched it disappear. A woman checker at the other end asked Clara to remove the object in the pocket of her backpack. Clara fought back panic as she quickly took out the seashell and held it out to the woman.

The checker touched it with a scanner of some kind, then gave her a quick smile. "That's nice. Wish I could be on the beach where you found it right now. You can put it back." The woman ran the scanner up and down Clara's body and directed her through an X-ray checkpoint that probably showed her bones and everything else. Luckily, she had given the pork *pasteles* that she'd taken from the refrigerator to the woman sitting next to her on the bus. She'd looked hungry, and Clara was glad now that they were gone even though her stomach rumbled for food. She smiled at the checker woman and wished she could tell her about the beach and Puerto Rico. But she had to move on.

After the X-ray, she stood in a huge room, turning in a circle to take it all in. Arches led to areas she couldn't see, and the walls of vibrant murals held her gaze. Voices echoed. She walked ahead under the vaulted ceiling that went on forever.

She was told by a guard, who must have thought she looked lost, to go to the waiting room. She thanked him and walked briskly toward where he'd pointed. As she entered, she took a number, thirty-seven, from a machine with a sign that read, PLEASE TAKE A NUMBER.

The room had at least two hundred chairs, and most were filled. She sat in the first empty chair in the third row. The man next to her, probably around Papi's age, was reading a magazine. He glanced at her and said, "*Hola*." She nodded, happy to hear Spanish. A few children sat with parents, and babies cried somewhere behind her. She couldn't believe all these people had arrived even earlier than she had. Her heart beat faster, as if it knew she was out of her comfort zone.

In her mind she rehearsed what she would say to the person she would talk to. That she needed to find out anything about her father, who was in Puerto Rico helping to rebuild. The recent earthquakes had put him in more danger. Could they help her find him? She would wait to hear the answer before asking anything else. Like, did they have any special phones that worked during emergencies? And would it be possible to go there to find him herself? Did they have any emergency planes flying to Puerto Rico, and could she go on one of them? She glanced at her watch every few minutes and checked it against the big clock on the wall. Her heart thumped in time with the second hand moving the minutes forward.

People got up and wandered around, probably trying to pass the time. Why were they all here? What kind of help did they need? More people came in looking confused, and others, who were seated, got up and went into the restrooms on the left side of the big room. She wasn't going anywhere until thirty-seven was called.

She had been watching carefully to see how it worked. A voice on a speaker called a number, and the person holding that number jumped up and hurried over to a long counter with a sign on the front that said EXAMINERS. She counted them. Ten examiners. For all these people waiting. She figured thirty-seven would never get called.

She kept her eyes on a woman who looked Latina, standing before Examiner Five. After a few minutes, the woman walked away and disappeared. Where to? Clara fought back a wave of uncertainty even after thinking she understood the process. How long was it supposed to take? She kept track of the numbers being called but couldn't keep up with where the people went after talking to the examiners. She pulled her social studies book out of her backpack and flipped to her bookmark. "Chapter Fifteen: Immigrants."

Nearly an hour after she checked in, when number thirty-seven boomed over the loudspeaker, she jumped. She'd almost missed it. Her heart thumped. She reminded herself why she came. She rehearsed it again. *I'm here to see if you could help me get in touch with my father.*

Her knees buckled as she leapt from her chair.

"Sorry," she blurted after she tripped over a little boy's foot sticking out next to her. Her face grew warm as she hurried to the counter where a man with a serious face was motioning her over.

"How may I help you?" he asked.

She swallowed, then started to explain. She only got the words, "Get in touch with my father," out when he stopped her as if he had heard this story before.

"First of all, how old are you?"

Clara swallowed. She pressed her lips together then said, "I'll be fifteen soon." She didn't tell him her birthday was five months away.

The man frowned. "Are you by yourself? Does somebody in your family know you're here?"

She gave a slight nod, so it didn't feel like a complete lie. She hadn't counted on these questions. She hadn't rehearsed this.

"You should be in school." He motioned to the left. "Wait over there." He spoke into a phone.

Clara's stomach knotted. Was he calling the police? Would they arrest her? She shouldn't have come. She needed water but probably shouldn't open her backpack or call attention to herself.

When the man hung up, he took a swig of water from a plastic bottle and called out, "Next." Clara shuddered. She stood exactly where he'd motioned, feeling like a trapped mouse.

A few minutes later, a woman holding a clipboard walked up to her. "Please come with me."

Clara nodded, remembering after María how her family had been dependent on people at Rescue and Recovery. That was her now, dependent. It wasn't a good feeling, not knowing what was happening, but she needed others right now. She followed the woman to a row of cubicles—not rooms, but open spaces with walls. The woman stepped into the opening of a cubicle where a younger woman sat at a desk. The woman behind the desk motioned for Clara to come in and sit down and went back to her folders. The clipboard woman continued down the hallway. Clara wished she had thanked her, but as she sat taking everything in, everybody seemed so busy and in a hurry.

"I'm Isabelle," the woman behind the desk said with a warm smile. "I hope I can help you. You're so young. Did your family come with you?"

Clara shook her head. "I need help finding my father in Puerto Rico." She started telling Isabelle about María before the woman could ask her anything else. She'd learned from the man at the desk and the clipboard woman to say her purpose fast. But only the most important facts. She told Isabelle about Empire Relief and Recovery and how they couldn't help. That's why she had come today. To see if another government person could.

When Clara had finished, Isabelle nodded. "I sympathize with everything you've told me, but I'm sorry. We can't help you with this now. So many people are trying to get in touch with family in Puerto Rico. We might have some emergency lines through next week or the week after, but right now, we don't. We're not in communication with anyone on the island because of the new earthquakes. That's probably why you haven't heard from your father. Everything has been disrupted."

Clara bit her lip as her hope faded to discouragement. She swallowed hard to keep from breaking out in tears. Isabelle looked through a folder on her desk. Clara searched her mind to think of something, anything to allow her to stay.

"Could I get an appointment with the governor? He brought help after María. I saw him on TV. Maybe he has a special phone that gets through."

Isabelle smiled. "I'm afraid that's not possible, Clara. There's so much state business to take care of from the governor's office." She paused and looked kindly at Clara, as if she wished she could help. "You had better get back home now. Do you have a way to get there?"

Clara nodded. "The bus."

"Good." Isabelle slid a sheet of lined paper to her. "Write all your information here."

Clara wrote it all—her name, phone number, address, email—and put down the pen.

Isabelle placed the sheet in a folder. "I'll contact you as soon as we know anything that could help you. But right now, we can do nothing."

"Nothing?" Clara whispered, more to herself. Had she come all this way just to hear "nothing"? What now? She wouldn't give up. She never did, no matter what the situation. This was the biggest challenge she had ever faced. Papi was somewhere in Puerto Rico, probably right where the earthquake had ripped the island apart. She had to talk to him.

She thanked Isabelle, picked up her backpack and left. Walking through the huge room with the high ceiling made her feel so small. She felt even smaller when she thought of going home with nothing.

At the bottom of the wide stone steps, she stopped and glanced back. She clicked a photo of the State Capitol. She'd show Mami and Diego, but not today. She'd show Papi too. And when he was back home, the photo would remind her that she had tried her best.

The big clock on the State Capitol said eleven fifteen. She should be in social studies right now. She sat on the bottom step to catch her breath and think what to do next. She took a drink of water. She longed for one of the pork *pasteles*, but they were gone. She hitched her backpack on just as a dark blue car pulled in front of the building. A man in a dark suit rushed over and opened the door, and another man got out. For a second his eyes met Clara's. Her jaw dropped. It was him. She stepped forward and took a few steps toward the car. Another man, also in a dark suit, blocked her way. "Stand back, please, Miss."

"Yes, sir," she said obediently, and backed up so fast that she fell. She scrambled to her feet, amazed that nothing hurt, and kept moving back. She stopped at a pillar and leaned against it to catch her breath. Her lips were dry. Her heart beat so fast. Her legs shook. She thought she would pass out any second.

When the governor walked up the three steps and toward her, she did her best to stand up straight and smile. Her face twitched. She had never been this nervous.

"Are you all right, Miss?"

"Oh." Her cheeks burned. She swallowed hard. "I'm fine. Yes. Fine." She glanced down to see if she was presentable after the fall, swallowed again, moved an inch forward and stretched out her right hand. "I'm Clara Montalvo. I came to see you."

He smiled and shook her hand. Clara couldn't believe this. *Say it*, she told herself. *Just the important part.*

"Please, Mr. Governor. My father is helping build houses in Puerto Rico after María. We don't know where he is after the recent earthquakes in the south. Everybody says all lines are down. Nobody can get in touch with the island. Can you help me?"

His face grew serious. He nodded, keeping his eyes on her, but his hand motioned to the man who had blocked her. The man ran over, and the governor said something to him. The man stood at attention, as if ready to do battle.

"Well, we can't take no for an answer without trying after you've come all this way, can we, Miss Montalvo?" the governor said. "My assistant will take you to someone who might be able to help. We're not sure how the communication lines are in different areas of the island now, but we'll have someone look into it. Thank you for coming to see me. I hope you'll come back. Goodbye, Clara."

He walked the rest of the way up the steps. People standing and waiting applauded him. He waved to them, then disappeared into the big State Capitol building. She would never forget him.

Clara and the assistant rode an elevator to the third floor. She noticed all the brass buttons marked one to five and how old-fashioned the wooden panels looked. They reminded her of old government buildings in Puerto Rico. She followed the assistant down a long hallway and wondered where he was taking her. Big paintings of past governors lined the walls. She read their names fast. Their footsteps echoed on the floor's dark wooden squares, like the ones in the elevator.

The assistant opened a door with a paper sign taped to it that said PUERTO RICO LIAISON OFFICE. It might have been a different office before the sign went up.

"Hello, Juan," he said to the person sitting at a desk. "The governor would like you to help this young lady. She'll tell you what she needs."

"Give me about fifteen minutes," Juan said to them. "We're swamped with telephone calls, and I have to return a few."

The assistant glanced at her and said, "We can wait out here."

Clara followed him and took a seat, grateful that she'd gotten this far. She crossed her fingers, hoping the man he called Juan wouldn't be too swamped to see her.

After twenty minutes, he opened the door and told her to come in. "Please, have a seat. And you can call me Juan."

The assistant said, "I'll be out here."

Clara nodded. "Thank you." She told Juan everything. He asked for her grandparents' names and their address. In minutes he was on the phone, speaking Spanish. He mentioned a government office and Guánica, the town in the south where her grandparents lived, so she knew she was close to getting what she'd come for. He told the person on the phone her grandparents' names and address and asked the person to send someone there to ask about her father. Juan had all the details, including Clara's phone number, which he gave to the person on the phone. She couldn't believe her ears. Someone in Puerto Rico had her phone number. And they would help her. Mami would be so happy, once she got over being so upset with Clara for going.

Juan clicked off the phone and repeated to her in English that if they located her father, they would bring him to the government office by six thirty so he could call her on their official phone.

Clara let out all the hopeful breath she had been holding in for hours. "Thank you." Tears streamed down her face. "My papi will call us. Thank you." She stood to leave.

"Just a minute, Clara," he cautioned. "Remember. I said, *if* we locate your father. We won't know anything until our people down there get over to Guánica. It'll take an hour or so." He looked at his watch. "So, if they find him, they'll bring him to the government office to make the call." He nodded. "Let's hope they do."

She liked that he didn't shake his head. What a perfect job for him, helping people like her to have hope. She thanked him again, picked up her backpack, and left the Puerto Rico Liaison Office, a new person. She nodded to the assistant, who was waiting as promised. She followed him downstairs and out into the bright sunlight. The clock chimed two.

Clara's buoyant mood plummeted. "Diego," she gasped. "Oh, no!"

Chapter Thirteen

Thunder rumblings

Jamie couldn't take his eyes off Clara's empty seat in class. She was never absent. Their debate had gone great yesterday. He had focused on his points, even though Clara had definitely brought up strong arguments about Tambora's destruction. He should have felt terrific afterward with all the applauding and laughs from his classmates, but he didn't. He knew why but forced that thought away.

Where was she? He thought he knew her. She wasn't sick the last time they'd talked. And she wouldn't miss school because of his joking. Of course, she was kind of sensitive. He had completely forgotten his promise the night of the pizza parlor-selfie disaster to be nice to her during the debate. How could he have let it slide?

He might have convinced her the selfie was dumb and that he'd had nothing to do with it because Clara hadn't mentioned it yesterday morning. He still wondered if her being out today had anything to do with that. It couldn't. She wouldn't miss school for such a stupid thing. And she wouldn't stay out because she thought he'd won the debate. The avalanche of thoughts weighed a ton. He wished he could take back all the jokes he'd made about her facts.

But Clara wouldn't miss school for something thoughtless that he'd done. She could see right through him. He liked that she understood him. The biggest thing that bothered him was that he really liked her. She was the kindest, most caring person to ever come into his life. And he had no idea where she was.

Mr. J started class. "As you may know, an earthquake hit Puerto Rico yesterday morning. Tremors are still shaking parts of the island. People have moved to shelters because their homes are collapsing. Imagine if that were your home. Think of how you would feel. That island used to be Clara's home. She moved here to Albany because a hurricane did a lot of damage in Puerto Rico. And now, this earthquake."

Gasps and, "No way," and, "Poor Clara," broke out in the classroom. Mr. J's hand went up for quiet.

"Is Clara okay?" Jamie asked. He turned to her seat and wondered if her books were still in her desk. He'd look later. "How long will she be out?"

"Thank you for asking, Jamie. We're not sure. She's with her family. All we can do is keep up with the news and send her our good thoughts. I hope I don't have to remind you of these disasters happening more and more in the rest of our country. Floods in the southern states. Fires in California. But I *am* reminding you to read about them in your newspapers or online and watch the news."

Jamie made a mental note to tell Mr. J that he watched the news every night, but now wasn't the time. And it wasn't enough to send Clara good thoughts. Mr. J didn't say how long she would be out of class. It sounded pretty bad.

During the rest of class, Jamie wrestled with an impulse to call Clara. How would he feel if he were in her situation? He'd love a phone call, but Clara wasn't like him. Independent and courageous described her. She didn't want anyone to feel sorry for her. He wouldn't mind people feeling sorry for him sometimes. He shrugged, defeated about so many things. There was nothing he could do to help Clara. It felt worse than disappointing his dad.

At lunchtime he paced back and forth in the hallway, hoping for an idea, anything to help Clara. What did he know about Puerto Rico? Nothing.

He headed down to Coach's office to take his mind off it all. At least he could find out whether he might still have a chance to take part in the last two competitions if he got his science grade up. The team was kind of like his family at school, and he really didn't want to let them down.

He reached the sports office just as Coach was coming out. Nick, Max, and Joe, other teammates, followed behind him. Nick smiled as he passed by. He held up his hand to fist bump. Jamie bumped weakly. His eyes were on the other two guys, whose heads were down.

"Jamie," Coach said, seeming surprised to see him. He glanced at his watch. "Too bad about your science grade. We really needed you for this competition, but rules are rules about grades. Hey. Keep up your spirit. We've got some major push-ups to do."

Jamie took the news like a punch in the stomach. "But, Coach," he called as Coach moved down the hallway. He yelled a little louder. "I had my first debate yesterday morning in science. I think I did a decent job. There're two more to go. It'll help my grade."

Coach turned. He nodded. "Keep up the diligent work." He moved on but called over his shoulder. "Better get some lunch." He motioned ahead to the guys.

"Yeah, lunch. Um . . . see you." Jamie called and started down the hallway in the opposite direction. He glanced back. Coach and the guys were heading for the gym, but he could still hear Coach. "We have to go into this competition with a plan. Our rival will definitely have one."

So he definitely wasn't competing. And he wasn't the rival. Why did he feel like one, now? Coach hadn't even asked him to come along for push-ups or even to watch them work out. He glanced back again. They had turned the corner, but the answer was loud and clear. Jamie's hope of turning things around with the debate disappeared. Dad was right. For him, the season was over.

———

After school he started for home, filled with disappointment over Coach and the guys going off without him. They didn't want or need him. He stopped at an intersection and looked both ways. Home or to Clara's? He'd never been to her house, but he knew her address and that she lived close to the pizza parlor because they'd talked about their favorite pies there and how she could run over any time to buy a slice. He'd even once or twice thought about asking her to go get dinner there some Friday evening. They could sit and talk and get to know each other better. He'd never gotten up the nerve to ask her out, though. Now with the debate pitting them against each other, he didn't stand a chance.

Just as his head filled with *didn't stand a chance*, his phone pinged. *Molly*. His finger hovered, ready to delete, but something made him accept the call.

"Jamie, can you believe Clara was absent today? Do you know where she is? I told her I'd like to help with your climate project and now she's not even here to talk about it or make plans. That's not very responsible, is it?"

Jamie frowned. "I don't know where Clara is, but she's probably doing something important. Maybe it has to do with her father. Clara's the most responsible person I know. I'm sure she'll be happy to have you help. She's got things under control. Don't worry. I've got to go." He clicked off, a little surprised at Molly's new eagerness to help but put off by what she'd said about Clara.

The closer he got to Clara's street, the smaller the houses and the more broken the sidewalks. He stepped over shards of concrete pieces, crumpled as if a mini earthquake had rumbled underneath. Grass grew in between the slabs so he knew the sidewalk had been like that for a long time.

As he got to Cedar Street, he glanced around for any cedar trees but all that stood in front of him were a fire hydrant and a line of telephone poles with paper signs tacked on describing a lost cat, stop signs at the corner, and a few plastic garbage pails against the fences in front of the houses. When he came to number 141, plants in colorful pots formed a small garden on one side of the steps.

He opened an iron gate and went up three steps to the door. He inhaled a few breaths for confidence before ringing the bell. His feet shuffled from side to side as he waited. He hoped Clara would answer.

He heard a rattle, then the door opened a few inches. A woman with dark hair and eyes who looked a little like Clara peered out at him.

"Hello. I . . . I go to school with Clara. She's my friend. My name is Jamie. Are . . . are you her mother? Is she home?" he managed to get out.

The woman opened the door a little more. "I am her mother. Clara is not here," she said with accented English. "Still in school."

Jamie hoped he didn't show her his shock. "Oh, okay." He struggled for something more to say, anything except that she wasn't in school. "Maybe she stayed for something after classes. Can I come back later?"

"Yes, come later," she said.

He nodded and pressed his lips together. That stopped him from showing her his surprise or letting out anything about Clara not being in school. "What time do you think she'll be home?"

The woman shrugged.

"Okay," Jamie said, trying to sound normal. "I'll call her later. Nice to meet you." She nodded after he did and closed the door.

Jamie headed for home. Then he turned back. He should probably tell her about Clara. They could go to the police. No. That could make trouble. He'd go back to school. Maybe Mr. J was still there. What would Mr. J do? Call Clara's mother? The police? His mind spun in circles.

He'd go home and ask Mom what to do. He kicked at a stone as he walked. Where could Clara be? Why didn't her mother know? Why hadn't Clara told her? He realized he didn't know much about Clara. Maybe she had a secret place she went when she was worried, like to her Latina friends' homes. Maybe she had a boyfriend but didn't want her mother to know. Any boy would want to be her boyfriend. *He* sure did. Clara must be really worried about something to totally disappear.

As he walked, thoughts swirled in his mind. He didn't want to trouble his mom with all this, but she seemed the best person to ask. As he neared his house, he saw cedar and maple trees and mowed lawns. He walked on smoothly paved, unbroken sidewalks. Something clicked in his mind as he walked . . . like a light switch. Off. On. Neat sidewalks and mowed lawns meant nothing. Neither did winning debates or even getting back on the snowboarding team.

Clara mattered. And she was missing.

Chapter Fourteen

Winter storm advisory

She had to catch that bus. It was sitting at the bus stop and Clara sprinted toward it, but it pulled out just before she reached the stop. She checked the schedule on the sign as she caught her breath. Fifteen minutes until the next one. Two-twenty. She wouldn't be home until at least three fifteen, maybe later. She wouldn't be there for Diego. Her spirits deflated as she thought of him sitting on the steps waiting. Mami would be furious. She hoped that Mami's joy when she learned Clara had spoken with the governor and that they'd be talking with Papi in a couple of hours would overshadow her anger. Should she call Mami and say she was on her way home? No, better to wait until she got there. Once she explained everything clearly, Mami would understand why she'd had to go.

On the bus she closed her eyes, worn out from the long but exciting day. She felt the bus moving, leaving the New York State Capitol where—she loved saying it over and over—she had talked to the governor. She relived those moments as they passed through parts of Albany she'd never seen.

After forty minutes, familiar street signs appeared. She had been paying so much attention to the scenery that she almost missed her stop. She grabbed her backpack and hurried out.

Her watch said three forty-five as she ran up the steps to her house. She hadn't even turned the key when the door burst open. "*¿Dónde estabas?* Where were you?" Mami grabbed her. Clara wasn't sure if it was a hug or an angry squeeze. Mami pulled away and stood at arms' length, staring at Clara and sobbing. "Where did you go after school? What is happening? *¿Que pasa?*"

Clara caught her breath. "Mami. Everything is good. *Todo esta bien.* Papi . . ." Clara's eyes welled. "He's going to call us soon." Clara began explaining as fast as she could to calm down her mother.

Diego wandered over. "Where were you? I was waiting on the steps." His little face filled with worry, resembling Papi so much Clara's heart hurt.

"Diego, I know. I know. I had to go to find out about Papi. He's going to call us in a little while. You can talk to him." She hoped that would explain enough for now.

He grabbed Clara around the waist. "Can I talk to him first?"

"We'll all talk. Everything will be okay again. We'll know Papi is safe." She'd tell him later about Tita and Tito and the earthquake, once she knew they were okay. She tried to eat the snacks Mami put out, but she had no appetite. She watched the clock, then smacked her head with her hands. "Oh, no." She dug her phone out of her backpack. Her low battery indicator flashed. "I have to charge it." She ran to her charger. Her hands shook so much she could hardly connect her phone.

All three of them sat around the table watching Clara's phone. It was taking forever to charge. Clara's heart raced. 6:28. She watched the seconds hand on her watch moving. 6:29. Her phone battery was still low—20% charged—but that would work. 6:30. She glanced at Mami. Her eyes were on their kitchen clock. Diego's eyes were too.

"It's six thirty," he announced.

They waited. And waited and glanced at each other. Could Mami's hands, folded, in prayer, bring in the call? Diego placed his hands on hers. Little comforter. Clara's promise wasn't happening. It had sounded so perfect.

She turned to Mami, hoping her explanation would help Diego. "Papi had to get from Tita's to the government office. Maybe it takes longer with the roads out and everything . . . you know."

She repeated to Diego, "Papi had to travel to a phone. The roads are really bad down there."

His nod told her he'd accept any reason.

At six forty-five, Clara picked up her phone, charging slowly. But still, she could receive a call. She tapped the phone again, as if that could bring in the call. Mami's shoulders slumped. How much more waiting she could take?

When Mami's phone rang, they all jumped. Diego leaped across the table and pushed his face as close as he could get to Mami's.

Mami's shaky fingers pressed the button. "Hola." Her face lit up. "Carlos, *mi amor, mi amor.*"

It was Papi. Chills covered Clara. Mami sobbed so much she could hardly get words out. Finally, she sat up and pulled herself together. "*¿Estas bien?*" She nodded, so Papi must have said he was fine. Mami nodded again and again.

"He's coughing a lot," Diego said to Clara.

Mami moved the phone closer to her ear. "Carlos. *¿Que pasó?*"

Clara's fingers drummed the table. She tapped her feet, unable to wait her turn, but she couldn't rush Mami. Her fingers drummed faster.

Finally, Mami said, "Adios, Carlos. *Cuídate. Te veo pronto.*" Clara reached for the phone after Mami's final words in Spanish: "Take care of yourself and I will see you soon."

"Papi, Papi," Clara screamed into the phone. That's all she could get out. Papi said he had been staying with Aunt Beatriz and some days with Aunt Blanca and her family. His work in San Juan was nearly finished, but the earthquake surprised them. He couldn't reach Tita and Tito by phone from San Juan. All lines were down, so he had taken a bus to Guánica to make sure they were safe.

Papi told her how Tito had said to him, "'We took care of you as our young son and now you take care of your old mother and father.'" Papi laughed, then he coughed and coughed some more. "But Tita and Tito are fine," he said.

"Papi, you're coughing. Are you okay?" she asked. She listened differently now. Something in their conversation had changed.

"*Si, si*," he said in her ear. "There is so much dust in the air. It makes everybody cough. Don't worry, Clarita."

"Papi, go to a doctor there. She can give you something for the cough." Mami was waving her hand, wanting the phone again. Clara didn't want to give it up. "Papi, I have to say goodbye. Mami wants to talk. When are you coming home?"

He said something about planes and schedules, then static took over. She shouted, "*Adios*, Papi," and handed the phone back to her mother.

Mami said *hola* a few times. Another person must have come on the line because Mami handed the phone to Clara. It was the person at the government office who had let Papi use the phone. He said they'd better end the call because the connection was bad. Clara thanked him, then asked for his number—just in case, she said. He kindly gave it to her but told her he probably wouldn't be able to find her father once he left Guánica. She gave the man Papi's number anyhow. She gave him her aunts' numbers too.

The man clicked off, and her connection to Puerto Rico was gone. She smacked her head. She hadn't even told Papi about the governor, how he had helped her to get in touch with Papi. How could she have forgotten? Papi hadn't said when he'd be home. She had to trust that he would come home as soon as he could. And he was fine, except for that cough.

"We will prepare," Mami said, interrupting Clara's thoughts. Mami began taking out all the ingredients to make a pineapple cake. She seemed a little frenzied, like when she started cleaning to get over her anxiety and worry.

They set everything on the counter except for fresh pineapple, which they didn't have. Canned would have to do. Clara sifted flour with spices and mixed the butter and sugar while Mami chopped the pineapple rings into small pieces. She added vanilla and other flavors to them, then mixed. "*Ay, mi amor*," Mami said, dropping the big spoon. "I forgot to tell you. Clara, your friend . . . nice boy . . . Jamie. He came here today. He worries for you."

Clara dropped her spoon too. "When, Mami? What did he say? What did he want?" It had to be because she wasn't in school. He was probably afraid she wasn't going to be able to finish the debate and that he'd fail science after all. "Did he come inside, Mami? Did you speak English?"

"He came after school. I said come back later. I thought you would come home from school like you do every day. I spoke English."

Clara grabbed her phone. Half charged. She wasn't even sure what she'd say.

She punched in his number. Voicemail. She'd try later. His coming over was the worst and the best thing that could have happened: the worst, coming to her rundown house and talking to Mami, who he probably didn't understand, and the best, coming to her house because he was worried about her. Those were Mami's words. "He worries for you." Clara didn't know what to believe. She put the Jamie worries aside. She'd deal with them later.

While their pineapple cake baked and sweet aromas filled the kitchen, they went over and over what Papi had said and how he sounded, and they talked about memories of eating Tío Andrés's pineapple cake in Puerto Rico. Things seemed to be working out for now. But Clara couldn't forget the sound of Papi's coughing.

Chapter Fifteen

Foggy

That night at the dinner table, Mom asked Jamie and his father questions to keep them talking. "Do you think what you're learning about this disaster will lead to another interesting project, Jamie?" She always asked how what he was doing could lead to a good result for him. And she always smiled when she asked.

"I'm not sure," he said, glancing at Dad. "But it'll help my grade. And the kids in class are psyched about all that happened after the eruption. Me too. I do wish we had more projects like this one." He pulled out his phone, which vibrated on silent, but got a disapproving look from Dad so he slid it in his pocket again. He'd missed the caller's name. Might have been Clara. He thought better of bringing her into their conversation. Too many questions to answer about her disappearance.

"Got to get to my homework," he said and carried his dishes to the sink.

"Sure," Mom answered. "I've got to get back to the news. We're trying to get a peace agreement with the Taliban. That's what I want to hear."

Jamie turned back toward the table. "Would that mean Lucas gets to come home?"

Mom's eyes teared up. "Wouldn't that be wonderful?"

He instantly regretted asking. The last thing he wanted was to make Mom feel worse, but when she'd said wonderful, he'd wanted to say, *It's probably not going to happen for a while.* Wars were long. He'd accepted that fact after seeing how stuck the Americans seemed over there. Instead, he repeated, "Homework" and left the room. He scrolled to Clara's number and hit "call."

"Hey, Clara," he said when she answered. "Where are you? Are you okay?" He made a face. What a dorky thing to say. Of course, she wasn't okay. "Where were you today? I almost told your mother you weren't in school. I didn't, though, I thought she might call the police and—"

"Jamie! Stop. I'm fine. You won't believe this. I talked to the governor at the State Capitol." She caught her breath, then added, "Thanks for coming by today. So you met my mother."

"She's great. What do you mean you talked to the governor? Are you joking? What's going on? You have to tell me everything."

She told him how she had fallen and how the governor had come over to her and shaken her hand. And that she was so nervous, she thought she'd pass out. She told him all about Juan and his phone call to Puerto Rico. Then, talking to Papi. Everything.

"I can't believe you went to the Capitol, Clara. I mean I definitely believe it, but . . . but you talked to the *governor*? Wow. How did you even know where to go? I could have gone with you and—"

"Jamie, it's okay," she interrupted. "It was easy. It was just a bus ride. Look, I'm really tired from this whole day. I've got to get some sleep."

"Clara, wait—"

But she'd clicked off. At least she was okay. Someday he'd tell her how he'd panicked at her house when her mom said she was in school and how he'd worried that she'd gone to a boyfriend's house. What a relief. They had so much to talk about. He couldn't wait. She amazed him. She'd gone to the Capitol. All by herself. "Just a bus ride," she'd said, but she'd accomplished what she'd set out to do.

What if he could get on a plane and fly to Afghanistan to save Lucas? He'd do it in a second. Would he, though? Did he have Clara's kind of courage, to do what she had to do like Lucas had done? Jamie hoped he did. He and Clara were so similar— their independence and good senses of humor—even though they were different. She always reminded him of important things like family, things he mostly pushed aside. Ever since they'd met, he'd tried to tell her in little ways that she was pretty cool, but his messages didn't always get across—maybe because he mixed in too much joking. He needed practice.

He needed Clara to like him, but he needed to know other things that mattered too, like if his science grade would move up. If it didn't, he would be in the same situation—Dad on his back, the snowboarding team history, and repeating eighth grade next year. Either way, Lucas would still be in danger, and Clara, still a mystery.

That evening all Jamie could think about was Clara's courage. He wished he had even a handful of it. He could use that to tell Dad about the first debate and how well it had gone and how the kids had laughed at his great points about Tambora. Well, maybe not. He'd hear about focusing for sure. But Dad wasn't home yet. First, he'd ask Dad what he thought about the credit article. Then he'd tell Dad what he'd said about credit in the debate. Maybe Dad would say, "Great job, Jamie. I'm proud of you." Well, maybe not the proud part, but he'd wait and see.

Dad got home later than usual that evening. He went straight to the TV and turned the news on. The earthquakes in Puerto Rico were the first story. During the commercial, Jamie told his parents about Clara and that her dad was in Puerto Rico. He still didn't mention her trip to the State Capitol or that he'd gone to her house that day. He didn't think Dad would approve. Mom hugged him and asked if they could help in any way.

"I'm not sure, Mom. I think Clara's working things out. Her family wants her dad to come home, but I don't think planes are leaving the island. She's so worried about him, and now this earthquake. It's hard to believe that disasters are happening right now when we're doing this project on natural disasters from the past. They don't seem as important."

He turned to Dad. "I finished my first debate and talked about credit and how business affects people's lives. For the next debate, I'm going to talk about how climate affected weather and credit saved people. You know . . . the article I gave you." Jamie pictured it still on the shelf in the garage, not too far from Lucas's motorcycle. He took a chance that Dad had read it. "What did you think about it?"

"I found it interesting," Dad said. "What collateral would you put up to receive credit for your grain if you had lived back then? You had to give the bank something in case you couldn't pay it back."

Jamie thought for a moment. "I'm not sure what I would have to pay it back. Maybe my house."

"You would be prepared to lose it if you didn't sell your crop?"

"I don't know," Jamie said. "I never thought about it before."

"Well, you'd have to move out, find another place for your family to live, get back on your feet with another job. Not easy."

"But Dad, that was way back when. We're in a different world today. I'd think about it before I asked for a lot of credit."

"That's fair. But people back then probably thought about it too. They had a lot to lose."

"Sure. So how do you do this every day at the bank? Give people credit and hope they make money on their business? You can't be sure it will work out, and then if it doesn't, you must feel bad about it." He wished he could go sit with Mom, still glued to the TV news about the earthquake, but he had to finish this credit thing. "I think I'd rather be a sergeant like you were in the army. You'd do your job but wouldn't have to feel bad about some soldier not doing something right."

Dad shook his head. "I don't think you would like to be a sergeant. It's no fun giving orders. And it wasn't pretty. I saw friends injured in Iraq and sent home very different from when they arrived . . ." His father's voice faded.

Jamie nodded, trying not to think about his brother. He'd read about injured and stressed-out men coming home from war with PTSD. They were never the same. He remembered the coffins on TV the other night. Those images were etched in his brain. The big surprise though was Dad's saying it was no fun giving orders.

"Were you scared?" Jamie asked. "Did you wish you hadn't enlisted once you got there?"

"I never wanted to kill," Dad said. "But I wanted to serve my country. That's why I settled for the Quartermasters Corps. It's an office job. They're the supply people who arrange to get everything to the troops at the right time and place. They take care of things that really matter in a war, especially to the men.

"And Jamie, I always felt bad when something went wrong with any soldiers under my command. All I wanted was to see that they were safe, get myself out of the service with body and mind intact, find a good job, raise a family, and pass on to my sons how to be a man in life."

Jamie nodded again, wondering how they'd gotten to "how to be a man in life" from credit, where they'd started. He wondered if his father had gotten even a little of what he had wanted in life.

Dad's eyebrows closed together. His expression darkened. "Lucas couldn't hear me. He wanted to do things his own way, and he did. He enlisted." Dad shook his head. "Stupid kid didn't know what he was doing."

Jamie's shoulders went up and his stomach knotted. He wanted to do things his own way too but didn't say so. He didn't want to start an argument or hurt Dad's feelings or remind

Dad that he was an obstacle in his father's dream. He had never pictured Dad with a dream, only saw him as a dad with a lot of commands and expectations.

Jamie wondered if surviving the service, having the job at the bank, marrying Mom, and raising Lucas and him were turning out to be what his father had wanted. And if Dad thought he was passing on to Lucas and him how to be men. How were they supposed to get the message and be like Dad? That was a tough order for a dream. Jamie wasn't sure it could come true.

Chapter Sixteen

Change in air pressure

For only the second time in his life, Jamie couldn't wait to get to school early the next morning—mainly to see Clara. The first time was when he'd wanted to talk to Coach and find out if he were still on the team. Clara had clicked off without even saying goodbye last night. He missed her. Behind his concern lurked something else: whether he'd be ready for their second debate next Monday. Could he find more good stuff that happened because of Tambora and convince the class and Mr. J that the world was better off because of these things? He'd have to if he wanted to win the debate and boost his science grade.

Some kids stood in the hallway, talking and fooling around with their phones. He hurried into the classroom. His racing mind settled. She was there—up front, waving her hands and talking excitedly to Mr. J, probably telling him about the governor and her trip to the Capitol. She'd never looked so happy.

Jamie hurried up to them. "Hi, Clara. Am I glad to see you!" He turned to their teacher. "Hi, Mr. J." Their expressions told him he'd interrupted the conversation, so he stepped back a little and toned down his excitement. "That earthquake was pretty bad. I saw all the damage."

"Another disaster, right?" Clara shrugged. "It's great that you're here early so we can get organized. Mr. J said we could finish our debates this week. We can do our second one today and—"

"Today?" Jamie swallowed hard. "Like right now?" He'd lose the debate for sure. Of course, Clara had prepared. He pictured his notes at home and wished he'd thought to bring them. He'd have to improvise. He had to nail this second debate or forget about the team the rest of this year, and maybe even next.

"Yes, if we could," Clara said. "With all these new quakes occurring, I don't know what could happen next. I might have to miss some days when my father comes home. I don't know how our lives might change." She nodded expectantly as if that would make him agree.

Jamie frowned. How could Clara spring this on him? She could have mentioned it on the phone last night. Was she getting even for the stupid selfie or maybe for their first debate and how he'd joked about points she'd made? Hadn't he apologized? He couldn't give up now. He had to do it—convince the class about the benefits Tambora brought. But she'd just convinced the governor to call Puerto Rico for her. He didn't have a snowball's chance in summer against her.

Mr. J turned to him. "Are you prepared, Jamie?"

He tried hard not to let his panic show. "Um. Sure. I'm ready." The lie came so easily. But he had to keep up his front. "I'll just check my notes." He headed for his desk. Kids were coming in now. Class would be starting in minutes.

As he scrambled for paper and a pen, he felt a tap on his shoulder. He turned. Coach was standing there. "Coach. Hey."

"Yeah, Jamie. Wanted to catch you before class started. Can we have a word?" Coach motioned toward the hallway.

Jamie followed him out, expecting the worst.

"We found a spot at Killington for our competition on Saturday. No snow around here . . . unpredictable weather this year." He shook his head. "I can't offer you a competing spot— you know the grades policy—but we'd love your support. You'd be a big help if you came with us. The team hasn't practiced on snow since the last competition. Hope all the push-ups and squats helped. We'll see, right? Anyway, we're leaving around six that morning. We'll get to Vermont and the starting line by nine, ready to win. Are you on board?"

Jamie could feel his smile getting wider. Relief calmed him like a cool winter breeze. He answered like a true teammate. "Um . . . yeah, sure, Coach. I'm on board. You can count on me."

As he answered, he forced back the thought that Dad would say no. He'd already told Jamie that for him, the season was over. He'd have to ace this debate and tell Dad about it tonight, then tell him how Coach wanted him to go with the team and convince Dad that it was all working out. His grade would go up, and he'd definitely pass science. Dad wouldn't have to bug him any longer. Jamie couldn't disappoint Coach and his teammates. It was his one chance for officially getting back on the team.

"Great. See you then." Coach high-fived Nick and Burly, who were heading into the room.

Jamie grabbed his notebook and a pen. He had to at least look like he was ready.

Mr. J started science class by asking if the students scheduled for their reports that day and the next would mind holding off until the following week to accommodate Clara and Jamie.

Molly nudged Katy, her project partner. "Sure. We'll help Jamie."

Jamie sank lower in his seat. He wished he could tell Molly to keep quiet, but he couldn't afford more trouble. He hoped Clara could see that. She was her biting her lip.

Mr. J said, "Thank you. Well, then, let's move ahead with debate number two."

Clara didn't even wait for him. She walked to the front of the room with her packet of notes. Jamie followed, empty-handed except for his pen and notebook covered with snowboarding doodles.

She whispered, "You start."

He froze. He had hoped she would start, and that what she said might remind him of what was on his notes at home. "Um . . . that's okay. You can."

Clara shrugged and took the floor like a pro. "The earthquakes in Puerto Rico in the last few days show us that natural disasters are still happening. The tremors are rumbling and destroying homes even now, and people are struggling to find shelter. It's very scary."

Jamie watched and listened to her closely. Something must have distracted her for a few seconds because she stopped talking, like she was thinking about those tremors. He wished he had a point to make and wracked his brain, but she recovered fast.

"I will present facts that prove even more strongly the Tambora eruption was a disaster, resulting in loss of life in the immediate area and so much loss too, in other parts of the world. We already know that famine led to diseases like cholera that killed millions. But the change in climate that Tambora caused brought new strains of the disease that spread to Western Europe and North America."

Jamie waved his hand to say something he remembered about medicines that were developed as a result. He had to get that in, but Clara kept talking. He waved again, but she ignored him. His impatience almost made him erupt and interrupt, but he pictured standing on the snowy Vermont mountain with the team on Saturday and cooled himself back to classroom normal.

"Scientists have predicted that new volcanic eruptions could occur within a thousand years and could be even worse than Tambora because the world population will have naturally grown.

"Finally, for today at least, I'd like you to listen to the pessimistic poetry that Tambora inspired back then. This is by Lord Byron: 'All earth was but one thought—and that was death.'"

Jamie listened as Clara emphasized the word *death*.

"'Immediate and inglorious; and the pang / Of famine fed upon the entrails—men / Died, and their bones were tombless as their flesh.'"

She paused to emphasize the words *died*, and *bones*, and *tombless*, and *flesh*. She was good. How could he beat this?

"I won't read the next part because it's too depressing, but these are the last lines: 'The rivers, lakes and ocean all stood still, / And nothing stirr'd within their silent depths; . . . / And the clouds perish'd; Darkness had no need / Of aid from them—She was the Universe.' It sounds as if the writer thought the end of the world was at hand." She stepped back and nodded at Jamie. "Your turn."

He scratched his head. "That was incredible, Clara. Yeah, those earthquakes in Puerto Rico are bad, but I don't think you'll see any more after they stop rumbling." He didn't want to downplay the earthquakes since they happened where Clara used to live, but other thoughts overshadowed that—his science grade, and which one of them Mr. J found more convincing.

"There are lots of small earthquakes happening where the earth shakes for a while, then goes back to sleep. So I wouldn't worry. I read in my research that scientists are studying conditions today that might be similar to those back when big disasters happened so they can predict when a big one is on the way. And like you said, Clara, we have a thousand years."

Much as he wanted to, he didn't dare glance at her. His guilt would show, betraying their relationship. He cared about Clara. He liked her a lot. More than a lot. But right now, he had to think about himself. He knew how to entertain his classmates and maybe Mr. J. He had to do whatever it took to convince them he was right.

He walked to the window with strides of intention, as if he really did know what he was talking about. He looked both ways, then turned back to the class. "All clear. We're safe. I don't think we have to worry about another volcanic eruption happening soon."

Kids laughed. Molly cheered, "Go Jamie! A thousand years."

He glanced at Clara, who stared straight ahead, looking like this didn't matter. But he knew it did. He could imagine how she felt, probably that he was such a jerk for putting up with Molly's remarks. He'd talk to Clara about that later. For now, he had to stop joking, even though having everyone agree with him felt amazing.

"And about the cholera spreading, Clara—" He turned to her, glad he could finally get this fact in. He told himself to be nice. "That got scientists to invent new medicines that they still use to cure people today. So that's good, right?" He hoped that would get a nod from her, but she still stared straight ahead. He wondered if Clara knew how effective that strategy was, acting as if nothing bothered her. He'd have to try it sometime.

He wished the debate were over and they could go back to being how they had been, but he still had to argue her points about writers, had to use any facts he could remember. His grade depended on it. "I'm not a big reader, but now that I know about these books that were written as a result of Tambora, I'm going to be busy reading."

He addressed Mr. J. "The writer who wrote that poem, Lord Byron, traveled with all these other writer friends in 1816 to Switzerland for a vacation. The skies were still covered with ash a whole year after Tambora erupted. It rained, and nobody could hike or be outdoors. So they stayed inside next to the fire and had a contest to see who could write the best horror story. Amazing, right?" He glanced at Clara, who stood with her arms crossed, impatience on her face.

"That's when Mary Shelley won the contest. Everybody loves Frankenstein, right?" He walked on his heels and made like a monster. Kids laughed. Clara looked up at the clock, then blew out a puff of air as if she couldn't wait to get out of there. Mr. J watched, his hand cupping his chin.

Jamie went on. "I'm psyched to read it. And a guy named Percy Bysshe Shelley" —he could hardly get out the name—"probably her husband, I'm not sure, wrote something called . . ." He thought hard, searching his mind and was stunned that he remembered the title. ". . . 'Hymn to International Beauty.' That's about beauty in the world.

"See, Clara? These writers weren't all writing doom and gloom. I never read that one either, but I might now." Another glance at Mr. J, who seemed interested, then at Clara, who hurried forward to say something.

"I'm sure you're going to tell us that Charles Dickens wrote his stories because he remembered how gloomy it was when he was growing up," she said skeptically.

He grinned. Just what he needed. "Yes, Clara. That's exactly what I was going to say. Look at how many novels he wrote. I never knew that before I did my research."

Mr. J's face was serious, but his shoulders shook as if he were holding in a laugh.

Jamie's spirits brightened even more. "I can't wait to read *A Christmas Carol*. You know, Scrooge and Tiny Tim?"

Clara rolled her eyes. "You're going to be really busy reading, Jamie, with all these books that have been classics long before your research. You might not have time for snowboarding."

"Ooohs" came from the class. Clara smiled, almost as if she liked joking, too, and getting a response. Jamie knew that she didn't want to hurt his chances for a good grade but that she was struggling to stand up to him and his joking. She never liked to make a scene. He sensed the hurt that the other kids couldn't see. Maybe he shouldn't have mentioned all those books that he said he wanted to read but probably wouldn't. Another lie. He didn't know how he could fix the damage he was doing. He tried to think of a couple of books to mention or at least one he'd read in fifth grade, but he couldn't come up with any other than a picture book called *Snow Day*, so he scrapped that idea.

He really wanted this battle to end but he had to prove he'd done research. He held up his hand to stop the *ooohs*. "Something else. Great art came about as a result of Tambora. William Turner, just like Dickens, Clara"—he glanced at her—"remembered how it was in 1816. He remembered the sunsets with all the strange colors in them, and years later, he painted those sunsets like no one had ever done before. His art is in museums all around the world. Maybe there's one of his paintings in our own Museum of History and Art. Can't wait to go and see."

He glanced at Clara sheepishly. He could tell she knew exactly what he was doing. She frowned at him and smirked too. Mentioning Turner, who he'd just learned about last night, was a big mistake. But he was simply presenting legitimate facts. Why was he so afraid? So what if she thought he was a fake?

Even as he reassured himself, he searched for some sliver of confidence inside to go on. "The very last thing I'll say about results of Tambora is totally new to me. I didn't know anything about Napoleon, but now I do. So here it is: The rainy days and muddy fields that Tambora caused where they were camped out"—he glanced up and put his hand to his chin to fake trying to bring a fact to mind—"somewhere in Belgium I think, fooled Napoleon into thinking his enemy—the British and their allies— wouldn't attack. But they did attack, and Napoleon was history. That was the Battle of Waterloo. Isn't that amazing? I wish we would study Napoleon. I don't know if he's a good guy or a bad guy or whether it's good or bad that he lost the Battle of Waterloo. You can read about all this and decide whether that was good or bad. That's it."

He bowed again and the class broke into applause, fueling his enthusiasm. The attention felt so good. He could have gone on longer.

Jamie wondered how he'd remembered all those points in the spotlight. But it was easy. His research had been interesting and made him wish he could have more projects like this one. School should be amazing research and debates all the time. Kids would love school then and really learn something. For a few seconds he saw himself in front of a classroom assigning a project on Napoleon or maybe famous battles that were won or lost because of curious events like volcanic eruptions thousands of miles away or other anomalies. He pictured himself telling students the meaning of anomalies, a word he had learned in his research. The word was full of so much possibility. Imagining himself up in front of a class of kids who were interested in what he was saying thrilled him. Like a great snowboard run.

"Good job," Clara said to him as she walked briskly to her seat. She said it like she had to but didn't mean it.

"You too," he whispered back. How could she even say good job when he'd attacked her? She had to defend herself against him. He wished he could erase the last thirty minutes. "You were awesome, Clara."

She faintly smiled. "Thanks." She gathered her stuff together and sat, ready to bolt.

She didn't really mean that either. He knew Clara. He had attacked her researched arguments by joking and had made the class think he knew more than he did. Sure, some of it was true, but he didn't have to walk to the window and make his dramatic prediction. He pictured her face when the class laughed as he belittled some of the other points she had made, simply for the applause and, he had to admit, for his grade. He knew it wasn't fair. She'd looked hurt. But at the moment when he could see his grade going up, he couldn't help himself. Making people laugh was like pats on the shoulder. He'd gotten a lot of pats from Clara—not physical pats, but her confiding in him and helping when he needed support in school. She was always cheering for him. That got him thinking maybe she didn't take his joking during the debate so badly. Maybe it was all in his mind. Maybe she knew that was just how he was. He didn't want to imagine it any other way. He'd convince her that he didn't mean it.

Clara hurried out of school after their last class. Jamie ran in the direction of her house but didn't see her, so he figured she didn't want to be found. He'd done just what Mom had warned him about; he'd acted without thinking about the results. She always said it with a smile on her face, though. Dad said it too, but in a different way; that Jamie had to learn to take responsibility for his actions. And Dad never smiled when he said it. They were both right. What he had done during the debate against Clara was proof that he'd acted without thinking about the results. He had only himself to blame for feeling bad now. He'd figure out what to say, something to convince her that he was sorry. He knew how to debate, how to convince, so he'd explain everything to Clara. Things between them would be okay again. He turned and headed home.

He was surprised to see Mom's car in the driveway. When he walked inside, she stood in front of the TV in the family room. She pointed to the screen. Lines of people were hurrying along a dirt road, carrying packs on their backs and pulling loaded carts. He moved closer to the TV. "What happened? Where is this?"

Mom motioned him closer. "The Philippine Islands. A volcano erupted. I think it's called Taal. It was a level four out of five. People are saying it's like the end of the world. Six thousand people were evacuated and told not to come back. Those poor families." Her hands flew to her ears and covered them as if she could keep out more bad news. She'd had plenty of practice from watching scenes in Afghanistan. "They have no place to live. No flights are going out. People are trapped."

Jamie couldn't believe what he was hearing. They weren't talking about a thousand years from now, like the scientists had predicted for the next big one. He had been joking about new volcanic eruptions just a couple of hours ago. Then he'd made things worse with that scene at the window and saying the class was safe. But the people in the Philippines weren't safe. And there was no sun out. Just like after Tambora. Chills ran all over his body. This couldn't be real.

"Mom, I have to call Clara." He gave her a pat on the shoulder and headed to his room.

He punched in Clara's number. "Clara, hi. Did you hear about the volcanic eruption? Yes, in the Philippine Islands. I don't even know where they are. Yeah. It's on TV now. My mom is so upset. I can't believe we just talked about eruptions today." This was his chance for the big apology, and he was ready, but she started in before he could tell her he was sorry.

He listened for five whole minutes and didn't say a word while Clara pointed out all the jokes he had made about her important arguments.

"Yeah, you're right. I-I-I'm sorry. I wanted to tell you after class but you'd—" It was hard trying to explain to Clara when he couldn't see her reactions. "I was wrong to talk about eruptions and how they wouldn't happen. You said it could again, and I made fun of that. But it happened today. I shouldn't have joked about disasters. I'm such a dork." She wasn't saying anything, probably thinking how messed up he was. "Hey, Clara. I'm not good at apologizing."

He waited for her response. When she didn't say anything, he added, "Clara, listen, and please answer me. Don't be mad at me. Please. You wanted to finish our debate tomorrow, so let's do it. I don't want to argue anymore. I mean, I don't want to argue like we're doing now, but we can argue in the debate. You know what I mean. I don't care who wins."

Shut up, he told himself. He drummed his fingers on his desk and waited, hoping she would believe some of what he'd said. He couldn't even imagine how he had come out of this second debate so well, with all the applause and kids laughing. How was Mr. J grading them? Was Clara worried? She wasn't giving him any clues.

"What are we going to talk about, though?" he asked. "Do you still have more stuff . . . arguments?" He didn't say that he didn't have any more. "Can we get together later so we can make a plan? I can meet you halfway. Maybe we can talk about all these disasters happening right now, like that earthquake in Puerto Rico and this new eruption in Philippines and—"

Clara interrupted, as if she'd had enough of his rambling. "It's *The* Philippines. And don't worry about tomorrow," she said. "You're right. We have to talk about these current disasters."

Jamie sucked in a breath and felt a tingling inside. He'd done something right for a change.

"Just get to school early," Clara said. "I have enough stories about all these new disasters for ten reports. We only need thirty minutes' worth. But you'll have to read some of the articles before we report. I'll bring them tomorrow. But meantime go online or on your phone, and you can read about them. Current Disasters."

"Okay. I will. Let's go for it."

"Then after tomorrow," she said, not even acknowledging his enthusiasm, "we'll be done with our debate project and be ready to move to the next stage."

"Yeah, great. Next stage." He waited for more and when nothing came from her, he asked, "What's that?"

"What we—all of us students—can do about some of these disasters that are actually man-made because we're living in ways that are making our climate change for the worse."

"That's good," Jamie said, feeling they were on good terms again. Maybe even great. But maybe not. Clara's serious voice was back.

She spoke as if she were still debating in science class. "We have to start with our class, convince them to help. I found out online that there's a big climate rally downtown on Saturday. We can go. It'll be great to see how people, right here in Albany, are working for change. Maybe kids like us will be there. We'll get ideas and be able to tell everybody in class. It's our future. And I have the whole day because my mother's not working on Saturday."

Jamie gulped. Vermont. The bus. Six in the morning. Coach. The team. Thoughts spun in his mind. "Saturday?" Of course, it *would* be on the same day. "Um, yeah. Our future. Sure." He was glad she couldn't see defeat all over his face. He couldn't tell her. Not yet. He'd just go along with her for now. A big part of his brain was saying, *So much for the trip to Vermont. It's not important.* Yes, it was. He had to go. Another part was saying, *Rally, rally.* He forced a smile. Maybe Clara wouldn't hear his confusion and fading enthusiasm. "What time should we meet?"

"Early." Her big cheery answer told him she couldn't wait. "We have to get a bus downtown. I have the schedule. Got to go now. See you tomorrow. Early, remember?"

Jamie's hope and optimism disappeared along with Clara after the click. He didn't know how he would tell her when the time came, but he'd think of something. Say he had an emergency, like he had to go someplace with his dad. He couldn't imagine her face when she heard he wouldn't go with her. He didn't want that disappointment. He loved her smiles when she was happy with him. He loved her smiles any time. Maybe he loved *her*.

She wouldn't have that smile on her face after he told her. He erased all his romantic thoughts. No time for them now. There was one thing he knew he loved beyond a doubt: snowboarding for his team. He wasn't sure what excuse he'd make up, but he had to be on the bus to find snow in Vermont.

Chapter Seventeen

Good weather ahead

J amie got to school early even though he'd barely slept. He thought he had made his decision. He had to go to Vermont and his plans were in the works, but he kept imagining Clara's face lighting up when she'd talked about the rally. He'd wrestled most of the night with deciding between them: Vermont or the rally. He was cracking up, picturing himself with the team on the bus. What a blast. But how could he disappoint Clara? He'd already done enough damage to their friendship.

He hurried downstairs to Coach's office. Locked. He jiggled the door again, out of frustration. Nobody in there. He had to see Coach. Maybe hint that he might not be able to go on Saturday. Ask if he could go with the team for the last competition instead. He could always say he was still trying to get out of . . . what? An emergency? If only he had one. He didn't even have a good lie.

As he trudged up the stairs he heard "Hi" from the top. Clara peered down at him.

"Hey. What are you doing up there?" he said as he took the stairs two at a time.

"Waiting for you. Good, you're early." She handed him a stack of newspapers, and they marched on.

Alone in their classroom, he waited for her to say something about Saturday, like, the rally was off. But she didn't.

"Before we start on this stack of papers," she said, "I want you to know you can do this research on your computer or your phone. All of these stories are there."

He remembered how she had said "just google it" a few weeks ago, when he'd felt so hopeless about his project, but she didn't say it now.

"I like reading them in the newspapers because I can see them all together," she explained. "And the large photos add so much."

She showed him the first headline: "California Fires Spreading Fast." Then the next: "Australian Fires Out of Control."

He read for about ten minutes, totally captivated by the photos. He finally raised his head. "These fires. Scary, all because it's getting hotter here and in Australia too. I saw something about this on TV, but I thought, okay, a fire, someone threw a match. Or lightning had struck. I had no idea it was the weather changing like it describes. So who's doing something about it?"

Clara rustled through the stack of papers and pulled one out. "Here. Look at these kids. They're staying out of school on Fridays and marching and texting their leaders and protesting that the government and governments all around the world aren't doing enough to stop global warming." She stabbed at the newspapers. "Here's the proof—all these current disasters. And it's mostly kids trying to do something about them."

Jamie was listening so hard that he didn't realize his mouth was wide open. He closed it fast. "Yeah, I saw this girl on TV too. Greta something, right?"

Clara nodded. "Yes, Greta the Great. She's from Sweden and so young and courageous. Just google her. She wants kids everywhere to spread the message about climate change and what it's doing to our planet." Clara opened another newspaper, and both of them gazed at the words in bold print: "Heat wave

. . . ten degrees higher than normal in Greenland. Glaciers melting as never before."

For a split second, glaciers reminded him of snow and Vermont. He pushed the thought away. "So that's why the sea level is rising," he said. "My dad said there were lots of people applying for loans to repair walls. I never connected that with glaciers melting." He looked straight at Clara. "Credit, right?" He thought about their debate and how they had argued about it. "But this credit isn't for wheat."

"No. It's for keeping all that water out. We have to rally our class and other classes and schools, like Greta did. Kids in Albany probably don't even know how close we are to another disaster. We have to send them online links. Then maybe we can march to let people know what they can do and text our state leaders. I'll text the governor."

Jamie smiled as he thought of her new friend, the governor. He scratched his head. "Great idea to text him, but how can we stop new volcanic eruptions like the one in the Philippines and that earthquake in Puerto Rico a few days ago?"

Clara shrugged. "Most of these experts say the new disasters are happening because of global warming. You have to read, Jamie. They say the seas are higher from all the melting. Hotter weather is causing the normal hurricanes to be stronger and more destructive because they carry more wind and rain. And a lot more hurricanes are forming because of that weather. Hurricane season starts all over in June. Puerto Rico and other places that get hurricanes are in big trouble."

Jamie kept his gaze on her. He knew she was thinking about her father and relatives and friends who still lived there. He wanted to ask her how they were doing, but he didn't want to upset her. Better to stay focused on their topic. "So are we going to talk about all this new disaster stuff today? What about our final debate on natural disasters? We told Mr. J that we'd do three. Will this count?" He was also thinking, *What about Saturday?* She hadn't mentioned it so far.

Clara cocked her head. "Jamie, I don't know who won the debate, but I think we covered what we had to. We have more important disasters to talk about—these current ones, and they're probably not natural but mostly man-made."

The way she said that gave him the shivers. "You're right, Clara, I don't care who won, either." He meant it. He'd often called the war that Lucas was fighting a man-made disaster. Those were the disasters to talk about today.

The first bell rang, and kids took their seats. Mr. J announced that Jamie and Clara would give their final presentation that morning. Clara had told Mr. J that they would cover new information and that they wouldn't debate. Mr. J said it was fine with him. After the second bell and getting kids to quiet down, Mr. J said, "So without further ado, Clara and Jamie."

Jamie mentally noted "ado" to look up. Why did people say that, anyhow? He couldn't take his eyes off Clara, who seemed so confident, so prepared. He was readier than he would have been, thanks to her. He forced away the nagging thought about wanting to get the best grade that day, for Coach . . . and Dad. Most of all, for himself.

They walked to the front of the room. Clara brought her stack of newspapers and set them in two piles. They hadn't talked about who would start, but he was psyched to begin. He wasn't sure where that confidence had come from, but he was going with it. Still, nerves made him twist the bottom of his shirt. She nodded, and he began.

"Um . . . Clara and I are done with the debate on natural disasters. We don't care who won." A few kids laughed as if they didn't believe that, and it stopped him. What was so funny? He continued. "But we'd like to talk about how all of us right here, right now, are losing the world we're living in because of disasters happening today."

Clara nodded so he opened a newspaper.

"Did you know that this eruption, Taal, that blasted out yesterday—can you believe that?—and Tambora, that erupted in back in 1815, are in the same part of the world, really close to each other?" He put his fingers a little apart. "Just an inch apart on the map. It's actually fifteen hundred fifty-one miles. They're both in Indonesia. Remember when Clara showed us where that was? I guess that's not a good place to live, right?" He reminded himself—no joking. "And I guess that's a place where more volcanoes could erupt any time. I found out all this on my phone. You can too. The only thing we can do about volcanic eruptions happening now is do all we can to keep the planet from getting hotter. The experts say that's what gets the gases started."

He glanced at Clara for approval. She nodded.

"And there are lots of things we can do right here about fires and floods that are happening across the country almost every week now." He held up another newspaper. "Did you know that it was almost sixty-five degrees in Antarctica a few weeks ago? That's the South Pole. More ice is melting, so there's more water in our oceans. And we wonder why all these floods are happening now. I wondered too, until I read all this." He pointed to the newspapers. "Come on, guys. You have to help with this bad climate change thing." He figured that was all he had and stopped.

Clara stepped up to the whiteboard and listed the disasters Jamie had described. She also printed Siberia—one hundred degrees last week—next to it. "Never before," she added.

Jamie sputtered a few words, then caught his breath. He had more to say. "And did you know that the Arctic is the refrigerator for the world? Well, it used to be. But now it's a lot warmer up there because of this climate change, and it can't do its cooling job. Just picture your refrigerator at home heating up. What would that look like?"

"Or smell like?" someone called out. Some kids laughed. Others said, "Ewww." Kids sat forward and listened.

"We have to move," a student named Greg said. "My dad lost his job over at the nuclear plant. We don't even know where we're going. Someplace where there's a job. That's what my mom said."

Jonathan spoke up. "I don't want to move to Florida. But that's where my dad got a job selling solar energy. Guess that's good, but leaving here sucks."

Jamie nodded. "We'll miss you, big guy," and kids started in about missing him. Jamie couldn't believe his classmates were blurting all this personal stuff out. "We're probably going to have to do a lot of things we don't want to do," he said. "Like the snowboard team driving all the way to Vermont to find snow this Saturday." He glanced at Clara and flashed her a quick smile.

"Hey, Jamie." It was Chuck. "You're right. No snow. That's why we're moving. My dad lost his job up at Rugged Mountain. Even if they make snow like they did all these years, it doesn't last now. It's not cold enough anymore. I think skiing and snow-boarding around here are history."

Jamie winced.

Someone was crying. Molly swiped at her eyes, then fake-brightened, Molly style. "Too many things are changing. It's not fair." Her voice shook.

Kids started moving around, talking to their neighbors. Then Lucy stood up, and kids got quiet. "I know how you feel, Molly. I always wanted to go to the Great Barrier Reef to surf and scuba to see the amazing coral." Jamie couldn't believe how Lucy never said a word in class, but here she was, speaking up. "They say all the coral in the reef is getting bleached out and dying because the water's too warm. Our generation is going to miss out on all the good stuff. It's sad. What generation are we, anyhow?"

Jamie shook his head. "No idea, but we'll get a Gen letter soon enough. I think they have to start over in the alphabet. Maybe we'll be Gen D for disasters." He couldn't believe so many of their classmates were moving away from Albany because of climate change. He felt the sadness burn in his throat.

He opened another newspaper. "And last of all about these disasters, the United Nations Intergovernmental Panel on Climate Change wrote that we have less than twenty years of environment stability before we've crossed the point of no return. Less than twenty years." He paused to let it sink in, then went on. "We're all going to be adults, maybe with children by then, and our world will be really messed up."

Clara thanked Lucy for her comments and added bleached out coral reefs to the whiteboard. She told the class about the forests being cut down around the world. "Trees are so valuable because they capture toxic carbon. They're being cut down faster than we can count them. We're the ones who will have to breathe poisonous air."

"Yeah," Jamie said. "And I read that people can taste the fire and smoke in their throats. Ugggh."

Kids gasped and sniffed the air and coughed.

Clara wiped her eyes and glanced at Molly. Jamie waited with Clara. He knew she didn't want Molly to cry again. "Clara, do you want to add anything?"

She nodded. "Thanks. I don't even want to tell you about the orangutans being killed when their forests are cut down, but I have to. Illegal loggers slash the trees so they can plant palm trees for the palm oil just so companies can use it in potato chips and soap and peanut butter and shampoo and other things. Think of that the next time you pick up a potato chip. We'll probably never get to see a real live orangutan swinging from trees. Everywhere you look, the news says that the mass extinction of animals is driven not by a catastrophe but by humans. *Us.*

"The animals and creatures that we love are disappearing. I'm going to name just a few of them. If you would like to, you can lower your heads out of respect." She lowered hers for a moment then faced the class and began naming them.

"Tigers, reindeer, kangaroos, koalas, gorillas, giraffes, songbirds. All the parrots in Puerto Rico are almost gone. Emperor penguins, butterflies, sea turtles, bees. There are a lot more." She stopped and took a breath to give the message time to sink in. "Just google them, you'll see. Experts call this time we're living in the end of nature. They say there is no Planet B."

Jamie gazed at Clara in amazement at all her knowledge and how much she loved nature. He might have aped an orangutan before but not now. He was done joking about serious stuff. He thought about all those animals being lost and lowered his head again. He wanted to walk over to Clara and stand next to her, but she started in again. He stayed where he was.

"The reindeer in the Arctic are starving because the grass and greens they eat is under ice called permafrost that thaws because of the warm rain. Then it freezes again, and the reindeer can't get to the food. Or the temperature gets warm and everything melts and floods. Same thing. No food for the animals. If we don't care if our children never know these animals, we'll sit back and let global warming destroy their chances for a happy life and healthy planet.

"I'd like to read one last thing. It's what Jamie Margolin said to Congress in Washington, DC. She's seventeen, and founder of the climate activist group Zero Hour. You can google her report too. 'Everyone who will walk up to me after this testimony saying I have such a bright future ahead of me will be lying to my face. It doesn't matter how talented we are, how much work we put in, how many dreams we have, the reality is, my generation has been committed to a planet that is collapsing.'"

Clara stepped back, which surprised Jamie because she always had more to say than he did. He swallowed and continued. "Yeah. Wow. So what I think Clara's saying, and me too, is that we have to act now, tell kids in school here—really young kids too—and in other schools around Albany and the state that it's up to us to keep our planet from going up in smoke or disappearing into the oceans. Wouldn't it be great to have classes on climate and keep up every day with how it's changing our planet? I'd be psyched for that class."

Kids laughed.

"No kidding. Maybe we can get our school board to do this. Mr. J would be the best teacher, right?"

Kids clapped and said, "Go, Mr. J."

Jamie held up a folded newspaper in one hand and his phone in the other. "It's all in here and here. I'm ready to go to the school board if you are."

Gasps and mutterings came from the class.

Lucy asked, "Are we allowed to?"

Jamie shrugged. "We have to if we want to save our planet."

More applause. Mr. J stood and paced around the classroom. "Comments on the presentation? Opinions?"

Kids' hands shot up.

"Awesome."

"It *was* awesome," Molly said.

Jamie noticed Clara turning to her, about to say something, but Molly kept talking.

"Awesome about the climate causing all that. Katy and I saw this animated movie on Friday night about a place where it wouldn't stop raining. A girl finds the sun and when she sings, the rain stops. She meets this homeless boy and together they sell the sun to drenched people. Wouldn't it be cool to be able to change the weather by singing?"

"Yeah," Nick said, "but that's not going to happen. "You know those big fires they can't put out in California?"

Molly and other kids sat on the edge of their seats.

Nick kept talking. "We have relatives out there, and guess whose house burned down? Yep. Theirs. So they're coming to stay with us. Five people. We don't have a lot of room, but we've got to share. That's what my mom said."

"Whoa. That's going to be hard," another kid said. "My mom said the fires started because it's way hotter than it used to be out there."

Lots of yeahs and nods came from the class.

"My parents had planned to take me to Paris for graduation," Katy said. "But my dad read that the temperature was over a hundred and ten degrees, so they canceled the trip." She let out a big sigh.

"I heard about the floods on the news, but I didn't pay attention," another girl said. "I figured they're not in Albany so why worry?"

"Yeah, but you should worry," Chuck said. "Look at the temperature today. It's like summer out there, and it's only March."

"Clara, I'll go to the school board with you," said Lucy, who'd spoken up earlier about the coral.

Clara nodded. "Great, Lucy. You'll be a great representative."

Lucy beamed a huge smile—one Jamie had never seen before. She looked like a different person.

"Jamie, do you have some last words?" Clara asked.

He gulped. He hadn't expected that. She sounded like Mr. J. "Um, yeah, sure." He stalled for a few seconds, standing with his chin in his hand like Mr. J did sometimes as he tried to come to some conclusion about disasters. "Okay. Some last words. It's kind of the perfect ending to our presentation," he said. "Here we are right now in twenty-first-century Albany, in the Year Without a Winter, right?" He waited for the nods. "Clara and I started out our debate about the Year Without a Summer that happened back in the nineteenth century.

"If we hadn't had this amazing assignment"—he glanced at Mr. J—"I wouldn't know anything about volcanic eruptions and what they caused. I thought some things that happened afterward were pretty cool. Clara told us the real facts, though, about how disastrous conditions were." He waited to see if there were any comments. Kids were quiet, probably from information overload. "We have lots of work ahead of us, so we don't have another Year Without a Summer—or a Year Without a Winter."

Kids clapped wildly. Jamie bowed. Clara waited for the applause to end, then bowed too. They took their seats, and Jamie breathed. Finally. His heart thumped. Not from fear, from excitement. He'd finished his assignment.

As Mr. J got to Jamie's desk, he leaned over and whispered, "You taught us so much. I'm proud of you." He patted Jamie on the shoulder. Then he moved over to Clara.

Jamie sucked in a breath, then a second one. Mr. J was proud of him. Chills ran through him, but the feelings he sat with were warm. Maybe Dad would say the same when his grade went up. Their presentation had been the best.

Then the warm feelings fizzled. How could he have forgotten? Saturday. Clara and the rally.

He didn't get much work done the rest of the day. He'd heard the term *perfect storm* and thought it sounded like what he was in the middle of—unpredictable, bad things coming together at one time that would end up even worse. How could anyone call that perfect? Sometimes words confused him. He'd just had a perfect presentation. Now he had to figure out his next predicament— getting to Vermont. Or not.

He headed home fast. Clara jogged up to him and slowed to a walk alongside. "Jamie, stop. Wait."

He turned, happy to see her.

"How can you be so, so unaware?"

He looked at her, dumbfounded. What was she talking about?

"Of course, you're going to be on that bus on Saturday morning. Do you think I can't hear you or see you up close? I saw your coach talking to you today. You looked like you were ready to jump out of your skin. And I talked to Nick at recess, so I know the team wants you to go with them. Why didn't you tell me about your trip last night when we spoke?" Clara stared at him with a questioning face like she was deciding their whole future right then. "We can't be true friends if you can't tell me honestly that Saturday is important to you. Do you think I don't understand?"

Jamie's stomach did flips. He held back a big *yay*. Then he wanted to scream at her. He wasn't sure if he was like a little kid-on-his-birthday happy or raging mad. She had known all day that he wanted to go. She had known last night too, on the phone. She could have told him. Maybe she thought he wouldn't focus on their presentation if she'd confronted him. Maybe she just wanted him to sweat and be miserable. It had worked. He'd been a wreck. But now she was doing a full turn in midair, giving him a gift. Vermont.

He couldn't help himself and lunged to hug Clara. She took a step back, blinking in surprise. They swayed, then stumbled, laughing and blushing. After a few more stumbles they found their balance. Another laughing spell came on.

Clara untangled herself and said, "Hey. See you next week. Have a great trip."

"What about the rally?"

"Oh, I'll be there." She waved and left.

Walking home, he thought about all that had just happened. He leapt into the air. "Yes!" he shouted. He should have been able to tell Clara how he felt, but he'd had too much practice holding in his feelings. Those bad feelings still churned inside. He wasn't sure how Clara had brought these memories up in him, but happy thoughts about how Dad used to be when Jamie was little surfaced. They'd played games. Jamie remembered really loving him. He stopped. He couldn't trust those feelings. That was long ago. Then Dad turned on him and started to yell for no reason and to expect so much once Lucas left.

It had started even before that, when Dad and Lucas argued so much. And it kept getting worse. Then somehow it seemed as if it were Jamie's fault that Lucas had enlisted. That's how Jamie felt every time Dad looked at him with disappointment and anger. So how could he ever tell Dad anything he felt? That was scarier than boarding down a monstrous mountain he'd never faced before. Someday, maybe. And maybe he'd tell Clara how he felt about all the things she'd said to him and also how he felt about her. He couldn't take a chance that she could turn on him too. He had a lot of hard work ahead of him with this feeling stuff. But he didn't have to think about that now. Clara had said he should go to Vermont on Saturday. And he was going.

Chapter Eighteen

Seismic

*J*amie ran the rest of the way home. He couldn't get there fast enough, couldn't wait to tell his parents, especially Dad, about the best day of school ever. About his last debate, although Mr. J had called it a presentation because it was about current disasters like floods and fires and he and Clara were no longer debating but agreeing. He'd tell Dad that Mr. J thought their project went really well and that Mr. J would tell Coach, and Jamie would be back on the team. Finally, he could give Dad the news he wanted to hear, that he wasn't failing science.

He rushed inside. Mom was slumped on the sofa, Dad next to her, with his arm around her, close.

"What happened?" His voice caught in his throat as he read the shock on their faces that said things would never be the same. Mom glanced at him, tears running down her cheeks.

"Come sit down," Dad said. "Everything's under control."

"Control? No, it isn't. Is it Lucas? Tell me!" Jamie insisted, his voice rising to almost a shout.

Mom wiped her eyes and patted the sofa. "Come, Jamie. Sit here." She made room for him and waited until he was next to her and had stopped breathing like he'd just raced downhill. "We

159

don't know exactly how Lucas is. There was an explosion at the base. He rushed into all that . . . it must have been bad . . ." She broke down again. Jamie hugged her. ". . . to pull men from the flames. That's when another one . . ."

She stopped again. Her head dropped into her hands. She sat like that, not even moving, probably holding everything in that wanted to come out. He knew that feeling. But Mom always made everything okay. *Make it okay, now, Mom. Please.*

Finally, she choked out a sob and stroked his arm. "They're bringing him home."

Jamie tried to speak but nothing came out. Weakness overtook him. "When?" He got up, tried holding himself together by smacking his palm with his fist. Hit. Hit. He stood in front of Mom. "Why, Mom? Why?" he asked, but she didn't answer. "Lucas was always careful. He's probably just exhausted, right?" He tried to assure himself. "He was at the base, in a safe place, right, Mom? You can tell me, Mom. Did he lose a leg or arm? I need to know, Mom." Mom could make it better. Couldn't she?

Dad rubbed his forehead and stood in front of him. "Stop it, Jamie." The defeat in his eyes was almost more than Jamie could bear. "The officer mentioned head trauma." Dad winced. He wiped his eyes. Jamie had never seen him cry before. Dad finally said, "They're putting him on a medical transport plane out of Kabul. They think he's stable enough."

"So that's good news, right? He's stable and he's coming home," Jamie pleaded, trying to find any shred of hope in the war words. He forced a picture of Lucas and him, maybe next season, boarding to the bottom of a steep slope in no time. "At least he doesn't have shell shock, right? And he's stable, right? They said that, right?" He sounded ridiculous babbling on and on, but he couldn't stand the ominous silence that filled the room. He'd give up all his dreams about snowboarding forever just to have Lucas be okay and for Dad go back to being the regular strong dad he knew, not a scared, crying dad.

Dad shook his head wearily. "He said trauma, Jamie. Shell shock, PTSD . . . they're the same thing. However bad it is, we'll have to wait and see."

Trauma. Shell shock. PTSD. All bad news. Mom covered Jamie's hands and motioned for Dad to join them. "But *we're* here for him," she said, probably holding back a flood of tears. The determination in her words lifted Jamie's spirits for a few seconds, though.

Under his mom's warm hands, he moved closer to Dad's hand, closed his eyes and pretended that they were in a shelter like the one Clara and her family had been in during the hurricane. They were safe. Nothing could hurt Mom, Dad, Lucas, and him while they held onto each other. Tears rolling down his cheeks burned and brought him back. Dad pulled his hands away and gripped his arms. Jamie sat up and told himself to face it. Facts were facts. He had learned that working on his project. Facts were what really happened. He couldn't make up a story about them or joke to convince his audience about something else. He couldn't do anything about his brother's trauma. He didn't know what to hope for in case it was the wrong thing or it wasn't possible. He tightened his fists. He had to be strong.

"All three of us are here for him," Mom said again, like it was for good luck.

Her tears were ready to roll again. He squeezed her hands to help her hold them back, and she tried to smile—for him, Jamie knew, but it wasn't her normal smile. Nothing was normal since he'd walked into the house.

Suddenly things in front of him looked blurry. His ears were ringing, his head spinning. He felt weak and dizzy, then everything went dark.

———

Sound came first . . . buzzing, then quiet. His eyes stretched open. Where was he? Mom's face came into focus. She was patting his forehead with a wet washcloth. He felt the smooth fabric under him. He was lying on the sofa. His parents' faces were in front of him. Dad held a glass of liquid out to him. Jamie licked his lips. So dry. He reached for the glass. "Did I zonk out?"

"A lot of people do," Dad said. "You took in a lot of serious news. The ginger ale will make you feel better."

He lay still for a while, mind blank, waiting for the room to stop moving. He'd fainted. He took a sip of the ginger ale. Ahh. He was okay. Maybe. In his house, on their sofa. But Lucas. He sat up fast. Mom had said there had been an explosion. Lucas was coming home. But there was something else, some reason he couldn't wait to get home from school and talk to his parents. He recalled talking about global warming with Clara in front of the class. Then he remembered what she'd told him after school: Go to Vermont. She'd been serious. She wanted him to go. He'd almost kissed her again. He remembered it all now. Vermont. Saturday.

Coach's instructions, "Be at the school Saturday morning dressed for the slopes," echoed in his mind. He rubbed his head. What day was it? Thursday? Friday? Maybe he still had time. He pressed his temples, tried to think. He couldn't go. Not when Lucas was being shipped home any time. Anger coursed through him, then disappointment, then fear. What was he thinking? The trip wasn't important. Yes, it was. He couldn't think straight. His brain was all mixed up. Maybe Coach was still at school. Jamie slowly sat up. He felt dizzy but he had to call Coach. He reached in his pocket for his cell, then patted the other one. No phone.

"Mom," he said, sounding like a five-year old asking for a cookie, "Do you see my phone? I have to call Coach and tell him I won't be going with the team to the competition Saturday." Her questioning look reminded him that he hadn't told his parents that Coach had asked him to go. Everything had happened so fast.

Mom's response, "I'll look for it," surprised him. He would have bet all his season lift tickets that she would have said, "Go with your team," that it was okay, that he'd see Lucas when he got back. She didn't. His thoughts were tricking him again. He didn't know the right thing to do.

Jamie had always trusted Mom, believed that anything she said was the right thing. But now, the last thing he wanted her to say was that she'd find his phone. Things must be bad. He wanted her to understand how much he wanted to go to Vermont and to tell him to go. He shouldn't want to go to Vermont. He was being selfish. A strange feeling ran through him, the sense that his life was changing fast but he couldn't see even an inch ahead.

Chapter Nineteen

Overcast

That afternoon Clara googled the American Red Cross and saw that Albany was listed under the Northeastern Chapter in New York State. Maybe they could help Papi to get home or help her get in touch with him like Mrs. Thurber had said. She punched in the number with high hopes.

"American Red Cross," a man said.

Clara composed herself. "Hello. My name is Clara Montalvo. I'm in eighth grade here in Albany." She waited.

"Yes. How can I help?"

"Thank you. My class is worried about all the disasters happening here and in lots of other places like in Puerto Rico. We want to help. Can you tell us how?"

"Thank you, Clara, for your interest. I'm Edward Morris. That's what we try to do—help."

He stopped and in those few seconds Clara couldn't hold in her excitement over connecting with the American Red Cross. "Oh, yes. You're so welcome," she said. She imagined him smiling on the other end.

"You mentioned Puerto Rico," he said. "Your class probably knows about the most recent earthquakes there. It's all over the news."

"Yes, we know," Clara said. She mentioned living there during María and couldn't resist telling how her family had been rescued and her father was down there rebuilding and not being able to get in touch with him. Talking fast so she could slip this question in, she asked about their helping to find her father and fly him home.

"I understand your situation, but we don't have planes carrying passengers out of Puerto Rico," he said. "I'm sorry, but that's not the work we do. We're on the ground in disaster areas. But you seem to understand the situation there very well, Miss. Many people in Puerto Rico still can't go back to their homes. They're in shelters and they don't have basic supplies like toothbrushes and batteries, towels, and things like that. The shelters are devastated too."

As Clara listened, hope for getting in touch with Papi or getting him back home drained from her.

"And people here in California and Mississippi, Louisiana, those areas that have suffered fires and floods and tornadoes recently—they need supplies too. Your class is very thoughtful to worry about these people whose lives are devastated."

She hadn't thought of that word, devastated. In her mind it was all disasters. But devastated meant no hope. The end. Most people gave up when they were devastated. Clara didn't know if she or her class could make much of a difference to devastated people, but she wanted to try. Her efforts might even help Papi in some long-distance way. The people in Puerto Rico after María had nothing left. They had been devastated, but supplies from volunteers had saved something to keep hope alive.

"Maybe our class could collect supplies," Clara said. "But I wouldn't know how to get them to the people. If we collected lots of things that . . . um . . . maybe things kids in schools could use, could you send them to the places that need them?"

"Thank you, Clara," he said. "Yes. We could help you coordinate your efforts."

"Thank you so much, Mr. Morris. I can't wait to tell the students in my class. They'll work hard once they know their collections will definitely go to help somewhere."

"These are rougher times than we've seen in many years," he said. "Working together, which is what you are suggesting, is how we'll all get through."

Clara's heart filled with pride and gratitude at the chance to help someone, even if it wasn't her papi right now. Maybe another person was helping him in some way at that very moment. Maybe that's how life worked. Yes. She had to believe that. "Should I call you back when we've collected things?"

"I'll be here. We're getting items from lots of people, but we can earmark your student collections for wherever you want them to go."

We'll collect school supplies, Clara thought. *For all those places. Maybe for Puerto Rico too.* "Mr. Morris, I'll call you as soon as we're standing next to boxes of pencils, erasers, notebooks, and lots more, okay? And thank you."

Their conversation made Clara think about eighth grade students like them in all the disaster areas, in the mainland United States where floods and fires had destroyed lives, but also in Puerto Rico after María and the recent earthquakes. She couldn't imagine kids even going to school there with the new damage. The leaders wouldn't allow kids to go into buildings that were dangerous. She remembered huddling under their desks when their teacher received an alarm about a big storm coming. They knew all about the hurricane dangers but had never thought winds or storms would topple their school. But after María taught that lesson, kids in island schools couldn't think like that anymore.

So what did they need? Everything she used here. She would make lists, and she hoped her classmates would feel as she did and make lists too. The needs seemed endless, but she hoped they could be a small part of the solution.

She read online about schools in Puerto Rico. Her school

in San Juan had closed after Hurricane María like schools all over the island. Most schools in the southern part of the island were closed again now because of new earthquake damage. She realized after all her research that schools in Puerto Rico weren't built to withstand earthquakes and hurricanes, even though they were required to be. She shuddered at how kids trusted grown-ups to do the right thing. Kids couldn't imagine that builders didn't build their schools with the best materials. Kids were kids and thought about other things—friends and fun. She stamped her foot hard. How could professional people—grown-ups—get away with being irresponsible?

She sat back and closed her eyes. At least the debate was over. She thought about Molly and her ballots. It all seemed so far away and small compared to serious problems in the world. She considered Jamie too smart to be fooled and tricked by Molly. She imagined him being really angry if he found out. But maybe not. Maybe he would be happy winning the debate with Molly's ballots.

If Molly thought she could get Jamie to like her for telling kids to vote for him and if he fell for it, they deserved each other. Clara couldn't do one thing about it. Her attempts to forget about Molly trying to cheat off her math test last year and resenting her for being Jamie's friend always failed, but she kept trying. Molly's tears when Chuck had talked about his dad losing his job and his family having to move had puzzled Clara. She didn't understand Molly.

She reminded herself that there were people who didn't cheat and who were nice. Like Mr. J. She had to believe he would grade them fairly.

She punched in Jamie's phone number.

"Hi. You okay?" she asked when he picked up. "I called earlier. What? Say that again. No! When? How is—" She sat on her bed and listened. Jamie said they didn't know how badly Lucas was hurt, just that they were bringing him home. She didn't want to ask too much. She knew how hard it was to not know.

Jamie told her everything that had happened, how he'd passed out, and how he had called school to tell Coach he couldn't go to Vermont. He had to be there for his brother whenever he got home and for his mom and dad.

"I'm so, so sorry about your brother." Clara tried for a cheery voice. "Maybe it won't be bad. Sometimes they send soldiers home to rest up."

"Yeah." He sounded unconvinced. "I hope so."

She wished she hadn't said that. It probably wasn't true, but she had to say something positive. If only she could send him some hope. Maybe she could. "Hey. Want to meet up . . . take a walk?" she asked. Did Jamie really want to leave his house after that bad news? Now that she'd asked, she had to leave it up to him. He probably needed to talk. "We could meet halfway, take a short walk. Um . . . unless you can't . . . I understand."

"No. I mean, yes. Yes, I'd like to," he blurted. "I need to get some air. I'll leave now. Halfway."

———

When she saw Jamie approaching, Clara hurried toward him. She had always been the serious one, but now she wanted to cheer him up, so she started to dance, probably the salsa, as she inched ahead. Jamie walked as if about to face a big test, but as they got closer, a smile broke out and he held up his fist. She moved closer and bumped it.

"Hey," he said.

"Hey," she answered, and they started off.

"You saved me with your phone call," he said. "I didn't know what to do next."

Clara turned and faced Jamie. "What would your brother want you to do right now?"

Jamie shrugged. "I don't know. Do you?"

"No, but after fighting and saving lives in Afghanistan, he has to know a lot more than he did when he first went . . . a lot more about war than we know. He might have changed in some ways, Jamie. But, still, I think that he would want the best for you, for you not to have to go to war, and he would mainly want you to be glad to see him. That's all you have to do. Let him know you're happy. I don't know, Jamie. I'm just imagining. He's really brave. That's for sure."

Jamie walked, head down. "It's scary not knowing how he'll be. I don't know if I can handle it if he's not my same Lucas."

Clara hooked her arm around his. "He'll still be your Lucas."

He glanced at her, as if she had said something magical. He stood straight, head up, and kept walking. "He used to love snowboarding. He taught me to love it too even though I was really scared of going down those steep slopes." Jamie laughed. In seconds, he got serious again. "Then I remember him always arguing with Dad. In the kitchen, in the den, in the garage, in the front hall. I know why they argued. Lucas wanted to do things his way, and Dad tried to stop him. Dad argues with me too. He always wants me to do things his way. I fight to get him off my back, but it causes more trouble and makes me angry and . . . I don't know, Clara. You're asking me things that I can't answer." He twisted the edge of his jacket.

She held onto Jamie as they moved ahead. "You'll be a really strong brother for Lucas when he gets home. That's what I know, Jamie. Look how you talked your way through the debate when you didn't think you could." She reminded him that he'd said he couldn't do research but got so many convincing facts. "You presented your information in such a professional way. And the way you joked was really effective. I didn't love it at the time, but now I see the advantage. Kind of like you convincing me about some of the good things that came about because of Tambora. Maybe you can teach me how to do a little of that joking." She glanced at him. He was smiling at least.

He stopped and pulled his phone out of his pocket. Clara saw the caller's name flash: Molly.

Clara pulled her arm from Jamie's snug hold. Her insides crumbled like a building on shaky ground. It wasn't any of her business who called Jamie, but Molly's selfie from a few nights ago came to mind. Then Molly laughing and talking about the ballots in the bathroom. Maybe Jamie knew all about them. Maybe they were teamed up in the secret voting. No. She would bet anything that Jamie wouldn't do that. Clara thought of all the help she'd given him before the debates. And now she was trying her best to make him feel better. Seeing Molly's name on his phone hurt. She released his arm, turned quickly and headed for home.

"Wait, Clara!" Jamie called as she sped away.

So what if Molly called him? Why should she care? This was a free country. And besides, Jamie was having a hard time now. That's all that mattered. She would want someone to be kind to her if she were in his situation. She'd forget about Molly. Before she could decide what to do, he caught up to her and grabbed her coat sleeve.

"Clara, look." He held up his phone. "I don't have a clue as to why she called me. I'll put a block on it. I never want to talk to her again."

"Jamie, I don't care what you do. We ... I have too much on my mind. I can't think about you and Molly."

"It's not me and Molly," he insisted loudly. "Want me to call her back and tell her to lay off? Never come near me again or call me? I'll do that just so you ..."

Clara faced him and faced the fact that maybe this was the end of their friendship. "Jamie. You're fourteen years old. I can't tell you what to do."

He smacked his head hard. "Okay."

He paced in a circle, then took hold of her arms. Their heads nearly bumped.

"Since you won't believe me, I have to tell you this. I screamed at that stupid girl. I wasn't going to tell you because I didn't want you to feel bad or hurt or any of those things you feel when Molly says mean things in class, but I have to, now. She started some stupid ballot thing, trying to get kids to vote and say I won the debate. It's so unfair, just like she is. I told her that if she didn't stop, I was going to tell Mr. J because it was wrong. It's cheating. You won if anyone did, Clara, but it doesn't matter." He peered into her eyes. "Does it?"

She held in a giggle, unable to believe he could make her care for him even when they were arguing.

"I didn't want any more trouble for us. I got you into enough already. There. Okay? Now you know. I have no idea why she called me. I clicked off as soon as I saw her name."

Clara blinked and took it all in. "Thank you. That was the right thing to do, Jamie, about Molly's ballots." She had to think about all this. By herself. But before she could leave, her phone vibrated. She pulled it out. *Molly.* Clara stopped and clicked on. "Molly."

Jamie did a double take. He kept close alongside her as she walked with her phone to her ear.

"Thanks, Molly. We need all the help we can get. I'm glad you called. I'm not sure when we'll meet . . . maybe Monday after school. I'll let you know." She clicked off.

"What was that all about?" Jamie stared at her as if she had two heads.

"Molly wants to help with the disasters. She asked what she could do and when we were meeting. She said she had called you just now to ask but you didn't answer. She didn't think I would want to talk to her." Clara gave him a cynical look. Could Molly be sincere about wanting to help? Was she really moved by what climate change was causing, especially close to home in her classmates' lives? Was she sad about the animals? Did she feel even a little guilty about all she had done to hurt Clara's feelings? She probably wanted another chance with Jamie. That had to be it. Clara shook her head. She didn't have time for nonsense. And she had no answers.

"I don't get it," Jamie said, frowning as if he were totally bewildered. "How girls think."

"Some girls," Clara corrected, hoping he could figure this out himself.

"Look, Clara, can I call you later? I have to get home, see if my parents know any more about Lucas. I'm so sorry about all this. I really am. It's not easy ."

Clara gave him a gentle shove. "Go home. Get your strength up for your brother. You can do it." She continued on her way, mentally sending him strength. He said he'd call later. She would listen and help him to believe in himself.

She arrived home before Mami, who had taken Diego for a dental appointment. She fried some onions, put potatoes on to boil, and mixed up a batch of muffins. Mami and Diego walked in just as she slid the muffins into the oven.

"Mmmm. Smells good," Mami said. Diego glanced in the sink for any batter left in the bowl. He took off his jacket and turned on his video game.

Clara whispered something to Mami so Diego wouldn't hear. "Do you think Papi will come home with . . . injuries?"

"Why do you ask that, *mi amor?*"

Clara told Mami about Jamie's brother being brought home from the war. "He probably won't be the same. It must be so hard for his family."

Mami reached for Clara's hand. "I am sorry. Yes, very hard for a family to see a child hurt. What a nice boy, Jamie. He will be sad."

Clara didn't know what she would do with her own sadness if it weren't for Mami. She thought about Molly's complaint that her mother didn't listen to her and squeezed Mami's hand in gratitude.

Mami had tears in her eyes. "It is hard to help someone to not feel sad, Clara. Maybe tomorrow you talk to your friend . . . but listen more. He will feel better."

Clara smiled, then told Mami how she and Jamie had taken a walk and how she had listened to him. "Mami, you're so wise.

It did make him feel better. And you always listen to me, Mami, and to Diego." She hugged her mother.

"You are wise too, my daughter."

———

That night, Clara began planning for the Red Cross Drive. She would ask for volunteers, have them make lists of supplies and stores and places that might donate. Sending some items to Puerto Rico would bring her as close as she could get right now to Papi.

The rally on Saturday might give her ideas about their climate change work at school. The class had to save time for that too. There was so much to do. Disaster work. Climate change. Were they two different things? She wasn't sure. What she was pretty sure of was that she couldn't count on Jamie for help. He had more important things to do right now. She couldn't imagine counting on Molly.

Or could she? Molly seemed to have stopped attacking her ever since they'd talked about Molly's relationship with her mother. Then there were Molly's tears when Chuck talked about moving. And how she'd called Clara to say she wanted to be involved in the climate project. She might want to go to the rally. Clara wouldn't know unless she asked. She hadn't texted or phoned Molly for months but nervously punched in her number.

"I'm glad you want to help with the climate project," she began when Molly answered. "Just a thought I had . . . I'm going to a big climate rally on Saturday downtown. Want to go? We could find out what other people are doing and get some ideas on how to move ahead." When Molly said yes, Clara reached for the rally announcement for details. "Great. Let's meet at the bus stop right in front of Town Hall. All the buses stop there and it's close to where the rally is starting. Say, eight fifteen, and we have—" Molly agreed. Then Clara heard a click as her words "—each other's phone numbers in case . . ." were drowned out by the dial tone.

Chapter Twenty

Unseasonal warnings

No way was he going to school today. He had to be here. Jamie had set his phone for six o'clock Friday morning. This might be the day. Mom had said that an officer would call when Lucas landed. She promised to phone or text Jamie at school if she got the call, but he insisted and finally convinced her to let him stay home. He wasn't sure what Dad would say when he found out, but he pushed that thought aside.

He wondered how his brother would arrive. In a regular car? A military jeep? An ambulance? Would he be sitting up or lying down? He erased the ambulance from his mind. He thought about what Clara had said, that he would be strong for Lucas. He dug deep to find that strength now and believe in it. He hadn't asked Clara where the strength would come from. That would have sounded weird. So, for now, he tried to imagine Lucas arriving, sitting Marine-straight in the passenger seat of some military vehicle.

Dad and Mom sat at the kitchen table. Jamie stayed within hearing distance, mostly out of sight. The last thing he wanted to hear was Dad telling him he should have gone to school. He peeked into the kitchen as both parents stared at their phones. His thumbnail, bit to the quick, throbbed. His frantic pacing that he couldn't help would upset Dad.

The call came at eleven forty. All Jamie heard Dad say was, "I understand. Yes. Yes. Of course." Then, "Thank you."

Dad put the phone back on the table. "He landed."

Jamie and Mom almost pounced forward. "What did he say?" came as a whisper from Mom, as if she could barely get the words out. Her hand was pressed against her heart. Jamie swallowed all the worry in his throat and fought back tears. *He landed*, words he might have given up a whole year of snowboarding to hear before, but now, he'd give his favorite activity up forever if Lucas could be okay. He squeezed his fists to hold onto any strength he had pulled together as he checked each window that faced the street.

The doorbell rang at ten minutes past one. Mom and Dad were already at the door. They'd been staring out of windows too, waiting. Jamie hung back at first, then moved up and stood with them as Dad opened the door.

A Marine in full dress uniform like the kind Jamie had seen recently on TV stood on the landing. "Mr. and Mrs. James Fulton?" he asked.

Jamie glanced around the Marine, hoping to see Lucas.

"Yes, Sergeant," Dad answered. "We're the Fultons."

Dad called him "Sergeant." He knew the man's rank because he'd been one. The sergeant stared straight at Dad and said, "Sir, I'm returning Marine Lucas Fulton home after injuries sustained on duty."

Jamie leaned in so he wouldn't miss a single word. He squinted to see the name on a brass bar. Sergeant Hamilton. Three stripes on his sleeve told Jamie his rank, just like Dad's. He asked if they would wait where they were, not rush to the car, that he would escort Lucas to them. Jamie's stomach knotted even tighter. That must mean Lucas can't take excitement, maybe he's not stable, maybe . . . Jamie shook his head. *Stop.*

Dad's hands were trembling. Jamie watched his father move a step forward when the sergeant turned and walked back to the khaki-colored military car parked in front of their house. Their eyes were riveted on the car.

Jamie followed the soldier down the steps even after his dad called, "Jamie, come back." The sergeant turned and said, "Stand back. Wait with your parents." Jamie stopped in his tracks. He fidgeted with the edge of his T-shirt. The sergeant opened the trunk and slid out a pair of crutches.

Jamie's breath stopped. He waited. "Crutches aren't so bad," he mumbled to himself. He felt a hand on his shoulder—Dad's.

The sergeant disappeared with the crutches around the other side of the car. A door opened and a figure got out. All Jamie could see were feet. And the bottom of the crutches. His heart thumped. He thrust himself forward ready to run, help his brother walk. But Mom was right beside him, touching his hand. Dad held onto his arm. None of them could bear to wait. Jamie bit his lip, bit deeper.

The sergeant walked Lucas slowly around the car. Jamie watched every move. They did a wide turn then headed toward them. Jamie winced at the painstaking, careful steps his brother took, as if every move hurt. Lucas was walking. He had his legs. And arms. Was anything missing? His right leg, bandaged, maybe in a cast—Jamie couldn't tell—from his hip to his ankle, and his pant leg was cut all the way up the side because the camo flared out. He tried to read Lucas's face, really pale, rising out of his dark patchy camouflage. Lucas's gaze was straight ahead but Jamie couldn't tell if that's how Marines were supposed to look or anything else from Lucas's expression, which was kind of blank.

Jamie pulled away from Dad and moved toward his brother. He stood in front of Lucas. Jamie heard Clara's voice: *"You'll be strong for your brother."* He nodded as if she were there.

"You're home!" Jamie lunged forward to hug his brother, but Dad, who waited right behind him, pulled him back. Mom held out her arms. Lucas's head fell onto her shoulder. Jamie could hear Mom murmuring, "Our Lucas. We love you. Thank God you're home." He couldn't catch what Lucas was saying. His brother's voice was thin, flat, with none of the liveliness Jamie remembered in it. He had a million things to say, but there was no space. Dad moved toward Lucas like he might be waiting his turn and didn't know how.

Mom held onto Lucas a long time. Dad put out his hand. He held it there until Lucas got out of Mom's hold. Lucas shook Dad's hand as if to say everything was good with them. Jamie watched Lucas closely. He faced Dad and held his gaze. Dad looked away after a few seconds, pressed his lips together, probably to get back in control, then again faced Lucas. Lucas seemed to have the edge. Jamie rooted for him. He could tell that it wasn't easy for Dad. Were they making up? Or still angry? Jamie focused one hundred percent. Dad would say, "Good job." But focusing wasn't helping now. It didn't tell him what he needed to know.

Dad turned. "Thank you, Sergeant," he said, as if he were dismissing him, but the sergeant only moved back a few feet. Dad walked next to Lucas the rest of the way to the house.

Lucas was as tall as Dad. Seeing his big brother in full camo made Jamie's heart swell. He followed closely behind them, not wanting to miss a second. He wanted to touch his brother, pat his shoulder, or do something to signal that he was right behind him, but he thought better of it. He wouldn't barge in. Dad and Lucas needed this time. He recalled how they had argued in the days before Lucas left for Afghanistan, Lucas slamming doors, saying he had to get out of this house, and Dad yelling back that Lucas didn't know how good he had it. The same things he told Jamie these days. He told himself to stop thinking of the past. Maybe now things would be different.

They reached the front steps. The sergeant who had been following behind moved to Lucas's other side and tried to assist him.

Lucas turned to him. "I'm good to go, Sergeant." He shook his sergeant's hand. Jamie got chills. He could see why young people enlisted. Uniforms, shaking hands, saluting, and all that formal stuff made you feel respected. Everybody wanted that. As he watched his dad and his brother make it up the steps, these thoughts stuck with him. He wondered if respect was what Lucas had wanted when he'd enlisted and if Lucas felt it had been worth it. Right now, he couldn't tell anything. And he knew to not say anything. The military feeling around them was too strong.

The sergeant came back from the car, set a long duffle bag near the steps and handed Jamie a cane. "For later. Just a bit of support for your brother," he said. "Good luck to all of you." He did a sharp about-face, headed for his car, and drove away.

Dad moved toward the front door, but Lucas shuffled in front of him. "Can I open it, Dad? I slammed this door when I left home." Something silent passed between Lucas and Dad, and Jamie sensed they were both thinking about that day and how they'd left things. He wondered if either or both of them regretted the way they'd said their goodbyes, trying to out-yell each other.

Dad moved aside, and Lucas leaned on one crutch. He opened the door and took a step in. Dad edged in before him and started moving things out of the way so Lucas wouldn't bump into anything. Jamie couldn't help thinking they should have done this before so Lucas wouldn't see.

Lucas stood in the foyer, staring at the floral wallpaper and sniffing the air. He looked normal, not that stare he had when he was walking. "Lemon . . . cinnamon . . . vanilla. I remember those smells. Soothing. Every time I came into the house." He leaned against the wall, then took a big breath. "Those homey smells kept me going over there." He shrugged.

Jamie sniffed. His parents seemed to be doing it too. Mom was closest to Lucas. Dad stood near the door. Jamie edged closer to his brother but stopped when Dad shook his head.

"Just memories, right?" Lucas asked as if he had to, as if he had been waiting for a long time to walk into his house and feel at home. "To think about smells." He closed his eyes and lowered his head. Mom and Dad glanced at each other. Jamie couldn't help sniffing again. He wondered if Lucas's remembering these smells now was good or bad for him.

"Funny what it took to keep from falling apart out there"— Lucas hesitated—"waiting for the next batch of wounded guys to be hauled back."

Mom and Dad seemed to be waiting for more. Jamie too. All of them stood in the front hall silently. Jamie wanted to yell at Dad, "Go and put your arm around him."

What else would Lucas say about what he'd lived through in Afghanistan? All Jamie could do was wonder. It was good that Lucas was talking, but maybe it was bringing back memories. For now, Jamie hoped Lucas would stop right there, just go in and smell the smells and sit down, and not be reminded of how it was before he left home, when Dad had laced into him. Jamie didn't want to relive their arguments again and hoped Dad didn't either. Mom took Lucas's arm and led him, hobbling on his crutches, into the den. Lucas leaned them on the side of the sofa and fell back onto it like he couldn't help it, not like he was excited to. Mom sat next to him and held his hand in her lap. Dad asked if anyone wanted something to drink, smiling awkwardly like it was a social occasion. Nobody asked for anything, so he nodded and sat next to Mom. Jamie wished he'd asked for ginger ale so Dad could feel useful, have something to do. He couldn't bear seeing his Dad turned down, defeated over drinks. They sat. Four, again. Lucas gazed around the room. His eyes would land on something and stay there for a long time. Was he remembering something or had his mind shut down?

"Lucas," Jamie dared in the silence. "How many hours did it—?"

Dad shot Jamie a look that said, *Don't ask anything.*

He wondered why his parents weren't asking Lucas about his leg. That's what Jamie wanted to know about. He had only been going to ask how long the flight was. Nothing about Lucas's injuries. Why wasn't Dad asking Lucas if he was tired and how he felt? That's what Jamie would want his parents to ask him if he'd just come home from war. Jamie couldn't tell anything about how Lucas felt from his expression. He desperately wanted Dad to talk to Lucas, to say something. Anything.

Mom patted Lucas's hand in between saying things like, "You're home now," and, "Everything will be fine," and, "You'll get plenty of rest."

In the silence in between, it didn't take long for Jamie's thoughts to rewind. He figured if you'd never asked your kids how they felt before all this, you wouldn't know how to ask now. Dad had only *told* them how they *should* feel or be. What he expected. Jamie could tick off the times Dad had told him he should focus, or he shouldn't procrastinate, a favorite Dad word, or he should apply himself, do something worthwhile. Dad had never asked him how he felt about anything. But now was the time for him to ask Lucas how he was feeling. Jamie's insides were ready to explode, but he had to hold everything in. He couldn't control a thing. The lemon, cinnamon, vanilla homey smells didn't help. Lucas was home. Jamie tried to reassure himself that things would be okay now. But even though Lucas was right there in the den, Jamie knew his brother wasn't back.

Chapter Twenty-One

Sunny with hovering clouds

*C*lara stood near the Town Hall bus stop at eight o'clock so that
Molly could easily spot her. Lots of people were gathering
there. She wished she had told Molly she'd be wearing red.

The sun shone, and the sweatshirt she wore was perfect for
marching. Crowds of people of all ages walked ahead. Band music
played. Clara's confidence zoomed as she marched in place, eager
to join in. Two buses stopped and people carrying signs got off.
No Molly.

At eight twenty, another bus pulled in. About twenty people
hurried off, but Molly wasn't one of them. At eight thirty, after
another bus dropped its passengers, Clara punched in Molly's
telephone number. It rang and went to message. Clara left
one, then texted her. People yelled slogans, and drum rhythms
tempted her to join the marchers, coming from all directions. She
couldn't let Molly's being late dampen her excitement.

She almost missed Molly's message but felt the vibration in
her hand. *Can't come. Mom emergency. Not serious. Sorry.* Clara
smacked her forehead. She had known somewhere in the back

of her mind that she shouldn't count on Molly being there. But she had. She might phone Molly later. She wondered if her trying so hard to make things better between them was worth it. Clara breathed in some fresh air and headed forward.

Most of the marchers seemed young, maybe early twenties. She counted thirty people right off, holding posters. She ran ahead to read them: "CLIMATE=DISASTERS." "MARCH FOR OUR PLANET." "DON'T STEAL OUR CHILDHOOD." The girl holding that poster looked about her age. Clara hurried alongside her and wrote down her name and phone number. The girl, named Heather, gave it with a smile. Clara's confidence soared.

She agreed with the posters' messages. "I WANT A FUTURE." "THE KIDS ARE NOT ALL RIGHT." "URGENT: OUR—NO, YOUR PLANET!" "HOPES AND DREAMS? NO. NIGHTMARES." As she jotted these in her small notebook, other warning signs she could have carried popped into her head: "WHERE HAVE ALL THE ANIMALS GONE?" "ACT NOW. WE NEED CLEAN AIR." She'd think up others later for their meetings in school. All around her, people moved forward in one big group. Families with young children, also carrying signs, cheered everywhere she looked. Clara introduced herself to as many marchers as she could and wrote down names and phone numbers. People eagerly shared. She did too.

When she saw "HELP SAVE PUERTO RICO" printed on a huge sheet held in front of them by a girl and a boy who looked about her age, she hurried over to them.

"Hello. I'm Clara Montalvo," she said to the girl with short brown spiky hair and a tattoo of a Puerto Rican flag on her arm. "I want to help save Puerto Rico."

They walked as they talked. "I'm Victoria. And that's Angel." The girl tossed her head toward the boy. "Proud Puerto Ricans. So you want to *ayudarnos*."

Clara startled at the Spanglish. "*Sí*. I mean yes. I want to help," she answered. She wouldn't mix, but she wondered if

Victoria would understand all she said in English about Papi and the hurricane and—

"The new earthquakes are taking a toll on those who are down there trying to help," Victoria said, settling Clara's wondering. Victoria spoke perfect English. "And we believe the climate heating up everywhere is causing the quakes. Eight people have been injured there. One person died. Eleven quakes shook the island in a few days, and more will surely come."

Clara agreed and tried to pull her thoughts together as she took in the news. She had talked to Papi after the earthquake. He was fine. And he'd said the other workers with him were okay too. But Victoria was probably right. More quakes would come.

The music and the cheering crowds made it impossible to get any more answers from Victoria, but still Clara shouted, "How do you know all this?" Loud music was her only answer. She scribbled her name and phone number on a piece of paper, showed it to Victoria, then tucked it into the girl's jeans pocket.

"Call me," Clara shouted again, hoping Victoria would. Victoria and Angel disappeared in the moving crowd, and Clara followed, waiting for what to do next.

The band music suddenly stopped, so she figured they were at their destination. A stage up ahead caught her attention. A rock group was making music now. People were finding places to sit. Clara squeezed her way to the front and thought how Molly would have liked all this. It could have brought them together again. A young girl was singing "Save Our Planet Earth," and the crowd sang along. Next, the girl sang "It's a Small World," and Clara joined in too. Everybody knew these songs. Clara felt teary at the words, "It's a world of hope / It's a world of fears," and at all these strangers coming together to sing and march to save their planet. The spirit of the gathering reminded her how strangers had helped her family and others to get a new start and rebuild their lives, just as all these people wanted to rebuild their planet. People coming together definitely made things better. She wished that Molly could have been part of it. She could have seen all these people warning about climate change, not only Clara talking in the cafeteria. Molly might have become excited about something other than herself. Clara knew it was kind of mean to think that about Molly, but it's what she felt just then.

Speakers came to the podium one after another. Each one spoke for about ten minutes on amazing facts about the planet. The crowd cheered, applauded, and shouted slogans. Young speakers, not much older than her, talked about the marches around the world and about Greta and Zero Hour and all the current action, started mostly by teens. She wished she could meet Greta Thunberg and Jamie Margolin and all the teens who worked so hard for change. Clara cheered too as her enthusiasm soared. She tried not to think of Victoria's warnings.

After two hours, the last speaker wound things up and asked people to take handouts, spread the word about the urgency of their heated-up planet, write and call congressmen and senators, tell people to vote for climate changers, and do all they could to wake people up about their climate.

Clara had so many ideas to share with the class. She couldn't wait. Maybe she would hear from Victoria and find out more about Puerto Rico. When her backpack was bulging from handouts and tiny souvenir giveaway key chains shaped like small glaciers and mountains and a free T-shirt saying, "Ask Me about Climate Change," she zipped up, ready to go home. The hundreds of people filing past her created a blur and no possibility of finding Victoria and Angel. Band music started up and a parade began, just like that.

As she made her way to the sidewalk, her phone rang. "Mrs. Thurber, hi." She covered her other ear. "It's hard to hear you. I'm at a loud rally. What? Can I call you back? Okay. As soon as I get away from this parade. Bye."

She called Mrs. Thurber back near the bus stop. Seven minutes till the next bus. Mrs. Thurber sounded teary.

"It's Gus," she said. "You're the only person he wants to see. He doesn't want to go to preschool or see his teachers. He misses his father." There was a short pause, then Mrs. Thurber continued. "I hadn't told you any of this because you have enough to worry about and it's our problem, but Gus's father decided this marriage wasn't for him. He moved out of the house two months ago, right after Christmas." She paused again, and Clara's heart ached for her. "Gus talks about his dad racing cars on the floor with him and giving him horsey rides on his crossed legs. He keeps asking when Daddy's coming home. Nothing I say helps him calm down. Now he's asking for you. He repeats your name over and over. That's why I called. I feel helpless." Her voice broke and Clara suspected she was crying. "You were probably having fun with your friends," Mrs. Thurber said. "I'm sorry."

"No. It's okay. I'm sorry too," Clara said, struggling to hide her sadness for Gus and anger at his father. "What would you like me to do, Mrs. Thurber?"

"I know you can't babysit any longer, but just for today, could you possibly come by, just for a few minutes, to say hi to him, reassure him that everybody he loves isn't leaving him?"

Fury at Gus's dad roared up. And disappointment. She'd always assumed Mr. Thurber was at work. She felt guilty too, for canceling her babysitting without telling Gus in person. That wasn't fair to him. Her watch said two twenty. She couldn't disappoint him again. "Sure. I'll come by at my regular time. Tell Gus I'll be looking for him in the window. See you soon."

———

On the bus, Clara thought about what exactly to say to Gus—the right words. What could she say about his father leaving? If he were older, she could talk about the different ways people leave. Some, like her father or Lucas, leave to help people for a while. But then they come back. She thought about Jamie and how he talked about his father being so hard on him and impossible to talk to, as though his dad had left or Jamie had left, even though they were still in the same house. But Gus was only four. He couldn't possibly understand these examples. She hardly could.

Gus was in the big picture window when she walked up to it. She waved and gave a medium smile, not too silly, just enough to make him smile and wave back. Mrs. Thurber waited at the open door. Gus ran to Clara as he always did. She bent down and hugged him. He hugged her back and held on.

When they parted and Clara had shaken the tears away, she asked, "So are we building today?"

He took her hand and led her to the playroom. He got his bag of blocks, emptied them onto the floor and fell to his knees. "The tallest?" he asked. He started building before Clara answered.

"The tallest." She started stacking.

When their towers were about the same height, Gus glanced at hers. "Keep going," he said, as if to boost her confidence.

"Okay."

She added a block. He did too, and both towers tumbled. Perfect timing. Gus laughed, his blotchy cheeks evidence of hours of crying.

"Gus, let's do something different." She gathered her blocks together. "Let's build pretend schools. Like yours or mine." She started lining up blocks and formed an outline of a building. He copied her. "We'll make them so strong that they can't fall down, not even in a big stormy hurricane. That's a big wind that blows roofs off houses."

While they built, she told him how the big hurricane came and blew off the roof of her school and parts of it fell to the ground. She told him that nobody was harmed, but the children couldn't go back into the damaged school. "We're going to build schools that don't fall down, okay?" She watched him carefully for any sign that she'd scared him.

Gus nodded as if hurricanes weren't new to him. He formed his foundation and sat, staring at it. Then he removed blocks from all the sides so that his foundation was smaller than Clara's. "It'll be stronger if it's not so big," he said, like a true builder.

"Good idea, Gus. We can see if that makes a difference when the hurricanes come."

He clapped his hands together. "Yes."

They built in silence, didn't laugh and challenge each other as usual. Gus seemed to need this quiet time. When his school stood about four inches high, he sat, head cocked, assessing it. He got up, took a box off a low shelf, and brought it to their work site.

"Legos . . . for the roof." He clicked Legos together, forming a perfect tile roof. "My school will have a red roof."

Chills ran through Clara. "What a great idea. Can I copy your roof?"

He beamed and slid the Lego box over to her.

Gus finished linking the Legos, then positioned his roof on top of the four-sided block opening. "There." He leaned in and pointed. "Next time, I'll put windows here and a door here so kids can get in. They can't get into this one."

Clara's heart melted. Warmth spread through her. Gus seemed to know exactly what was going on inside of him. Clara held back tears and forced a big, "Yes. Great idea." She decided to go one step further. "Now, should we see how strong our schools are?"

He nodded. "Yeah. Mine's really strong."

She gently urged him to move back a little from his school as she did the same. "Now let's blow hard, like the wind in a big storm. See if a hurricane can blow the schools down."

Their schools stood firmly. Even their roofs endured the storm. Gus kept blowing fiercely, trying his best to move a block or the roof with his breath. After a few more gusty tries, he stopped. "I told you. My school is strong. The kids inside would be safe."

Gus would be okay. No need to say another word about his buildings. Not about balance or gravity or how good his motor skills were or how building might be in his future someday.

When Mrs. Thurber asked what they had built, Gus said, "Really strong schools you can't blow down." Then he turned to Clara. "Can you come back like you always did after school?"

She had hoped he wouldn't ask. She had planned on the climate and disaster collections meeting after school on Monday. Notices were already posted. How could she not show up there for her class? But how could she not show up for Gus, who probably wondered every moment what he had done to make his father leave? Clara had no answers, but maybe through their building he could find some answers. Maybe she could too.

———

At home, she told Mami and Diego everything about the day. She gave Diego his choice of key chains. He reached for the mountain. Jamie would have chosen the mountain too. Jamie and Diego would like each other when she introduced them one day. Both were athletes, both twisted the ends of their shirts, and both thought school was boring. But Jamie would have loved the rally. No. He had harder challenges to face now with Lucas. She was dying to call him and find out how he was, if his brother was home, and how his parents were doing, but she thought it best not to interfere.

She twirled the glacier keychain that she'd snapped around a loop on her jeans. All the excitement of the day energized her. She was tempted to call Molly but decided against it. She would wait to see what Molly came up with on Monday. After all, Molly was the one who hadn't shown up. Clara had to admit she was disappointed, but it was easier to blame Molly.

She had to do something productive, so she dug out her markers and started printing slogans on blank sheets of paper.

She could tape them up at their first meeting on climate change. After that, she'd get the Red Cross collection drive going. Two projects. Could she handle them both? That thought landed another big decision right at her feet: Monday after school Climate and Collecting meeting or building with Gus?

Chapter Twenty-Two

Atmospheric pressure

J amie stayed close to Lucas's room. He wanted to be there in case his brother woke up and needed anything. He'd get Lucas back to normal. He pulled a chair from his room and sat against the wall so he could hear sounds coming from the other side. His thoughts spilled all over. What had happened to Lucas's leg? Would his mind be the same? Lucas didn't have any bandages on his head so the injury must be inside. Was he scared?

Questions about Lucas did him no good. He'd have to wait to find out. Jamie knew one thing, though. He'd be pretty scared to go fight in a foreign country. His whole body tensed up, as if his muscles and bones needed answers too.

One persistent thought had hung over him ever since Lucas had left: Why was Dad so angry that Lucas had enlisted? Dad had enlisted when he was young, too, so what was the difference? Why were they on different sides about the same thing?

And why was Dad so angry with him, too, about dumb grades? He wished he could see Dad's grades in eighth grade. Did Dad really mean it when he said he thought Jamie and Lucas were headed in the wrong direction? When Dad said stuff like that, the only direction Jamie wanted to head was downhill on his snowboard with clean white snow all around and frosty air and sun on his face. With Lucas right next to him. Actually, Lucas would be way ahead of him but waiting down the mountain, somewhere along the way. That's how it had always been. His brother was always there, just a little bit ahead of him on the slopes.

Jamie couldn't imagine it any other way. He didn't want to. Although he fought against the thought, something told him Lucas wouldn't be way ahead of him on the slopes any longer. He'd read a little about military people coming home disillusioned, so he'd looked that word up. It meant disappointed, let down, not what you expected. That made sense. You enlisted probably thinking one thing and then lots of bad stuff happened that you didn't expect. But what if Lucas did get better but couldn't concentrate or balance, and he fell or crashed on his snowboard?

Jamie's brain kept sending what-ifs his way. What if Lucas never went back to school, never found a job? Jamie's elbows dug into his knees as more what-ifs were coming on fast.

He listened for any sound from Lucas. None. He pulled out his phone. It was way past lunchtime. He clicked onto WatchMojo. com. Maybe he'd see some new snowboarding moves.

He mentally cheered the boarders as they triple turned or did backward flips off the track. When one boarder crashed at the bottom after a corkscrew, Jamie yelled, "No!" He dropped his phone. The crash as it hit the floor filled the hallway. Lucas screamed. Jamie jumped up and scrambled into his brother's bedroom. His parents were up the stairs and behind him in seconds.

Jamie froze inside the room. Lucas's face twisted in anguish. He was screaming, "No! No! No! No!"

"What happened?" Dad barked at Jamie. "What did you do?"

"Nothing, Dad. I dropped my phone. Sorry." Jamie shook so badly he dropped his phone again. It clattered onto the hardwood floor, and his brother shrieked louder.

His father scowled. "Give me that phone." Jamie fumbled it to his father. He was right. Jamie was wrong. He'd hurt his brother.

"You can't do that, Jamie," Mom scolded as she watched over Lucas. "Your brother is . . ." Jamie leaned in to hear what she would say next but instead of continuing, Mom seemed to change her mind. "Just stay away from him while he's recovering."

Jamie crawled off and crouched in a corner, away from Dad and Mom, who bent over Lucas, watching him. Jamie bit his lip harder. Had he really yelled that loudly? He vowed to be super careful from now on, to really think things through ahead of time, like Mom always told him to do. He sat with the hurt he had caused. He didn't know what the sounds had brought back, maybe Marines screaming or gunfire. Jamie only knew he'd triggered Lucas's bad memories.

Mom and Dad stayed next to Lucas till he closed his eyes. Mom checked his breathing and whispered something to him, and then she and Dad went back downstairs. Jamie sat, left out of the family, but it was his own fault. He waited for an hour, maybe more. Lucas didn't budge. Jamie's legs ached from being folded under him on the hard floor. So what? No facing Dad or Mom at least. He stretched and made his way to his chair outside Lucas's room.

He let his mind leave all this behind and go to the team and the competition yesterday. They'd probably won and had a great time, cheering and acting like the new champions on the bus back. He pictured it all. If he'd been there, he would have been right in the middle of all the fun. He'd have won his run, and Coach would have patted him on the back. "I'm proud of you," he'd have said. Jamie fantasized about being on the bus all the way back to Albany. He tried to picture Clara at the rally, probably right in the middle of all the fun too. They were alike that way. She'd tell him all about it when they talked. He couldn't wait.

About an hour later, a thump startled Jamie. Lucas stood in the doorway. "Hey, Jamie."

Jamie jumped up. He couldn't believe Lucas stood next to him, looking okay leaning on his good foot. "Lucas. Hey."

Lucas reached out and hugged him. Lucas's fingertips dug into Jamie's shoulders. Jamie couldn't keep his tears back but managed to wipe them with one hand. "Sorry," he said, brushing a few off Lucas's shoulder. He'd waited all morning for this. Now if only he could do something for his brother, help him settle in.

Lucas released him. Jamie stood statue still as Lucas assessed him. "You're nearly as tall as me, When'd that happen?"

Jamie shrugged and tried to hide another sniffle.

"I can still lick you, little brother." Lucas did a quick wrestling move with his arms. "Or I'll be able to once my leg heals." He raked his hand over his crew-cut head.

Jamie cheered inside and didn't say anything about the bad time he had caused. Jamie remembered yet again Mom telling him to think carefully before he spoke, to give himself a chance to imagine what the other person might feel. "I'll bet you can still lick me," he said. "After all that Navy Seal training."

Lucas shook his head. "Nah. I wasn't a Seal, just a regular old Marine with a rifle. Come on in here while I get dressed. Takes me a while with this leg." Lucas crutched over to the bed and sat on the edge.

Jamie stared at Lucas's injured leg. "Does it hurt?" Jamie winced. The words had tumbled out despite his resolve to follow Mom's advice.

"What? This?" Lucas used both hands to lift his bad leg. "Up you go."

Jamie stared. "Don't do that! You'll hurt it."

"Oh, it's pretty hurt already . . . burned to a crisp." Lucas laughed like maybe that would make it not so bad. "But it's med-icated right now. I have these pills I take when the pain gets too bad. Burns—they take forever to heal. But so far, I'm lucky. I could lose it."

"No!" Jamie covered his ears, then pulled his hands down. "It'll heal, Lucas."

"Sure," Lucas said as if he were dismissing that prediction, then got that faraway look. "I was that close to the explosion . . . mortar shell." He pointed from where they were to the doorway.

Jamie nodded. "Mortar shell? It exploded so close. Weren't you on security at the base? Wasn't that a safe area? How'd it happen?"

Lucas's pained face proved he was remembering. "Psssht. Boom!" he said, surprising Jamie. His brother's eyes went blank again. Lucas sat there on the bed, but his pale face and open mouth said he had disappeared.

"You were doing your duty at the base, right?" Jamie hoped the question might bring Lucas back.

Lucas didn't answer for—Jamie timed it—over a minute.

"Yeah," Lucas finally said, "but who knew they would attack the base? Our guys had been shelling the Taliban to shreds. We didn't think there were any more of them left. Then, no warning. Just *eeeee . . . Boom!* Then, flames."

Jamie imagined the crackling or whistling before the blast. "You don't have to tell me any more."

Lucas's gaze was on Jamie now. "I have to tell you, or you'll keep bugging me." Lucas reached over and messed Jamie's hair. "But right now, Bro, I need to put my head down again. I get dizzy even when I think I'm okay. My head kind of throbs." Lucas lay back on the bed. "I'll pull myself together . . . I'll be . . ."

Quiet took over the room. Jamie figured that he'd worn his brother out. "You sure you don't need anything? Your clothes?" He needed to help his brother. But Lucas's eyes were shut, his chest rising and falling.

Lucas's duffle bag sat in the corner. Jamie wondered what was inside. He pictured Lucas's helmet, but maybe that had gotten blown up. Maybe Lucas would show him his stuff when he unpacked. Part of him wanted to know all about his brother's experiences, and another part was afraid of what he'd learn and how talking about it might impact Lucas. Mom said talking about hard or scary things helped, but Jamie was beginning to think maybe it was better to leave them in the past.

The images of Afghanistan he'd seen in news reports showed a land that was completely different from their home in Albany. Nothing was the same. Maybe if Lucas focused on the present, he wouldn't get pulled back into what he'd left behind in the war-torn country.

For once Jamie understood Dad's favorite word: focus. Maybe he could help his brother do that. He covered Lucas with the blanket and left.

———

Mom and Dad sat at the table drinking their coffee. Nobody said a word. Jamie joined them to try to make up for what he'd caused upstairs. He hoped they'd let it go for now. After all the upset, breathing in the silence slowed down his heartbeat. If only the calm would last. Dad held onto his big blue mug with a shaky hand, and both of Mom's steadied her fragile porcelain cup. Funny how he'd never paid attention before to things like the kind of cups his parents used. Now he seemed to be really focusing, noticing everything, like how tired Dad looked. And how edgy his parents were.

"Should we check on him?" Dad asked.

"Let him sleep," Mom said, her voice as thin as her cup. "He needs all the rest he can get. I've been reading about head trauma. Soldiers with war injuries have a hard time sleeping. They keep waking up, recalling an explosion or an attack."

Jamie slumped down in his chair to block out what was coming.

"It's better if you don't read about those," Dad said. "It's bad enough without knowing all the details."

Mom always wanted to know the details. Dad told everyone in the family what to do. That had always bothered Jamie, but the more he thought about it, the more it sounded almost logical. Maybe Dad did want to protect them rather than let them learn the hard way, as he'd said so many times. But Jamie questioned if that were the right way to have your kids learn stuff. He wasn't sure, but all this time waiting for one thing or another made his mind go places it hadn't traveled to before. Lucas hadn't been allowed to learn things his own way, and look where it had gotten him. And Dad's anger hadn't gotten him very far either. When Lucas bought a motorcycle and Dad told him to sell it or else— another blowout. Lucas never paid attention to "or else." Jamie wished he could stand his ground with Dad as well as Lucas could. Maybe he'd learn. But now, because of an old argument about doing things Dad's way and Lucas's resistance, they were all dealing with the consequences.

Dad got up and poured himself more coffee. "Maybe I should call the hospital, mention that he had that scare, ask a doctor if it's normal for someone with his kind of injuries to sleep all day."

"Please, Jim. Let's wait," Mom said. "Give him a little more time. He's had a long journey home."

Dad frowned. "Well, I don't think it's a good sign. I've seen plenty of men with concussions. You can't let them sleep."

Mom's face was set. Jamie recognized persistence. Still, she let Dad pace around the kitchen. "The officer would have told us if he had a concussion," she said. "Let Lucas rest."

As Jamie sat in this arguing hopelessness, he heard Lucas. Really loud. "Jamie! Hey, Jamie. Can you come up here?"

Dad started first, then stopped and motioned for him to go. He couldn't get out of the kitchen fast enough. Lucas needed him. He could help him. Finally.

Lucas was sitting on his bed, rubbing his forehead. "Hey, thanks, Buddy. I tried to get up but when I do it too fast, the room starts spinning. Then, *boom!* I'm back down." Jamie recalled in a flash his own passing out, then coming to and the spinning room. Lucas pointed to the corner. "Over there. Can you open my duffle? There's a folder somewhere. Probably on top of my fatigues."

This was Jamie's big chance to see what was in the duffle. He unzipped the bag and smelled dust, scents like soap or shaving cream, and something flinty, maybe gunpowder. The folder was right where Lucas had said it would be. He picked it up and, while Lucas was looking away, took a quick peek inside. A letter stapled to a report said, "Lucas Fulton—Delivered home with injuries. Letters are being processed for bestowing honors for bravery." Honors. Bravery. Wow! He closed up the duffle and delivered the folder to Lucas. He wanted so badly to salute after handing it to him.

Lucas opened the folder, scanned the letter, then said, "I have to get to the Veterans' Medical Center on Monday. Hey, Bro. Can you believe I'm a vet now? Got to get these bandages changed." He ran his hand over some bloody strips of adhesive tape. "Guess I'm putting too much pressure on the leg. That's why it's bleeding."

"*I could lose it*" stuck in Jamie's mind. He shook the thought away.

"I need more pain pills too. Can you hand me that bottle over there?" He pointed to a small table.

"Leave it, Jamie," Dad announced, as he walked into the room. "I'll get it."

Jamie's heart sped up. Was Dad stressing Lucas?

"Hey, Dad," Lucas answered. "We're good." He patted Jamie on the back. "My buddy here gets me what I need."

Dad's head jerk indicated that Jamie should leave. Dad probably didn't want him to hear his lecture on drugs. Jamie knew more than he wanted to about drugs from school. For a second, he wondered if he should be worried about Lucas and his pills. Then he shook that thought away. He tried to sound upbeat. "See you in a while, Lucas. Call me if you want anything."

On his way out, he heard Dad say he'd take Lucas to the hospital on Monday. Jamie would make sure he got to go too. Lucas hadn't asked him anything about their old life or snowboarding or school. Nothing about how it had been before. Had he forgotten?

—

He found Mom in the kitchen still at the table and sat across from her. He always felt better when he talked with her. "Dad's up there giving orders. He never listens to anyone."

Mom took his hand. She held it for a few seconds as if she were thinking about something. "Jamie, do you remember when you showed Dad how to bend his knees when we were all skiing years ago? You must have been seven or eight."

He thought back to those family ski trips when Lucas had taught him all he knew about skiing and snowboarding. He shrugged and hoped Mom would go on.

She laughed. "Dad kept falling, even on the easy runs, and he couldn't get down that one slope until he started bending his knees like you showed him."

Jamie smiled and shook his head. Mom patted his hand. She knew what he was thinking. Dad and bending didn't go together.

"You came up on the lift and skied right next to him. You said, 'Like this, Dad, for balance,' and then bent your knees. I'll never forget that day. Dad won't either. You were the best teacher. A real natural."

Jamie filed Mom's every word close to his heart.

"After that, Dad couldn't believe he could ski down a hill without falling—well, without falling a lot—thanks to you. But then, once he got down, he couldn't relax till Lucas got back down from skiing the expert hills. He knew you were okay because you were right next to him, in case he wanted to do another run. What a boost for your father to learn how to ski with his sons."

"A boost? Really?"

"Of course, Jamie. Your father needs to be competent, and you gave him that. Oh, yes, of course he also needs to be in control, and he's a natural worrier. But he listened to you that day."

Jamie wished Dad still listened occasionally. Coaching Dad back down the hill years ago was no problem. But what would happen now when the controller got back downstairs?

Mom had blown him away when she said he'd helped Dad feel competent. Could he do it again—give Dad a boost? He would give up everything: snowboarding, the team, even passing science.

The more Jamie thought about that day on the slopes with Dad sliding and falling, then finding his balance, the more he was convinced that they might both have to bend a bit.

Chapter Twenty-Three

Calm before the storm

*A*t the Veterans' Hospital, Jamie didn't know what to expect. Veterans came in, some on crutches, others in wheelchairs, some limping. Jamie tried not to stare at men with bandaged heads or missing legs or arms. Two women vets were on crutches, another in a wheelchair. She smiled at him as they passed. He smiled back and said hi. Lucas had slept most of the way there and yawned and seemed groggy as he crutched in with Mom, Dad at his side. Maybe he'd had nightmares again. Jamie hoped not. He'd stick close to his brother. Lucas would get clean bandages, and his leg would get better.

"You stay here with Mom," Lucas told Dad in the big waiting room. "Jamie can come with me."

"No, I'll go," Dad said, and started off.

Lucas didn't move. "No, Dad. I want Jamie," he said, louder than Dad probably liked. "It's a first for me. I want it to be a first and last for him."

Dad stood in his spot like he wasn't convinced but not sure what to do next. Mom moved closer to Dad and put her hand on his arm. "Let's find some seats and wait for them."

200

Jamie grinned. His brother wanted his help. He glanced at Dad, who probably didn't like Lucas's defiance, then walked slowly with his brother to the information desk. Jamie felt a little sorry for Dad but wished he didn't. He quickly recalled almost losing out this morning when Dad insisted that he go to school. Jamie had argued that he belonged with his family. That had been the first time he'd stood up to Dad. Exhilarating as it was, his win had scared him.

At the information desk, they waited their turn behind a woman on crutches and a man with one arm. The man dropped a folder he'd been holding under his good arm and Jamie picked it up for him. Lucas smiled approvingly. Jamie almost saluted; that's how patriotic he felt standing between two military heroes.

When their turn came, the woman behind the desk said they were running a little behind schedule so the two of them should find comfortable seats. She would call Lucas in a short time.

Lucas sat next to Dad and started to say something. Jamie bent his head toward them. "Dad, listen to me." Tears shone in Lucas's eyes. "We were both military. You were in a war. Can't we be . . . I don't know . . . friends, talk about how it was for you and maybe how it was different for me? I think it would help us both."

Dad bowed his head without answering.

What Lucas said made sense. He was brave to say this to Dad. Jamie didn't think he could have. It was as close to an apology for enlisting against Dad's wishes as Lucas could probably make, and it was huge.

"You could have avoided all this," Dad finally said. "If you'd only listened to me."

Jamie couldn't believe it. How could Dad start in again? He wished Lucas would tell Dad to shut up. He wanted to yell at his father to quit being such a jerk. He balled his fists instead. His stomach knotted up too.

Lucas shrugged. "Guess I had to learn from my own experience. I wasn't headed anywhere else, so why not see the world?"

Dad huffed. "I could have told you about seeing the world." Mom patted Lucas's knee and gave him a proud-of-you smile.

Jamie remembered the expression "walking on eggshells." They were all over the floor around them right now, and if anyone made a move—crunch. He tried to think of something to say that wouldn't upset anyone.

"Will you see Tony or Mooch or any of your other friends from high school?" he asked. "Are they still around?"

Lucas stared off into the distance as if he were trying to remember. Uh-oh. Bad question. Lucas stretched out his leg like he needed to get life back into it. "Do you remember them? My memory's shot."

A sharp crack echoed. Lucas slid down in his chair. A man seated not too far from them reached down and picked up a book that had fallen. Lucas peeked out as if he were wondering if it were safe now. "All I remember are dirt roads in Afghanistan . . . the base . . . equipment and trucks bringing wounded soldiers in." He stopped as if he were seeing it all. "Yeah . . . driving new ones back out for combat." He shook his head. "I rode with the medics a few times . . . helped out in the field. You wouldn't believe the stuff I saw. Vehicles blown up, people inside . . . bodies on the road, little kids hunting for shell cases, seeing who could find the most."

Lucas kept talking, as if he were still there in the war.

"A mortar shell landed . . . smack in the middle . . . ten men on the vehicles, keeping them ready for action. Flames and smoke . . . I couldn't see anyone . . . fire spreading fast. I ran . . . found two men crawling out, their clothes on fire. I pounded out the flames with my jacket, dragged them as far as I could. A couple of guys showed up, carried them inside." He stopped again. "Headed back to look for more men."

He shook his head. "Eight others somewhere in the fire. Two security guys went back in with me. We found all of them. . . .Yep. Carried them out, in bad shape, but alive. That's when the second shell exploded."

Mom let out a distressed cry. "Oh, Lucas." Her hand flew to her mouth.

Jamie shifted uneasily in his seat. A book falling to the floor had started all this. He recalled his phone falling outside Lucas's room, crashing to the floor like the book, and Lucas's reaction. His brother's voice was as flat as if he were telling them the weather report. It gave Jamie the creeps to hear Lucas sound so matter-of-fact about something so horrific. He felt certain now that no matter how many questions he had about his brother's time in Afghanistan, talking about it could only hurt Lucas further. He was pretty sure he'd have nightmares about it tonight himself.

"Yeah, Mom," Lucas said, "I thought of you right then because I wanted my mom." Jamie winced as his brother's voice broke. "I figured we were goners. My leg was on fire, and I didn't even know it. A friend rolled me over. My leg was smoking like a chimney. All I could feel was heat, kind of like my leg was melting. You don't ever want to know what that feels like. I guess I don't remember anything after rolling. Everything went black."

Mom wiped her eyes. Lucas leaned over and hugged her. "Jamie has to know all this, Mom, so he'll never do what I did. Do you hear me, little brother?" Lucas's eyes narrowed to slits. "Think seriously if you ever want to join the armed forces."

Jamie nodded. He'd never forget this moment. "You don't have to tell us any more right now, Lucas."

"Yeah, I do, Buddy, but the next thing isn't bad. I was in bed in the infirmary, my leg up in traction, and my sergeant was saying my name." Lucas laughed. "I was really out of it, but I kept hearing, 'Lucas, can you hear me?' over and over. And I kept thinking, yeah, man, I hear you, but I couldn't pull myself out of that dark hole. Took me a whole day to come out of La-La Land."

Dad put his hand on Lucas's shoulder. Jamie hoped Dad would say, "I'm proud of you, son." But the words never came. Instead, the four of them sat together, huddled under the bright fluorescent lights of the waiting room. Jamie wished they could stay there forever. That way if anything bad happened, there'd be lots of help right there. And Dad and Lucas weren't likely to get into any more fights in front of all these other people. Yes, if he could freeze them all in time, Jamie thought, they could all stay safe. Dad's hand would be on Lucas's shoulder. Who knew? Dad might say Lucas was brave. Anything was possible. Jamie pressed his lips together so he wouldn't blurt out that Lucas had earned honors in the war. When the honors came, maybe, just maybe, Dad would tell Lucas he was proud.

———

The receptionist finally called Lucas's name. In the examining office, a young doctor shook Lucas's hand and Jamie's too. He said Jamie could come back in about forty minutes.

"I got this, Buddy," Lucas said, so Jamie left even though he really wanted to stay. He hurried back to Mom and Dad and told them what the doctor had said. Dad glanced at his watch. "Ten fifty. I didn't *think* you'd make it to school today."

Jamie nodded. He was in no mood to argue. It was stupid to fight about going to school. Being there for his family was a lot more important.

Mom broke the silence. "I hope these brave people get the services they need."

"You always see the positive side of things, Mom." Jamie needed to hear more from her. "This seems like a good hospital, don't you think?"

She nodded. "But so many wars . . . and so many men and women . . ." She didn't finish.

Jamie sucked in his breath. How many wars were there? He'd only ever thought about Afghanistan. Where else were they going on? He'd have to google.

"Dad," he said, taking a big chance. "Did you have any injuries after your war?"

Dad looked up and sighed. "No, Jamie. No bodily injuries, that is." He rubbed his forehead. "But I came home with mental pain and memories of men who were profoundly changed by war." He stopped, as if the rest was too painful. "So much that their families wouldn't know them when they returned home. That's what war does. Those men couldn't come back to normal lives. They had seen too much death and suffering."

Jamie wondered for the millionth time why his father had enlisted. He bit the bullet, as Lucas would say, and was about to ask when Dad started remembering again.

"And soldiers coming home from Vietnam long before I got back didn't get good treatment from Americans who should have been grateful to them. Hospitals didn't step up to the task."

Jamie glanced around. Was this hospital one of them? He sure hoped not. "Lucas will get what he needs here." He tried hard to sound certain.

Mom squeezed Dad's hand. Dad spoke as if he were proud of his service, but Jamie heard anger in his words. And sadness. Jamie wished with all his heart that he could say something kind to his father. Thank him for his service, a phrase he'd heard people say. But he couldn't seem to find the right words. He was afraid he'd screw it up. He remembered Mom's encouragement about his giving his father a boost. The way they were all talking about war and emotional stuff seemed to be opening a door to the past and maybe to the future too. It was what he'd always wanted: for them to talk about important things.

Maybe he could ask Dad more about the war when Lucas was with them, and they'd both find out why he had been so against Lucas enlisting. Two brothers and their father talking about their wars—Jamie tried to picture it. Not easy. Dad seemed to like answering questions about his service. He seemed proud of it. Like Mom said, Dad needed to be competent. Jamie would have to think hard about his next step. If only Dad and Lucas wanted peace as much as he did.

For now, though, Jamie would focus on helping his brother. He'd get Lucas stuff when Lucas needed something, listen to his stories, and not ask dumb questions. Jamie hoped that whatever the doctor was doing for Lucas would help him get back to his old self again. They'd play games, talk about high school and how Lucas got through it, and sports. Lucas would tease him about girls. Maybe Jamie would even tell Lucas about Clara. He'd get Lucas back to normal in no time.

Chapter Twenty-Four

Partly sunny

T he only thing Molly said to Clara Monday morning as she passed by was, "Sorry about Saturday."

Clara offered, "I hope everything's okay." Molly shrugged and moved off. Clara was disappointed that Molly didn't say more after all her sadness recently. She told herself all Molly could do was be Molly. Clara had made her decision, the one she had been wrestling with. She couldn't disappoint her classmates, whom she hoped would show up for the meeting. And she couldn't disappoint Gus, either. He expected her Monday after school. At three ten, she walked into the cafeteria where two of the servers were folding their aprons and closing up. Her stomach fluttered. She had counted on Jamie partnering with her when they had planned all of this. She'd feel more comfortable if he were here. But she would have to motivate kids to work to stop climate change and inspire them to collect supplies by herself.

"Thanks for cleaning up so fast for us," she said to the workers. She laid her materials on a table, but there was no *us* so far, just her. She set up the blank pad on an easel for brainstorming ideas, propped a few of her homemade climate change signs against the napkin holders on the table next to her and taped the rest to the edge of the table.

The rally on Saturday had shown her how people of all ages could get excited by hope for change. Their cheering and hundreds of big signs like, "WE CAN DO IT!" and, "ALL WE NEED IS YOU" proved that. But it needed the *we* to get anything done. Clara, sitting all by herself, though, wondered how she could make big changes.

She could make a big change for Gus. She could make him smile. That's what a four-year-old needed most: attention and something to smile about. She'd told Mrs. Thurber that she would be over there a little later than usual for another short visit with Gus. She planned to get the climate meeting started and then turn the brainstorming over to someone who might volunteer.

Clara pictured the notice about the meeting she'd hung on the classroom bulletin board. It was large enough to see from anywhere in the room. She wondered if kids had read it. They had sounded so enthusiastic about doing something to make people aware of the current disasters during Clara and Jamie's presentation. She glanced at the big clock ticking. She would wait for five more minutes.

To stay optimistic, she pictured the speakers at the rally and the parade. The enthusiasm for making the planet healthy again had been like a rushing river. It couldn't be stopped. Unlike here, where the river was dry.

Clara walked over to the easel and was about to take it down when shouting and laughing broke through the doors. A rush of kids from her class and some from lower grades, too, headed for the benches. Molly perched on the end of a front bench and shushed the group to quiet. Clara's heart lurched. Could Molly have rounded up all these kids? Maybe she gave them ballots to vote for Jamie, then brought them here to laugh at her. Was Molly really that cruel?

What mattered now was that Molly was here with all these kids when Clara needed it most. This felt like the same Molly who had befriended her when she first arrived in Albany.

Clara stood at the front of the room. She had to finish what she'd started. "Hi. Wow. It's great you all came. I thought nobody would. Um . . . uh." For the first time ever, she couldn't think of what to say but mouthed, "Thanks," to Molly.

Mr. J appeared at the door. "Hello, all. Just checking. Great to see so many of you. I'll be in my room if you need anything, Clara."

She nodded, grateful for his encouragement. Knowing he was just down the hall helped. "Okay. Let's start."

"So what are we supposed to do about all this bad climate stuff happening right now?" Nick asked.

"Where's Jamie?" Molly asked. "I thought he was in this too."

Clara's face heated up. So that's why Molly was here. After all those good intentions she had given Molly credit for. She fought to keep a straight face. She couldn't reveal Jamie's business. "Yeah, he is. He's doing a lot of the research, Molly. Maybe he'll be here the next time."

"Let's get back to these disasters and what we should do," a boy named Nate said. "I don't have all day."

"Yeah, me neither," added a boy Clara didn't know well. He sat in the back of the classroom and never said much. "So like, what's the government doing about all those floods and fires?"

"That's what we all want to know," Clara said. "Thank you for your question. There's so much we can do to alert people, tell them how they can help prevent conditions that might contribute to these disasters. We should write them all down. I went to a rally downtown on Saturday and came home with a lot of ideas. Thousands of people—even little kids—carried signs and wore shirts that said, 'You Can Do It,' and 'Change Now,' and so many other hopeful messages. Maybe there will be more rallies, and we can all go." She nodded cheerily at Molly. "People like us want to do something to make a difference for our planet. I'm sure we have more ideas. Will someone write them down?" She held up a thick marker.

"I'll do it," Molly said. "I have good handwriting."

Some of the boys laughed and talked behind their hands. Molly gave them a big fake smile. Clara wished she had that kind of confidence, even though she still didn't believe Molly cared one bit about the climate. She handed the marker to Molly anyhow.

"Okay," Clara said. "Why don't we start by naming all the disastrous things happening today?"

Ideas spilled out. Some kids were googling on their phones then reading headlines aloud.

"Floods."

"Fires."

"Big companies destroying forests, so animals don't have anywhere to live. It's what you talked about the other day, Clara. The orangutans. I looked it up."

Her heart warmed. People remembered.

"Glaciers melting."

"And waters rising from those glaciers. That's why there are so many floods."

"Yeah, you're right. Whoever said that during your . . . debate . . . or was it a presentation?"

"Slow down, people," Molly said. "I can't write that fast."

More laughs came from around the room. "You don't have to write every word," Nick said. "Just the main ideas. Bullet points. Get it?"

Molly shot him another fake smile. "Would you like to take over?"

He retreated. Clara held in a laugh.

"What about all the pollution?" a girl asked. "I saw a picture of people in India. It was daytime but it looked like night. That's how polluted the air was."

Kids shook their heads and started talking among themselves again. One girl had her hands over her face, as if she were trying to keep out the imagined pollution. Clara couldn't have been happier about the meeting. It was all that she had hoped for.

"The weather's messed up here too. Look how warm it is in Albany, and it's still winter."

"It's *supposed* to be winter."

"I just saw that it was a hundred degrees in Siberia. Isn't that where they sent people so they could freeze in prison?" Nate said.

Some kids laughed. "That's the wacky world we're inheriting," someone said.

Nate stood up. "You have to google all this, guys. It's not funny."

Nick stood too. "You know that we had to go all the way to Vermont for our snowboarding competition, right? The snow up there wasn't even so great. Who knows if there will even be a team next year? We're headed for real trouble. What happened to winter?"

"It's kind of like Jamie's debate—the Year Without a Summer," Molly added. "Except this is the reverse."

Clara almost blurted that a debate takes two people, but then she thought of the last few days and Molly's strange behavior. Instead, she said, "We have to be hopeful. It's easy to get overwhelmed with all of this and give up . . . do nothing. But it's good to ask questions like we're doing. After that, though, we need answers."

"Hey, Clara," Nick said. "You're pretty amazing to . . . um . . . get this project going. I'm glad to be involved."

Her face heated up again. She hoped nobody saw.

"Me too, Nick," Molly said. "We can be partners."

Nick shrugged, and Clara forced her attention back to the meeting. She wondered what Molly had in mind by saying they could be partners. Another Molly mystery.

"How can there be floods in some places when other people don't have water?" a student asked. "I don't get it."

"It's the climate, dummy," another boy said. Kids booed. "Sorry. I didn't mean that," he said. "We're all here because we care about our planet, but I have no idea how to stop floods from happening. There's a lot more water around from all the ice melting. It's logical, but what can a bunch of kids do?"

"Yeah," someone else said, "that melting's scary, but in some places, the hot weather causes a drought." He shrugged as if he could easily give up. "Either way, people are in trouble."

"And what about starving? A lot of people don't have enough food because of all these disasters," Katy said. "It's all because of the heat. It was a hundred fifteen degrees in Paris last summer. My dad said we'd be miserable if we went there now."

"Hey Katy," Nick said, "Yesterday you said it was a hundred ten degrees in Paris. Did it go up five degrees in one day?"

Kids laughed. Clara wondered if this was the time to talk about what they could do right now: collect supplies for people in disaster areas.

"Um . . . these are really good, or I mean, really bad situations, but they're good comments," she said. "We should be proud of ourselves for reading about them, for knowing what's happening so that we can inform others." She looked around the cafeteria. Kids were listening. She told them about her conversation with Mr. Morris from the American Red Cross about disasters happening right now and how he would send supplies they collected to disaster areas. They would go from store to store and ask for donations.

Kids started talking before she'd even finished. Some shook their heads. Clara didn't know what had scared them.

"We can start by making a list of what we think people need." She nodded at Molly. A few kids got up and said they had to leave. More followed. Clara's heart sank. Why were they leaving? She took a few steps toward them. "Um . . . we're almost done and . . ." But they kept going. Excitement drained from her. She'd failed to keep them interested in saving their planet.

In the middle of all this, Lucy suggested asking for inexpensive windbreakers. She'd seen them in a drug store. A few more ideas were thrown out as the large group dwindled to five. Molly handed Clara the marker. "I have to go too."

Clara stood, confused, wondering what had happened. Had Molly given a signal for them to leave? Had she planned it this way . . . bring the kids, then have them leave? For the first time Clara questioned her instincts about people, especially Molly. Just like a disaster—without warning, as Jamie had said when she asked if he knew what a disaster was.

Three students remained—Lucy, Megan, and Greg. Lucy held her hand out for the marker and wrote down more supplies they could request. Clara thanked them for coming. And for staying. But her heart wasn't in it. She couldn't show it, though. They looked to her for what to do next. She breathed deeply and said, "Right. Let's get to work." They agreed to begin visiting stores after school the next day. She hurriedly took down the easel and signs, stored them in the classroom, and thanked Mr. J. She told him she was late for an appointment and rushed out.

On her way to the Thurbers', she reviewed what had just happened. Kids had seemed interested—Molly too—and angry that all these disasters were happening because of climate change. Then she mentioned the American Red Cross, and how they could collect things that people needed. That's when kids started leaving.

It had to be something about the collecting. Were the kids scared to ask for donations? She'd told Lucy, Megan, and Greg that they'd start collecting tomorrow. Four students against the world of man-made disasters. She wondered if they stood a chance of succeeding.

Chapter Twenty-Five

Possible clearing

*G*us threw himself at Clara when Mrs. Thurber opened the door. Mrs. Thurber's smile, a little sad but still a smile, said thank you. Clara was so glad she'd come despite all she had to do.

Gus pulled a bag toward her. "Look, Clara. More blocks. New ones."

Clara bent down and peeked inside. "Perfect blocks for building schools and houses, Gus. I can't wait to start. Should we go?"

He dragged the bag, and she followed. She turned and gave thumbs up to Mrs. Thurber, who had tears in her eyes. She hadn't thought Mrs. Thurber could ever have anything to cry over. Clara gave a small wave to reassure her all was okay.

In the playroom, Gus already had the blocks scattered around him and was building.

"I'll be your assistant builder," she said, and he nodded, stacking away.

"A house," he said, more to himself than to her. He put another block into place and took his time adding more. Ten minutes later, he cocked his head as if checking for what might be missing.

"It's a really fine house, Gus. It looks strong."

"Yeah. A family live here. But they don't worry about hur-hur . . . those windy storms because nothing can hurt them inside."

"I can see that, Gus. They're safe inside from hurricanes because you built the house to be strong."

Mrs. Thurber surprised them with ice cream and different toppings. Gus poked his finger into the butterscotch and licked it. "That one."

Clara chose butterscotch too. After a spoonful of vanilla ice cream and butterscotch sauce, she tapped Gus. "Mmmmmm. Thanks. It's the first time I ever had butterscotch."

"Yeah. I like chocolate, too, and strawberry."

Clara licked the ice cream off her spoon. Gus was so wise for a little boy. "It's nice to have choices, isn't it, Gus? There are so many choices you'll have in your life."

She finished her ice cream, told Gus she'd be back soon, and thanked Mrs. Thurber for the treat. On her way out, she glanced back. Mrs. Thurber was handing blocks to Gus, who was concentrating on his building again. He looked like he was making important decisions.

———

As she walked home, she thought about Gus wondering about his dad and about her own father. All this mixed in with her perplexed thoughts about the end of the climate meeting. Her good intentions and plans didn't seem to be working. The one good thing that had happened recently was meeting the governor. She stopped walking for a moment, dismayed. She'd never written to thank him.

At home, she took out a sheet of plain paper and began.

Dear Governor,

I cannot thank you enough for arranging for me to talk to the kind man, Juan, in the Puerto Rican Liaison Office. He got in touch with government people there and helped me speak to my father. I know that you went to Puerto Rico after Hurricane María a few times because I saw you on TV, and my relatives there also saw you. My family lived through the hurricane. I was twelve and my brother, six. Thank you for sending the hundreds of students to help.

I know that there are more Puerto Ricans living in New York City than in any other city in the world. And I was surprised to learn that there are 1,103,067 Puerto Ricans in New York State. We are four of those citizens now.

One of your organizations made it possible for my family to come to Albany, where we are starting a new life. It will be perfect once my father is back from Puerto Rico. He has been there for almost eight weeks helping to rebuild houses. My mother, my brother Diego, and I wait every day for a phone call from him saying he is on his way home. Unfortunately, planes are not flying regularly, as I understand it. He has a round-trip ticket so he doesn't need money, only a seat to fly home.

Thank you again, for everything you do to make people's lives better everywhere you go.
Sincerely,
Clara Montalvo
141 Cedar Street
Albany, NY, 12205

She added her phone number as a P.S. She hoped the letter wasn't too long. She read it again, then couldn't resist. She added another P.S.

In case you are in Puerto Rico again in the next few months, if you could try to get in touch with my father and give him any advice, I would be forever grateful. Even longer than forever.

She thought that might be too bold a request, especially the last plea, but she sealed the letter before she could change her mind.

She addressed the envelope and ran out to the nearest mailbox. The letter was on its way, probably like thousands of others from people around the state requesting things. She tried not to think of that. She didn't want to dampen her optimism for something good to come.

Chapter Twenty-Six

Cumulonimbus clouds

*J*amie was back in his room at three o'clock, just as school was ending. He'd learned a great deal that day about disasters—family ones. But he didn't know how Lucas's checkup had gone. He'd have to wait until Lucas was ready to tell them when he woke up. But he couldn't wait for what he had to do—try to keep peace in the house—for Lucas—at least for today.

He was helping Mom set the table for dinner when thumping sounds coming from the hallway alerted him that his brother was up. By the time he rushed to the stairs, Lucas, pale as the white painted walls, was at the bottom, leaning on the rail. He seemed to be in a daze. He focused on Jamie and placed his hand on Jamie's arm to steady himself. "Hey, Buddy. You can't let me sleep half a day."

"Lucas. It's okay," Jamie said. "You went right upstairs and crashed, so we knew you needed your sleep. I do that too, sometimes," he assured his brother, who still seemed pretty out of it.

Lucas rubbed his crew cut, then hobbled into the dining room and collapsed onto a chair at the table. "Seems all I do now is eat."

Mom helped him get closer to the table and patted him on the shoulder. "But you really haven't eaten much at all today, just a sandwich. I hope you're hungry now."

Dad came in and took his place. Jamie sat across from Lucas, watched each move everyone made, and tried not to make a bad one. He was thrilled to have Lucas there after all those months staring at an empty chair.

Mom said the first words, the ones Jamie waited to hear. "Can you tell us what the doctor said?"

"So first off," Lucas said, then stopped as if he didn't want to tell them. "The doc said I should come in to talk about the stress. You know, the nightmares and flashbacks." Lucas rubbed his head again like that would make them go away. "They're bad at night." He lowered his head, as if he had used up all his energy. His dinner sat mostly untouched.

Mom touched Lucas's hand. Jamie could tell she was trying to lighten the mood, make things better. "That sounds like good advice, Lucas. We can drive you any time."

"What did he say about your leg?" Dad asked.

Jamie moved his potatoes around with his fork, but his appetite had disappeared. He felt too jittery to eat. But he listened like his life depended on it.

Lucas lifted his head after a few minutes. "They're more than just bad dreams," he explained, as if he hadn't heard Dad's question about his leg. He spoke so softly Jamie and his parents had to lean in to hear. "Explosions go off in my brain about a thousand times a day." His eyes closed, and his chin dipped to his chest again. Mom's hand swiped her cheeks while Lucas wasn't looking.

Nobody moved. Jamie had never thought about the power of silence, how right now it was paralyzing. The explosions that flashed to him were his and Lucas's fireworks in the backyard, all that fun.

Finally, Mom motioned to Dad to help Lucas into the den. "Lucas, why don't you get comfortable on the sofa in the den? You can put your leg up the footstool. I'll bring you some dessert."

Dad got up and stood there like a statue. He didn't hold out his hand or anything.

"Wait till he opens his eyes," Jamie said, on Lucas's side, not Dad's. Seconds passed, then minutes.

Lucas finally raised his head and moved his plate. "Thanks, Mom," he said. She glanced at his untouched food. "You know, what I need right now are my pain pills. The burning in my leg is bumming me out. Buddy, can you get them? They're in my pocket." He motioned to his khaki jacket, folded over the back of a chair.

Jamie hurried over and fumbled in the pocket. He brushed off all the drug warnings he'd learned and was about to do what Lucas wanted. On his way back, Dad gave him a stern look, along with a slight shake of his head. Jamie handed his brother the bottle anyway and wondered if he had helped Lucas or was hurting him.

Lucas palmed the vial, like it was something he counted on. "The doc said I have to keep my leg clean, so it doesn't get infected. These"—he shook the bottle—"help the burning and itching." Lucas made a weak attempt at a smile. "Wouldn't it be worse than a bad joke if I lost my leg here in Albany after surviving all that over there?" he said wryly. "The doc said I could lose it."

Jamie gulped and silently screamed *no!* Dad and Mom's eyes locked.

Then Dad asked, "What are those pills you're taking?"

"Painkillers," Lucas said. "They help . . . till they don't. I have to keep a good supply, that's all, maybe get something stronger."

"Are they addictive?" Dad's face went dark. "That's the last thing you need."

Lucas blew out an exasperated breath. Jamie did too.

"Yeah, Dad. I know," Lucas said. "Aspirin and ibuprofen, all those over-the-counter meds, don't do a thing. Don't worry.

I could have had all the pot and heroin I wanted over there." He tossed his head as if Afghanistan were right outside their dining room.

Jamie's insides knew the conversation was veering out of control, two racing cars heading around a curve before they crashed. He had to change the subject.

In a flash he had an idea that might help Lucas . . . and him. He blurted it out. "Lucas, when you feel up to it, maybe you could come to school with me and talk to my science class about . . . um, your experience. You know, about how war is a disaster."

Dad hollered, "What's wrong with you, Jamie? Of course, he can't go to your school!"

His parents' eyes darted first to Lucas, then to him. Dad's mouth opened to say more but Jamie kept going. "Our teacher Mr. J is really cool, Lucas. You'll like him. He assigned this huge project on natural disasters, like volcanic eruptions and hurricanes, things like that. My partner Clara and I found out so much about past disasters and ones happening now too, so that's what we want to focus on—man-made disasters like war and temperatures going up, and fires and floods, and all that."

He rambled on and on. If he stopped talking, Dad might say that Lucas couldn't go, and another argument would start. He had to speak up and ask for what he wanted. Listening to Lucas these few days had shown him that. Now he was doing it. "Maybe you can convince kids that combat isn't glamorous the way movies and video games portray it."

Lucas sat up and leaned forward. Something gleamed in his eyes. He seemed interested. It was so much better than the blank empty stare Jamie had noticed earlier, and the one Lucas mostly wore. "Sure, Jamie. Just say when. If you want me to tell those dudes to stay out of war, I'd be happy to."

Jamie's love and admiration for his brother skyrocketed. "Can you come this week if I get permission?"

Dad hit the table with his fist.

"Sure." Lucas shrugged, not paying any attention to Dad. "It's not like I have much else to do."

"It's too soon to expect Lucas to go out," Dad commanded. Jamie watched Dad changing tactics when screaming didn't work with Lucas. Dad's frown had grown deeper and deeper as they planned around him.

"Dad, this is important," Jamie countered. "He can discourage kids from enlisting." His excitement soared once the words were out. He'd spoken up about something that really mattered to him, helping his brother get back to normal, and for a few seconds, nothing else mattered.

Dad turned to Lucas. "You're having all these nightmares, and you need your rest. How can you say you're okay with going to his school to talk?" He looked to Mom for agreement. She nodded, then turned that into a slow shake of her head to Jamie. Two against two.

"Then it's settled," Dad said, like he'd won.

Lucas gave a loud clap, surprising Jamie. Was it Dad's speech? What was happening? "I'm good to go, Jamie, whenever you say, but now I'm starving."

Dad's jaw clenched. He'd lost.

Jamie helped Mom get the meatloaf and vegetables back on the table and they all dug in.

"So," Jamie said, borrowing courage from Lucas. "I'll check with Mr. J tomorrow, and maybe the next day—that's Wednesday—we can go in. Or it can be Thursday or Friday." He gave a sideways glance at Dad.

Lucas put down his fork after a few bites and rubbed his forehead. "Dizzy again. And my leg's throbbing. I need to go lie down. Great dinner, Mom." He picked up his crutches.

Dad got up to help.

"I'm okay, Dad," Lucas said and hobbled out of the kitchen.

Mom slowly piled the plates. Dad sat back down. Jamie didn't dare follow Lucas. He crouched in his chair, hoping for invisible.

A crashing sound roused them. They ran to it. Lucas was on the floor at the bottom of the stairs. He didn't move for a few minutes. Dad raced for his phone and called 9-1-1. Mom fanned Lucas with her hands. "Run. Get me a wet washcloth, Jamie." He ran faster than he'd ever run before.

Lucas moved, then opened his eyes. "What the . . . why am I on the floor?" He lifted his head and the washcloth fell off. "Oh, yeah. I was on my way up. Guess I blacked out."

They kneeled around Lucas until he drew himself up to a sitting position. Dad told Lucas the EMS would be here soon, but Lucas said, "No! Cancel them."

"EMS doesn't cancel."

Lucas said he'd had enough medical service. He didn't protest when Jamie and Dad helped him to his room.

Jamie's head was spinning. They'd just made a plan to go to school together in the next few days. Now Lucas was falling down, blacking out. Dad was probably right. Maybe it was too early for Lucas to go out in public. Lucas wanted to please Jamie, sure, but was he stressing Lucas out, like he had with the crashing sound his phone made when he dropped it, the crash that had made Lucas scream? An awful suspicion crossed his mind. By trying so hard to help, maybe instead he was hurting the person he loved most in the world.

Chapter Twenty-Seven

Sign of fair weather

When Clara walked into class just before the bell rang, Jamie was up front talking to Mr. J.

At the chime, Mr. J addressed the class. "Before we get to natural disasters, Jamie has an announcement."

Clara crossed her fingers for Jamie and wondered what he was going to say. He seemed nervous.

He stood next to his seat and ran his fingers through his hair like he'd done during the debate. "My brother Lucas came home from Afghanistan on Saturday." He stopped for a few seconds. "That's why I wasn't here yesterday. He came home with a messed-up leg from an explosion, and he has head trauma. You can't see it but . . ." Jamie clicked his ballpoint pen over and over. He seemed choked up, at a loss for words. The class was quiet. A few kids cleared their throats. Clara silently cheered Jamie on.

"He's a little different now," Jamie explained. "He gets tired and dizzy."

Kids glanced away. Clara could sense the unease growing in the classroom. Jamie's upset reached her. But he was doing okay. *Just finish, Jamie*, she silently urged.

"Lucas is going to come to class to tell you how it was in the war."

Kids shot looks at each other like they couldn't believe it and started chattering to one another.

"I wanted to tell you in case you don't want to hear him or if you think it might scare you. It scared me at first, and he's my brother. I love him so much and want him back to normal."

Nick raised his hand and waited for Jamie to call on him. "That's so cool of him to come. Can we ask him questions?"

"Yeah, sure," Jamie said. "He'll tell you whatever you want to know. And . . . um . . . thank you. Talking to you might help him get back to how he was before. I feel a lot better now that you know."

Clara watched Jamie changing right before her eyes. He seemed more certain of himself regarding Lucas, and of what he needed to do to be there for his brother. Apart from his joking, she liked how he'd handled himself during their debate. She liked this new independence and hoped it would carry over to the rest of his schoolwork. He might even start to believe he had the leadership abilities she saw in him.

The class was quiet again. As Jamie passed her desk, he glanced at Clara. She reached out for his hand and squeezed it tight as she whispered, "I'm proud of you."

———

Jamie walked home on air. He went over and over Clara's words. She didn't give out compliments lightly. And she'd even squeezed his hand! A tingle ran through him as he recalled the softness of her fingers wrapping around his. For a girl, she sure had a strong grip. But that was Clara, strong and steady in so many ways.

When he thought of how he'd joked at her expense during the debates, the feeling crept over him that he didn't deserve her friendship. But knowing her was as exciting as snowboarding down a steep slope.

He wondered if he'd experience the same satisfaction if Dad said he was proud of him. He wondered how pride worked. How could it buoy him up all of a sudden? Maybe because someone, Clara, had recognized that he'd said what was in his heart about Lucas. That must be where pride lived—next to truth and confidence. He was pretty sure Clara had a lot to do with awakening these qualities in him.

———

Lucas and Dad were talking in the den when he walked in after school. Dad was home from work early. A surprise. And another: Lucas looked good. Rested. Maybe he would be up for going to school tomorrow after all. Jamie waited and listened.

"And I didn't use anything I learned in basic training," Dad said.

Lucas waved Jamie over. "Come on in. Dad's telling me about his rigorous basic training." He laughed.

"It's not funny," Dad said. "It was hard. What I said was, I didn't use any of it in the office job I had."

"Why did you even enlist, Dad?" Lucas asked.

Jamie moved in closer to Lucas. That was the big question he'd wondered about for so long.

"That's a short story," Dad said, "as opposed to a long one. See, I wanted to travel, take some time off after high school, maybe join the Peace Corps or do service of some sort. When I told my father, he argued that I should go to college or get a job. I told him I wasn't ready for college, and know what he said?"

Jamie shook his head. "What?"

"'You want to travel? Join the army.' So I did. End of story. See? Told you it was short."

Jamie wanted more. How did Dad feel when Grandpa said that? Did Dad *want* to join the army?

"What about you, Lucas?" Dad asked. "How much of your

training did you use over there?"

"Well, I was responsible for keeping a lookout for anything suspicious," Lucas answered slowly. "I had to protect the Marines on the base and—"

Jamie couldn't help interrupting. "What about saving those men in the fire?" He remembered the letter in Lucas's duffle about honors for bravery. "You had to know how to go in and—"

All was quiet.

Lucas shrugged, like he was embarrassed to say anything about saving anyone. "Well, if I hadn't carried that hundred-pound load for a mile five times a week in basic, I wouldn't have been able to drag those guys out."

"Now that's training," Dad said.

Jamie waited, hoping his father would acknowledge his brother's accomplishments, which were huge. He knew all too well how much it hurt to feel that no matter what you did, it was never good enough for Dad.

"I'm proud of you, son."

The words he'd been waiting for. Goosebumps rose on Jamie's arms. It was a hundred times better than if Dad had said them to him.

"Me too, Lucas," Jamie blurted. "Really proud." His throat hurt from holding back more stuff he wished he could say like, *Dad, that was the best thing a dad could say.* "I checked with Mr. J," he told his brother. "He said, 'Please bring your brother to class.' So can you come to school with me tomorrow?"

"Tomorrow?" Mom said as she stepped into the room with some snacks. "Jamie, Lucas isn't ready to go out so soon. He needs a few more weeks at home. His blackouts are—"

"It's okay, Mom," Lucas said. "I can handle it. They come and go fast."

Jamie pumped his fist, unable to hold his excitement in.

Dad threw up his arms. "I tried. What more can I say? I sure wish I could be a fly on the wall and hear you talking."

Jamie thought he heard a sense of relaxation in Dad. He wasn't insisting that Lucas stay home, wasn't yelling at him. Something about Dad seemed different. Maybe tomorrow could be Lucas and Jamie day.

"Get some sleep," Jamie told Lucas when they got up the stairs. "We have to wake up early for school."

"You don't want to know about early when you're in the service," Lucas said and crawled under his covers. "I was up every morning at five."

Jamie sat on the edge of the bed, watching over his brother as he nodded off. Jamie almost did too, but Lucas startled awake and slammed his hand on the bed. "No! No!" An eerie gasping sound came from him, like he was trying to scream, but all that came out was loud air.

Jamie's heart galloped. He didn't touch Lucas, afraid that it would make things worse. Lucas mumbled something Jamie couldn't make out, then went quiet again. His breathing slowed. Jamie's followed suit.

Should he call Mom and Dad? Forget about tomorrow? He'd been so sure about Lucas being okay just minutes earlier. If they didn't show up, he'd disappoint his class and Clara. But now he was afraid of what might happen if Lucas did go speak to his class.

Chapter Twenty-Eight

Blizzicane

*M*r. J was waiting for them at the door. Kids took their seats even before the bell. Jamie walked in next to Lucas on crutches. Jamie hoped he was doing the right thing. The class fell silent. Then Mr. J clapped. A few kids did too. Then Jamie did, and everybody joined in.

Lucas forced a smile and moved next to Mr. J's desk. He leaned his crutches against it and sat in the chair set out for him. He stretched his leg out. Jamie took his regular seat, but Lucas waved him up. "Come on up here, Buddy. Bring a chair."

Jamie dragged one up and sat next to Lucas. They bumped fists. Lucas sat up straight. He told the class how he'd finished high school in town just like they would, and then, like a lot of seventeen-year-old kids, he didn't know what he wanted to do next. "Any of you think you'll feel that way?"

Nods and yeahs came back to him.

"I thought about college, but I didn't do so well in school. Couldn't do anything about it then, so I enlisted. That didn't go over too well at home." A few kids laughed. He paused, probably to let what he'd said sink in. "I figured serving my country was the right thing to do. But you people . . . eighth graders. Geez." He smacked his forehead. "You have your futures in front of you. Go out there and be whatever you want to be. You have so many choices."

Jamie glanced around. He and Clara locked eyes. Her smile reassured him he'd done the right thing bringing Lucas. A few kids leaned forward like they were waiting for Lucas's next bit of advice.

He spoke for twenty minutes about basic training and arriving in Afghanistan. "When you're deployed, you're with the same guys, maybe forty or so, for seven months." He smiled and glanced around. "Kind of like here—same people every day. Except we worked with them, ate with them, argued with them, gave and took orders, and slept in the same quarters. For seven months."

Everybody leaned in to hear more.

"The things that made your heart thump every second were the car bombs, roadside bombs, suicide bombers, mortars. Every second." His chin fell to his chest.

Kids glanced at each other uneasily. Jamie chewed on his thumbnail until it hurt. He silently begged his brother to talk about something else. But Lucas continued.

"I wasn't sure if the civilian . . . yeah, it might be a woman or a kid . . . like people I knew back home . . ." Lucas stared straight ahead again, as if he were trying to remember those people. "That person right in front of me . . . was either about to kill me or hand me a bowl of kebabs and flatbread." Lucas shook his head. "Unbelievable. You could kill the wrong person . . ."

He trailed off again. Was he seeing some kid he'd killed? Jamie squeezed his eyes shut. *No more, Lucas . . . please.*

"Or watch my buddy die while I screamed at him to keep his eyes open, to keep breathing, Buddy."

Jamie didn't want to open his eyes. His insides tightened knowing Lucas would keep talking.

"Yeah, Buddy said we'd get out of that place real soon, take care of each other. We got sent over together. I carried him out of the inferno. It was a . . ." Lucas's face twisted into a grimace of pain. "There was fire like you never want to see."

He stopped again. Jamie silently begged Lucas to come back into the room, back into himself.

"I was too late."

Jamie's heart clenched. Now he knew why his brother kept calling him Buddy. It wasn't a nickname; Lucas had carried his friend out of the explosion.

Everybody in class stared at Lucas and side glanced at each other and Mr. J for what to do.

Jamie thought fast. He tapped his brother on the knee to let Lucas know he was there with him. Lucas blinked over and over and shouted, "No! No!" He tried to stand, stumbled without his crutches, and nearly fell before Jamie leapt from his chair and got hold of him.

"Gotta go back in. Get the rest of them," Lucas shouted loudly and tried to walk, then drag his bad leg. He fell over and scrambled along the floor. He grabbed his head and screamed, "Hold it in. Hold it in."

Jamie quivered with fear and desperation as he kneeled next to Lucas. He placed a hand on Lucas's back and whispered, "Lucas, we'll be home soon. I'll call Mom. Don't say any more." He didn't care about what his classmates thought; his only worry was for his brother.

Mr. J rushed over and punched in numbers on his phone. "School nurse," he barked. Jamie fumbled for his own phone and left a message for his mom.

In minutes, the nurse arrived. She gave Jamie a quick glance, then told everyone to stand back so that Lucas could get enough air, kneeled next to him, and fanned him. She opened a package and placed a folded towel on his forehead. She checked both sides of his head, probably looking for injuries. Then she piled five books on top of each other, raised Lucas's bad leg and set it on the books.

Everyone watched in silence. Would all her first aid work?

Lucas slowly raised his head. His eyes settled on her. He smiled. A few kids tried to hold giggles in. Jamie thought it was kind of funny, too, now that his brother seemed out of immediate danger. Lucas lay his head back down.

"I'm the school nurse," Nurse Davis said to Lucas. "Don't try to get up yet."

Lucas obeyed. Not for long, though. He lifted his head and looked around as if trying to make sense of the room full of people.

"Oh yeah. I remember," Lucas murmured, like he hadn't just crashed. "Science class. I just need a minute. Blackouts come on fast. They go pretty fast too." He was breathing hard, as if he'd just done some heavy exercise. "Buddy didn't make it."

Jamie's stomach lurched. Enough about Buddy.

"Three men went home worse off than me." Lucas raised his good leg and winced. "I still have this, and two good arms. See," Lucas said, like he was on a roll.

Jamie didn't know how to get out of their bad situation with Lucas still remembering. He wished Mom would hurry up and get here.

"When you're over there, you're watching over your shoulder every second for danger, so you shut down every emotion that's not going to keep you and your team safe. No relaxing, ever. You're on high alert every second. No vacation. Then you come home. It's hard to laugh, hard to feel anything good, see, because you shut down that part of you. You're still waiting for another bomb to go off."

Lucas's expression was vacant again, his voice weakening. He repositioned his bad leg and struggled up. The nurse helped him. He leaned against Mr. J's desk. She sat next to him. Jamie sat on his other side.

Lucas smiled and glanced at the nurse. "This is the best time I've had since I got home."

Kids laughed, but not too loud. Jamie didn't want to get his hopes up but let out a laugh too. His eyes met Clara's. He hoped his expression told her that he got strength from her calmness during all this. He wanted to tell Lucas, *Enough. Stop talking about what gives you flashbacks*, but he'd brought him here to tell kids about the war.

Nick raised his hand. "Is it okay if I ask Lucas something?

"That's what I'm here for," Lucas answered, sounding like he was back again.

"Thanks. It means a lot. I'm Nick. That was awesome, Lucas. Thanks for telling us all this. What you said was what I needed to hear, 'cause sometimes I get this far out idea to enlist in a few years. You know, like you said, because I don't know what I want to do in life. I don't think I'll have any idea what I want to do even then. I scare myself and say, no way. I could be over there and not even know what I've gotten into, right? Did you know what you were getting into?"

Lucas shook his head. He didn't say anything for a good two minutes. Nobody did. Jamie thought, *Mom would have said, "You could have heard a pin drop."*

"It's confusing," Lucas said. "You want to serve your country, but you have no idea if that's what you're doing once you get there."

He said troops were being sent to faraway places like Afghanistan to hunt down the Taliban, but they couldn't tell the Taliban from civilians.

"The Afghan people were kind to us even though we were shooting up their country. They gave us water and food when we were out in the hills for days. *Their* hills, but we took them over, treated them like they were ours. Stupid of us when you think about it."

He glanced around the classroom. "If any of you found yourself over there, you wouldn't know what you were doing. Like Nick said. You thought you went for a reason, but when you got there, you couldn't tell what it was. How would you like that? You'd have a rifle, but you wouldn't know what you were fighting for. Your officers wouldn't know either. Ours didn't. None of us wanted to kill innocent people, but lots of times we didn't know who we were killing. In bed at night, I spent hours wondering who decided that American soldiers should be killing people in Afghanistan. We were just little guys sent to do big things we didn't understand. We were mighty thankful to hit our beds each night, thankful we'd survived another day." Lucas's voice wavered. He lowered his head again.

Jamie leaned over and hugged his brother. He'd brought Lucas to school way too early, maybe done him damage.

Mom arrived to pick up Lucas, and Jamie got to his next class a little late. He didn't need a late slip. Somehow, the whole school had heard about the Marine who'd come to Mr. J's science class to talk about war. And a flashing ambulance outside was big news too. Kids came up to him all day long, asking if Lucas could come to their class. Jamie hated to disappoint them, but he wouldn't ask Lucas to do that again.

Clara found him at lunchtime. "Thank you for what you did for all of us today." She squeezed his hand again. He almost hugged her, but he was afraid that if she hugged him back, he'd never let her go.

He nodded instead. "I learned my lesson, though. Lucas wasn't ready to come out. He's fragile. I'm going to spend as much time with him as I can, see if I can help him get back on track." He had no idea how he'd ever make it up to Lucas. Maybe he'd have to spend the rest of his life trying.

Chapter Twenty-Nine

Partly cloudy

*A*fter school, Clara waited in the cafeteria. The kids who had signed up to collect supplies were supposed to meet at three fifteen to get oriented. At three twenty, Lucy, Megan, and Greg came in. Clara looked at her list of twenty names. A few were scratched out. She smiled at her audience of three. "Thanks for coming. We're it, I guess." She tried to set aside her disappointment about the others.

She handed each of them a list of stores and supplies. "We'll cover different streets. It's probably best to ask to see the store manager. Then we can introduce ourselves, show our student IDs, and tell them about our drive for supplies. We can say the American Red Cross will send the supplies they donate to disaster areas. You can mention fires and floods."

"Should we ask for items like toothpaste and hairbrushes too?" Lucy asked, checking her list.

"I think we should request whatever people would need after a disaster. Maybe hand the person the list. Then, if they say they'll donate, write down the items and quantities. We can try to get them involved—ask them what they think people suffering a disaster need. Tell them we'll come back the next day to pick the supplies up. We'll carry the packages to a central location." Clara let out a big breath. She hoped the four of them could do all this. "Ready? Let's go."

Clara zipped her jacket as they walked ten blocks to the business area. It was colder than it had been the last few days. A snowflake landed on her cheek as they stood at the crossroads. A snowflake. Jamie would like that. He'd probably also like their challenge of being only four—or five, counting him—handling a big job. He'd make their work easier with his joking. She missed him.

"Good luck," she said, applauding the others to keep their spirits up. And hers. "See you tomorrow. Happy requesting."

As the others took off in different directions, she pictured the rally on Saturday with thousands marching, cheering, committed. Maybe they'd started out small-scale too.

———

By five o'clock, Clara had nine promises of donations: canned and packaged foods, plastic bags, toiletries, plastic windbreakers that didn't cost a lot—Lucy's idea—and other useful things like socks, underwear, and flip-flops in sealed packages. She headed for home, grateful for it all, and only hoped they would have enough time and strength to get everything to one place for the American Red Cross.

Nine donations. But what if her fellow collectors didn't get any donations? She'd find out tomorrow at school. Maybe they'd get a ton of donations. But they couldn't reach the numbers of items needed for so many disasters with only four workers. They needed more volunteers. She had to figure out what was scaring the rest of the kids away.

Chapter Thirty

Snow day!

The next morning, Clara sat up in bed. The house was usually quiet at that hour but Diego was jumping up and down next to her bed shouting, "It snowed! Yay! Snow day!"

She slid out of bed to see if Diego and his superheroes had woken up early and were playing a winter game. At least a foot of snow covered everything outside the living room window and flakes were still coming down hard. Clara opened her phone. Diego was right. Schools were closed for a snow day. Jamie was probably tossing snowballs already.

Mami was rummaging in the front closet. She pulled out her high winter boots. She'd go to work, snow or not. Clara waited until nine, then texted Lucy, Megan, and Greg to find out their donation request results.

All three had their sheets of donation promises, thirteen in all. How lucky, as Clara had hoped. And now, more luck—a free day to pick up the items. They planned to meet at eleven o'clock, downtown where they had split up yesterday. They'd collect the supplies and take them to Lucy's house. She had space to store the things in her basement, and she lived the closest to the stores.

Clara clicked off, letting her enthusiasm spill all over. "Diego, adventure today. Put on your snow gear, boots, gloves, and your warm hat."

He left his calendar that he'd made to check off days until Papi got home on the table with his superhero drawn in for today. The superhero was dressed for big time snow.

The team met right on time, all bundled up, lists in hand. Diego high-fived his new friends. Lucy thanked him for coming to help out when he could be home playing. Diego gave thumbs up, probably pretending they were all superheroes out on a mission. Lucy led them to the first store on her list. They stared at the CLOSED sign hanging in the window, then at each other. They rushed to the next store. CLOSED. They hadn't considered this. Lights shone inside the next store they approached. Lucy tried the door. Yes! They beamed at each other.

The manager had six boxes of products ready, so the five of them loaded their arms with as much as they could carry, thanked the people in the store, and slogged through the snow to Lucy's. After three trips back and forth and mugs of hot chocolate, they headed to more stores. Diego begged to go in first. His courage had soared as the first salesperson he talked to escorted him to the store manager. Now he knew the speech perfectly and couldn't wait to give it. And he thanked people. Clara knew Papi would be proud. She was, for sure.

The sun came out as they left the last store on their pickup rounds. The streets of Albany shone with white melting to gray. Parents and kids in boots plowed through probably the last big snow of the year.

Loaded down and tired, they sloughed through piles and slush. A woman holding a microphone caught up to Clara. She looked familiar. A man with a big camera followed her. "Hello. I'm Kathryn Quinn from Channel 10 News."

"Oh, yeah." Clara, loaded down with bulky boxes, recognized her from watching the news.

"This is John Lee. He and I've been following your group for an hour."

Lucy, Megan, Greg, and Diego hoisted up their packages and crowded in to hear.

"I've talked to the store managers, so I know what you students are doing," Miss Quinn said. "How thoughtful. Can I ask you some questions?"

Clara turned to her group. "TV news? Oh, no. I've never been on TV. I wouldn't know what to say. You guys can."

They did. And after a few minutes, Miss Quinn turned to Clara, who couldn't say no. She finished their story by telling how they'd accomplished their goal thanks to their gang of five, who stood clasping their packages.

"We'd love more collectors, though. We invite everyone watching to help. Or if you can donate just one or two new items for people who've been in a recent disaster, that would be so appreciated. And please do something to stop the heating of our planet. There are so many small ways to make a difference." She stated her phone number. "I'll give you more information on what you can do if you call me. Thank you."

Clara couldn't wait to watch Channel 10 news at six o'clock that evening. Diego stood superhero straight in front of the TV and told Mami to stay close so she wouldn't miss any action.

Mami held her hand over her mouth and hugged Diego. "You, *mi amor*, on TV?" she marveled.

Kathryn Quinn put the microphone to each of the collectors, then to Diego. He beamed proudly as if he'd just had a big soccer save.

Her little brother was such a superhero. Clara allowed herself to feel like one, too, just for a few minutes. The newscast ended and they sat, going over and over what they'd all said, until Diego fell asleep on the floor.

The next morning the streets were plowed, the snow mostly melted. Back to school. Clara didn't know what to expect that day. She had missed Jamie even though it had just been a day off. So much had happened that it felt a lot longer. She wondered if he'd seen her on TV. All she knew was that they had collected more supplies than she had ever imagined and had discovered the generosity of the people in Albany. Mr. Morris at the American Red Cross would be happy with this first load of supplies.

"You're amazing," Jamie said, and he kept talking as she took her seat.

Clara ignored his remarks to save him and herself from more trouble with Mr. J. She knew Jamie couldn't help himself, but she was trying. He won out.

"We saw you on the news. Clara, my mom thinks you guys are the best kids ever. My dad does too. Lucas saw you and said I had the coolest friends. I want him to meet you, get to know you. Can we do that sometime soon?"

Jamie was still talking when Mr. J interrupted. "Mr. Fulton. May I have the floor? I believe it's time for class to begin. Science class."

Clara groaned to herself. Jamie got quiet, fast. *Saved*, was the only word she could think of as she peeked at him. He had his hand over his mouth.

Mr. J asked Clara, Lucy, Megan, and Greg to stand. "I'm so proud of all of you." He turned to the class. "How many of you saw the six o'clock news?"

A few hands went up. Others looked bewildered.

"Good for you who watched the news. The rest of you missed an amazing interview with these brave volunteers, your classmates, who worked tirelessly on a snow day so that people in disaster areas might have toothpaste and clean clothes to wear. Towels too, right, Greg?"

Greg's face turned several shades of red. He nodded sheepishly. "It was fun. People really want to help if you give them the chance."

"Megan, Lucy, Clara. Brava to you all." Mr. J said. "And a

big bravo to your little brother, Clara. Please tell him that we all saw him carrying the biggest packages. Would any of you like to tell us how it was asking for donations and collecting supplies?"

Clara turned to the others, who shook their heads, so she stood up. "The people were so kind. They knew about the disasters, so we didn't have to say much about them. We just asked for whatever they could spare for people who were left with nothing. We have more stores to cover because the disasters aren't stopping. So many people are left without basic things that you don't even think about, like toothpaste and towels."

"And deodorant," someone said. Kids laughed.

"We'll make sure it's on the list. Thanks." She didn't say anything about the kids who had bailed out of collecting.

They sat down again. Jamie stood up and said, "I'm in for collecting."

"Me too," Molly said. "I would have come with you to collect. I'm good at that. Nobody told me you were going."

Clara didn't remind her that she had left their meeting early. "Maybe next time, Molly."

A few kids raised their hands and volunteered. Clara thanked the new recruits and told everyone to meet in Washington Park the next morning, Saturday. They would have the whole day. And time for training. But she didn't mention this.

———

Clara waited for Jamie after class and told him she didn't expect him to show up to collect since Lucas was home, but that if he could give their effort just one hour, he could make a big difference. She pleaded for him to think about it even before she told him what the job was. "Just trust me. You can do it."

"What? I'll collect stuff. No problem."

"Great. That will be a big help. *But*. You can help in another way that no one else can. You're an amazing teacher, Jamie, and you know how to convince people to do things. Remember, I've competed against you."

She explained how most kids left her first meeting after school probably because they didn't want to ask for donations—mostly guys. "They probably don't know how to be active for a cause. Like go into stores and convince the managers that they can be part of saving lives. So they just left."

"Yeah? I get it," Jamie said. "But what can I do about it?"

"You can show them how to go into a store, talk to the manager and request a donation for a good cause," she said. *"If* you believe people need help after the disasters they've been through, and I think you do, you could do a pretend session . . . show the guys how to go in and act out what to say so they'd feel confident. Sometimes, people just don't know what to do. My family didn't when we came here, but we had to learn how to even start. That's what you'd be doing. Showing them how to start."

She searched Jamie's face for his answer and hoped she got it right.

Chapter Thirty-One

Sunshine?

When she got to the park, Jamie was standing at the entrance with a clipboard. Twelve new kids showed up right after, and Jamie took their names and thanked them. Clara looked out for Molly but stayed focused. Once kids were seated on park benches, some of the boys confessed they didn't know what they would say and didn't know how to ask for stuff. A few boys said their parents told them to do this. They couldn't say no. Once they said that, other kids nodded. "Yeah. I've never done anything like this before," Nick said.

"That's because you never had to before," Jamie said. "We're living in different times now, and it's because our planet is heating up like never before."

Clara called out her committee's names. "Greg, Lucy, and Megan." They stood up. "These successful volunteers can tell you how they did it." The three pulled out their IDs and recited their short speeches.

"It works," Greg said. "And it's fun. If you don't try, you'll never know."

Clara turned to Jamie. He stepped up without any introduction.

"Thanks, Greg. That's what I needed to hear. Nick, come up here. You be the store manager."

Nick waited for his lines. Jamie told him to improvise, just pretend he was the store manager. Then Jamie, as student, came into the pretend store and requested supplies. Nick listened to him, then agreed to give him what he wanted. Their audience applauded.

"I get it," a kid named Toby said. "Doesn't seem too hard."

Armed with lists of requests, the students took off. They knew the drill. Jamie went with the group and did his part. He called Clara and told her he finished with eight promises of donations, then was hurrying home. He said he had another drill to do with Lucas.

———

Clara got her quota and went with Lucy to her house. Ten boxes were marked school supplies. "I don't think your basement can hold any more supplies, Lucy. I'll call Mr. Morris and tell him we're ready for their pickup."

Maybe he would send the supplies to Puerto Rico for the schools damaged in the earthquakes. She allowed herself the satisfaction of knowing kids there could start school with new notebooks and pencils.

Her joy spilled over as she ran the rest of the way home. She said hi to Mami and Diego and collapsed in her room. She and her classmates had done something worthwhile. She tried not to think about Molly not appearing after her announcement in class.

Never in her wildest, most far-out dreams did she imagine she would get a ping on her phone from the State Capitol. She fumbled the phone as she hurried to put it to her ear. "Hello?"

A woman's voice said, "Clara Montalvo?"

"Yes, yes. This is Clara."

"The governor would like to speak to you, Clara. One moment, please."

"The governor?" Her heart skipped a few beats. She sat down, stood up, sat down again. She licked her dry lips while she waited.

"Hello, Clara Montalvo. This is your governor. We met in front of the Capitol building. How are you?"

Clara answered fast. "Fine. Yes, I'm fine. I remember. Yes, Governor. How are you? I hope you're fine." She shook her head at her silliness. *Of course, he is fine. Oh no. My letter. I shouldn't have said all that about Puerto Ricans. Did I get the number of them in New York wrong?*

"I want to congratulate you and your friends for your heroic work collecting supplies for disaster areas . . . and in a snowstorm too. How did you manage that?"

Clara grinned. "Governor, sir, we . . . my classmates . . . well, just four of us started it but now we're about sixteen from our class. They did so much work. I just organized. And the American Red Cross is going to send the supplies we collected to places that need them. There are so many, right?"

Stop. Don't say anything else. Don't ask him questions. You're bragging. You're rambling. But she couldn't seem to help herself in probably the most important conversation in her life.

She thought she heard the governor's smile even though you can't hear a smile. Even over the phone she could picture him, so kind, waiting for her to find her way out of her long-winded, mixed-up message. *Just thank him. Don't keep him on the phone. He's a busy person. A busy governor. You're just a kid who happened to walk up to his car and get stopped by security men and told to stand back. So stand back, Clara.*

"Well, Clara Montalvo. You have a lot to say."

She couldn't believe he was still on the line. He hadn't hung up.

"That's good," he said. "I did too, when I was your age."

She could hardly breathe. This moment was definitely one million lollipops all rolled into one. It was better than anything she could have imagined.

"You reminded me of what's important, Clara—taking small steps makes big differences. You motivated your classmates to do that. I'll use your example when I talk to people about helping others. If each New Yorker took the action you took, people in disaster areas would have hope. Please write some of this down so you'll remember it."

Chills ran over her again and again. "I will. Thank you," she said, and repeated his words about small steps silently to herself. She would never forget those words. She tried to hold onto the rest of what he had told her too. She wanted every single word.

"I'm on my way to Puerto Rico again," the governor went on, "to see what we can do to help after these new earthquakes. You told me you knew about all this in your letter and how many Puerto Ricans are New Yorkers. I have all the details from Juan in the—"

Clara mouthed, "Puerto Rican Liaison Office" as the governor spoke the words. "My father. If you could . . .?"

"We have all the information you gave Juan about your relatives' addresses. My staff will do its best to find your father wherever he is and bring him home."

Clara sobbed into the phone, right in the governor's ear. She couldn't help herself. He knew exactly what she wanted. "Papi," she whispered. She shook away her tears. "Thank you, Governor. Those are the best words I could ever hear."

"Good. I can't tell you right now when we'll arrive, but you'll know as soon as our plane's wheels lift off the runway in San Juan. Your father will call you from the plane."

Clara choked up. Tears flowed. "Thank you. Thank you, Governor."

"And thank you, Clara Montalvo."

The dial tone sounded, and she sat with it ringing in her ear. The governor would bring Papi home.

Chapter Thirty-Two

Outlook change

"Lucas." Jamie tapped the lump under the covers on Saturday morning, hoping he wouldn't freak Lucas out. He waited.

Lucas spoke, his voice throaty from somewhere underneath the bedding. "Hey. Hi, Bro. What time is it?" Lucas pulled the blankets off his head. "What day is it? Am I blacking out again?" He groaned.

Lucas used to coax him out of bed in the morning. Sometimes when Jamie refused to get up, Lucas would grab him by an arm and a leg and drag him out and down the hall to the shower. Jamie always made sure to yell loudly, but both of them knew it was mostly for show. He pushed the memory from his mind. Lucas wasn't the same anymore. Jamie would have to get used to this new version of his brother and try his best not to compare Lucas to his former self.

He had an idea. He hustled down to his room, unstuck one of his posters and flew back with it. He taped it to the wall across from Lucas's bed.

"Lucas. Get up. Please. I need your help."

"No help here," his brother mumbled. "I couldn't even save Buddy."

"No, Lucas. Not Buddy again. You did what you could. It's me, Jamie."

Lucas lay there for another ten minutes, staring at the ceiling. Jamie sat quietly too. He decided he'd wait all day if he had to. He figured that at some point Lucas would have to get up to use the bathroom.

His brother finally inched himself up to a sitting position. "Hey, Jamie," he said, as if he were seeing him for the first time. "My little brother. When did you get here?"

Truth or lie? Truth, he decided. "About thirty minutes ago. I've been watching you sleep. It's Saturday, so you get to sleep in." He pointed to the poster. "See this corkscrew twist? Can you tell me again how you mastered it and won a competition?"

All of Lucas's ribbons and trophies were stashed someplace in a drawer. When Jamie begged him, Lucas would show him one or two, but he always hid them again right after. Jamie kept his two ribbons pinned to a wall at eye level in his room. No hiding them.

Lucas stared at the poster. "Yeah." He tossed the covers off and lifted his good leg. "You have to turn your knee like this and then like this . . ." He was imagining it from a sitting position, Jamie figured. "And at the same time, twist your upper body." He stopped. "Ouch. That hurt."

"Don't twist," Jamie said. "Sorry I asked."

Lucas ignored him and waved his arms. "Then you turn and soar through the air."

Jamie had always known it. Lucas was a natural teacher. "Could you coach me?" Jamie asked. "Tell me how to improve my moves? You don't have to show me. I don't want you to hurt yourself. I'm off the team right now and feel like a piece of . . . I don't even want to say what I feel like, but you could keep me in training till . . ." He stopped. There were too many *tills* to talk about. Right now, he just wanted to motivate Lucas to do something, anything. And what Lucas could do better than anyone was coach him on snowboarding moves. Lucas had that ability in his bones. "Can we start tomorrow after school? I'll be ready." There was no time to waste for either of them.

Lucas sat on the edge of his bed, maybe listening. Jamie couldn't tell. His brother stared off into space again, his hand rubbing up and down his leg. He winced as if it was hurting.

"Yeah, sure. But you know, Bro, my leg really hurts." He grimaced and Jamie found himself making the same face in sympathy. "I'd better get back to that doctor. He said I could lose this leg. Right now, it's burning and throbbing so bad I think I am losing it. I wish you had your driver's license. I hate to ask Dad to take me. He gets so worried, and it makes me even more nervous." He lay back down, and in a few minutes, seemed to be out again.

Jamie recalled how the nurse had taken Lucas's temperature at school to see if he was running a fever. He laid a hand against his brother's forehead and quickly drew it away. His brother was burning hot, his skin clammy with sweat. Jamie hurried downstairs and told his parents everything. Lucas saying that he thought he was losing his leg had really scared him. Dad was on his phone in seconds.

An ambulance came. Lucas fought the paramedics at first. He didn't want to go with them but finally gave in. They carried him out on a stretcher. Mom went along in the ambulance, and Dad drove behind. Jamie had to stay home. Mom said he could help most by waiting there in case they needed something from home.

Jamie paced the whole time they were gone, replaying every day since Lucas had arrived. He tried to distract himself with TV and video games, but he couldn't shake thoughts of his brother. He wondered whether the trip to school had been so stressful it had made Lucas sick. He'd never forgive himself if that were the case.

Around eleven that night his parents returned. Right behind them came the EMTs, who climbed the stairs and laid Lucas on his bed. Jamie followed after Dad and Mom. Lucas's eyes were closed. Did he still have two legs? Jamie was so afraid to look his insides hurt.

"What did they say?" he asked Mom while Dad walked the EMTs to the door.

"A doctor saw Lucas in the emergency room. We were there with him the whole time," Mom explained. She motioned for Jamie to follow her out of Lucas's bedroom and then turned off the light and closed Lucas's door.

"Yeah, but his leg?" Jamie followed her down the hall toward his parents' room, unable to ask about what he most wanted to know.

"It's infected." Mom paused in her bedroom doorway. She placed a hand against the doorframe as if she needed some help to keep her upright. Her hair, which she normally wore up in a neat bun or ponytail, was loose and scraggly around her face. Weariness filled her eyes. Jamie felt bad for her. It had been a hard day for all of them, and it showed. "The doctor cleaned the wounds, but Lucas had to be sedated. The doctor said it would be too painful without anesthesia." She paused and looked past Jamie, as if weighing whether to say something more. Finally, she added, "He also said he couldn't promise miracles. Lucas might lose his leg."

Tears sprang and streamed down Jamie's face. "Shouldn't he be in the hospital? Why'd he come back home?" Images of his big brother flashed in his mind: Lucas speeding down a slope on a snowboard and taking a curve on his motorcycle and horsing around with Jamie in the backyard. The next thought hit him like a sucker punch to the gut: Lucas couldn't do any of the things he loved with only one leg.

"He refused to stay," Mom said. "The doctor said he could heal at home just as well if he took care of the leg. We couldn't convince Lucas to stay, Jamie. We tried. Believe me."

"Can it get better?" He heard desperation in his words. "How can he take care of it? What did the doctor say about it getting better?"

Mom's arms circled him. She drew him in close, almost rocking him, but Jamie didn't mind. "It's a matter of time," she explained. "He's on antibiotics for the infection. He has to take them regularly, keep the wounds clean, move the leg when he can to keep the blood circulating. It's a lot to do. We'll all help."

Antibiotics, cleaning, exercise, time. Jamie's head was spinning. His whole body quivered with fear. The old Lucas would do all those things. But the new Lucas might not.

Chapter Thirty-Three

Warm and sunny

Monday after school, Jamie ran up the stairs. He wasn't superstitious, but his fingers were crossed anyway. Lucas was still in bed under the covers, head and all. Jamie bit the bullet and bounced lightly as he sat down on the bed, just enough to wake but not scare his brother.

"Lucas. Training time."

Lucas tossed the covers off. "What day is it?"

"Monday. And I have good news."

Lucas rubbed his eyes and yawned. "Good news. I like that. How long have I been sleeping?"

"Since last Wednesday." Jamie didn't mention the trip to the hospital. He hoped Lucas didn't remember.

His brother blinked. "Whoa. What a way to pass the time."

"How would you like to pass the time with a really pretty nurse?" Jamie said.

Lucas laughed and seemed to come to life. "Yeah, I wish. Like the one in your school who stayed with me after the big blackout."

Jamie's spirits leapt at Lucas's response. "Exactly right. Her name is Monica Davis. She's pretty great. She taught our snowboarding team exercises to strengthen the muscles we needed and how to limber up before competitions. I think she's also a trainer and does physical therapy. We're mega lucky to have her at school."

Lucas's eyes lit up. "I'd love to see her but why would she want to see me?"

"Lucas. Listen to me. I always listen to you when you give me advice. Now it's your turn. She's a nurse. She knows how to change bandages on a wounded leg. She can give you exercises for your leg and make sure you've taken your antibiotics. You'll be back in shape in no time."

Lucas shook his head. "Sounds like a good plan, little brother, but I don't want her feeling sorry for me."

Jamie made an exaggerated show of rolling his eyes so Lucas would know he thought that was a weak excuse. "That's why people become doctors and nurses. They don't feel sorry for their patients. We're just lucky that Nurse Davis knows what to do." He waited a few seconds and then added, "And c'mon man, she's totally *hot*."

Lucas laughed. Color rose in his face. "When can we start?"

Jamie grinned. "I'll ask her tomorrow."

Then he'd tell Mom and Dad.

Chapter Thirty-Four

Possible squall

*A*t lunchtime the next day, Jamie went to see Nurse Davis in her office, right down the hallway from Coach's.

"Jamie. Come in." She smiled warmly. "I hope your brother is feeling better."

"Actually, an ambulance had to take him to the hospital Saturday night." He told Nurse Davis the whole story, even about Lucas possibly losing his leg. "He could use your help, Ms. Davis. If you could spare maybe an hour a day to check his leg and change his bandages, show him some exercises, make sure he's taken his medicine, I think you could motivate him to do all these things that he has to . . . or he'll lose his leg."

Nurse Davis nodded. "Are you sure it's okay with your brother?" Her eyes narrowed. "Is this your idea, Jamie?"

He tried his best to look innocent. "Yeah. I saw how you took care of him when he blacked out and mentioned it to him. He asked when you could start. That's why I'm here." He confessed that he hadn't told his parents yet. "I'll tell them as soon as I get home," he promised. "They'll be happy. I can guarantee that. So when can you start?"

A new sign in the classroom announced the next Change for Our Planet meeting after school that day. Molly had posted it and signed her name in big letters, and Nick's too, as co-chairs. Clara couldn't believe Molly had taken over the project. She hadn't even mentioned that she wanted to hold a meeting after not showing up for the rally and not explaining. Clara clenched her teeth so she wouldn't shout, "You can't do that!" She'd survived María. Molly was just as unpredictable. Clara was tired of worrying about the next Molly disaster. She made up her mind to go to Molly's and Nick's meeting, see what she, or they, were up to.

"Let's do it now," Nick was saying to a few kids standing with him as she and Jamie walked into the cafeteria. "We're on a roll."

More kids filed in and took seats. Clara, surprised at the number of kids coming in, simply watched. She thrilled at her classmates' enthusiasm for the project, Molly's, especially, even though she couldn't believe it. She could hardly believe that a small science class project was turning into something big, maybe actually helping to save the planet. Maybe this was how change began: with one person at a time coming on board. She told herself to not judge, simply watch.

Molly was up front again with a big pad on the easel. She turned the filled-up brainstorming sheet over and held her marker ready. She wrote: "On a Roll. Our World—Adults today destroyed it—It's up to us to fix it."

Clara couldn't help envying Molly's ease at what she was doing. And she had a good message. Kids at the tables commented and gave their ideas. A few kids sounded angry. "Yeah. It's our world. It's not fair. So now what?"

Molly wrote those comments down and underlined them. "Okay, everyone. No more complaining."

Clara tried to forget her resentment and gave her thumbs up. Molly's lips curved into a smile as she turned to the easel. "Now let's get serious," she said, almost as if she didn't know how to deal with a compliment. Clara figured Molly would get used to it now that she was the official brainstorming leader. Clara's feelings were all mixed up about Molly. How would she figure her out? She glanced at Jamie sitting next to her and wondered if his puzzled expression meant that he might be trying to figure Molly out, too.

"Let's march through town," someone said. "We need big posters saying someone messed up our world."

Molly wrote it down but shook her head. "Be constructive. Who messed it up?"

"Our senators," Chuck said. "They could have voted for clean fuels. And the president. That's who I'm blaming."

"Yeah," Nick said. We should email everyone in our state government."

Kids started yelling out questions and more complaints and volunteering to work.

Clara watched, amazed at how kids were organizing themselves. She couldn't hold back her own suggestions even if they combined helping when current disasters struck and working to solve climate change. She still wasn't sure they were the same thing.

"Let's email all the senators in all fifty states."

"We need a list. I don't know who they are."

"I'll do that list," Molly said. "And another list of everybody who represents our state in government. We'll tell them we're going door-to-door to tell people not to vote for them ever again unless they wake up to what's happening and change the laws."

"Yeah. Laws about factories shooting all that pollution into the air."

"And drilling for oil and ruining our forests and animal habitats."

"We have a hybrid. My mom said we'll never buy a car that guzzles gas again."

Clara couldn't believe her ears. "How do you all know these things?" she asked her classmates. "You seemed so surprised a few days ago when we talked about them in class."

"You told us to go on our phones and to google," a girl named Kim said.

"Yeah, and my parents were like . . . not believing it when I watched the news with them all week. My mom asked me if I was feeling okay." Simon, a boy Clara had never said a word to before, couldn't stop talking. She couldn't believe all these kids were speaking up.

Jamie laughed. "News. I get that."

"And Mr. J said we'd better watch the news. I need a B in science," Greg added.

"Some of us can go to other schools here in town and around the state, too, maybe and tell them all this," a boy named Jerome said. "Get them to organize, like we are. Get names and phone numbers of the students so we can be in touch."

Clara had never heard Jerome speak in class, and now he was volunteering to go around the state and talk. She had never noticed before how many kids in class never spoke up. Now they were right in the middle of all the brainstorming and finding a way to participate. Her resentment didn't exactly go away, but it wasn't as strong as it had been with Molly taking over the project. Maybe it didn't matter.

Mr. J popped his head in. "Time to wrap for today. I have to lock up."

Kids moaned, "Awww," and started getting up to leave. Others closed their notebooks but hung around to talk.

"Thanks for starting all this, you two," Nick said to Jamie and Clara. "It's awesome to be part of it."

Molly put down the marker and took the pad off the easel. "That was fun. I'm getting really good at this."

"You are," Nick said. "And if you can get your lists of people to contact this week, that would be great. Kids are psyched to start."

Clara and Jamie helped move benches back to their places. The bathroom–ballot situation was still never far from Clara's mind. She'd been thinking about confronting Molly, even now as they worked together on the project. But what would that accomplish? After Jamie told Molly off, she'd be foolish to keep going with her ballots. Besides, Mr. J had probably already graded them for their project.

Clara waved to Jamie and headed home. She didn't have any lists to make or organizing to do. But she still needed a service project. She'd talk to Ms. Dunne tomorrow about the animal shelter.

"Clara. Wait up." Molly caught up to her. "You live down here? It's so far from school."

Clara kept walking. "Yeah. Did you want something, Molly?"

"I just wanted to say I love being the official note-taker in our meetings. Nick and I are great partners and so good at running the meeting. When we sign our names on the posters, kids show up. I hope you stay involved."

Clara nodded but didn't know how to think about all of Molly's organizing and taking charge. She had to call her on it, though, or she would never know how this all happened. She swallowed her pride and organizing abilities, thought about Papi doing what he had to do and Lucas's bad leg and so many people hurting in the world. So what if Molly wanted to be the leader? Clara wasn't sure where her ability to let Molly take over the project had come from. Probably Mami and Papi. They always put people and their needs before them. How could she and Diego have gotten these messages without living with their amazing parents? Clara gave one last try. "Molly, this is a big, big project and there's room for all of us. You're right. You can really bring kids in." Clara waited. It didn't matter who the leaders were. It simply mattered that lots of kids wanted to be involved and make change. Molly was trying her best, and Clara wanted to believe that.

Molly didn't respond, so Clara went on. "You are a really good group motivator and leader," she said and immediately felt upset with herself. Molly was still cheating in a way, and she had just encouraged her. But maybe sometimes what seemed like cheating wasn't. It wasn't hurting anyone, and the so-called cheater was getting something she needed.

Clara kept walking. Molly was right alongside of her, keeping up. Clara stopped, hoping to end this conversation. "Molly, I'm glad you're involved in the climate project. Really, I am. But I want you to know that I also have some other feelings you should know. Jamie and my meetings came about because of our debate."

"So what?" Molly said.

"So what? . . . because we didn't even want a debate. Remember how you were one of the kids in class that yelled, 'Do a debate.' That's why Jamie and I found ourselves in that predicament."

Molly nodded. "When we were friends, things were simple."

Clara bit her lip so she wouldn't say, "Sure. You weren't picking on me then." She didn't want to bring up Jamie but wanted to end this in a friendly way if possible. "Molly, I so wished you had come to the rally," she said. "We could have had so much fun. I did, and I missed you." She waited for Molly's rejection.

"I wanted to be there . . . I really did. I got up early and was ready. Then my mother started in about something stupid . . . always about my dad who's not around much, and she was upset that I'd forgotten to get her dress from the cleaners. It's too much. You can't understand. Anyhow, since I didn't get to the rally, I thought I'd work on meetings."

Clara turned to go. "I hear what you're saying, Molly, but you could have told me so we could have done them together. It hurt that you just went and took over. Do you get that?"

Molly didn't respond.

"There's more than enough work for us all. I don't care who leads the meetings, but you can't be so sneaky." There. She'd said it.

She gave another quick glance at Molly, then walked off. Molly stayed behind.

———

Jamie raced up the steps to Lucas's room. His brother's head was down . . . in a book. Lucas looked up as Jamie burst in.

"Lucas, remember how we talked about you training me in snowboarding moves? You were showing me when . . ." He stopped short. He didn't want to bring all that up again. "I'm ready."

Lucas put the book down. "Okay. So am I. On the mat."

"What?" Jamie looked around. A dark blue mat was spread out on the side of Lucas's bed. He hadn't noticed it before.

"Twenty push-ups. Then twenty back-and-forths. Twenty twists after that. The mat'll give you lift."

Jamie, surprised, blurted, "No way. Where'd you get it?" He eyed some other equipment.

"I ordered it, Bro. Mom picked it all up for me. No more questions. Let's go. Twenty push-ups."

Jamie dropped to the ground and began, growing more and more pleased with himself with every push-up he completed. And pleased with Lucas. After an hour of training, Jamie surrendered, out of breath. "Can we stop for today?"

"Sure," Lucas relented. "I have to save some energy for my exercises with Nurse Monica."

They both laughed, and that reminded Jamie of something. He told Lucas to get back to his book. He'd see him later.

He told Mom and Dad about Nurse Davis. Mom was all for a nurse, especially one from school, helping Lucas recuperate.

Dad had to have the last word. "I'll go along for now, but we'll have to take it a day at a time."

Jamie couldn't expect miracles. Dad's answer was as good as he could give, for now.

Chapter Thirty-Five

Brightening

T he natural disasters project was over. The reports were done. Back to science and chemical formulas, Jamie figured. He handed a note to Clara in class, telling her all about Lucas and his hopes for recovery. He wanted to reassure her things were getting better, then ask about her father. His attention was drawn out the window. The sun was shining. Buds on the trees promised an early spring. That was okay with him. Snowboarding was way over. He'd have to wait till winter to get back on track. But he'd be ahead of the game with Lucas getting him in shape.

"... and so, Mr. Fulton, as I was saying ..."

Jamie swung his head back to class from the budding trees. "I know. I'm in trouble again. You caught me thinking about springtime."

"Yes and no," Mr. J said, standing right next to his desk. "Yes, I caught you passing Clara a note but no, you're not in trouble."

He turned to the class. "'In the Spring a young man's fancy lightly turns to thoughts of love.'"

Everyone laughed. Jamie's face heated up. At least he wasn't in trouble with Mr. J. He dared not look at Clara and kept his eyes riveted on Mr. J, whom he hoped would stop talking about thoughts of love.

"That poem by Alfred, Lord Tennyson, may pop up again next marking period," Mr. J warned. "It's filled with science. Read it and you'll see. Anyhow back to springtime. Your class has survived natural disasters through informative reports and an original, illuminating debate. You've experienced how an injured Marine returned home, cheered our TV news class celebrities, participated in climate change meetings, and involved our community in awareness of current disaster needs."

Kids applauded and whooped.

"I applaud you too." And he did. Jamie heard and saw the class's pride. "I think we've covered just about as much as we can for this marking period."

More kids clapped. Some cheered.

"But . . ." Mr. J said.

Here it comes, Jamie thought. Another project.

"Don't you think we all deserve to celebrate?"

The class went a little wild. . . but under control. Mostly kids applauded and said, "Yes!"

"I'll offer my few suggestions and leave the rest to you," he said. "My suggestion is that whatever it is be: 1) a school day or evening; 2) that we invite our families; and 3) that it be held within the next two weeks. The school year is going by fast, and we'll have other activities like prom, graduation, and probably some extra celebrations. So those are my three suggestions. The rest is up to you."

Committee lists were posted for categories like invitations, welcoming, and refreshments. Jamie tried to guess who had organized so fast. All he knew was their class was ready—every kid, even in the back rows—for anything.

Nurse Davis was ready too. She said she could meet Lucas and his parents that day after school. Her only condition was that she be paid only if Lucas made progress. They would assess that in six months. She said she'd keep track of expenses for bandages and other supplies, and they would work things out later. Everything was businesslike. It sounded a lot like credit. Dad would be pleased.

Jamie called Mom as soon as it was settled. They would all be ready, she said over the phone. When he and Nurse Davis got to his house, Mom was waiting at the door. She welcomed the nurse in, and Jamie's heart swelled with pride over what he'd done.

Chapter Thirty-Six

Warming trends

Mami asked for a day off for the party. She held the invitation and read it to Diego. "You are invited to celebrate the Eighth Grade Science Class Achievements on March twentieth, the first day of spring. Please come to Albany Central Junior High School at four o'clock."

Diego clapped. "I love parties. Mami, you'll get to see Greg and Lucy and Megan. They were with me on TV. I can't wait a whole week."

Clara worked with four other students including Lucy on the activities committee, but most kids had signed up for refreshments. Everybody's name was listed, and they wrote in the dish or drinks they would bring. Clara asked Mami if they could make *pastelillos de guayaba*, another favorite that she knew everybody would love. She wondered if there would be time for anything besides eating. Mami brought puff pastry and guava paste home one day after work, and they were ready to bake.

The day before the celebration, Clara thought about Molly and what she'd bring. At recess she asked Molly if she and her mom would like to come over and bake with them. She had been thinking about this for a few days, working up the courage to ask. She had seen in Molly's eyes sadness about her mother. All Clara could do was try. If Molly said no, that wouldn't kill her. And Molly had admitted she'd liked it when they were friends. If she said yes, it could be a next step in their friendship *if* Molly still wanted it. Their moms would get to meet and maybe like each other.

Molly frowned at the invitation and Clara immediately regretted asking. But then the frown turned to a questioning look. "Are you sure? I'm not good at baking. I'll ask my mom, if she's in a good mood when I get home. Sometimes she's not. She used to bake. Can I tell you tomorrow? Or I could text you tonight."

"Great either way," Clara said and congratulated herself for taking the chance.

Greg and Molly were charged with getting the students to bring back their natural disaster reports to be displayed. Clara smiled, picturing Molly's and Katy's project in which she knew Molly would feature up front and center. Clara and Jamie would show some of their research on printouts and be prepared to talk about their debate.

Nick and three other boys made posters with original slogans about climate change. Nick suggested that they leave spaces for people to sign up to help. "What a great way for families to meet and see their kids' work and for them to help save their planet," he said to his group.

Megan, who had been interviewed for the news, had a great suggestion. "I can walk around with a microphone. Somebody can follow me with a camera, and we'll pretend we're News Eight— you know, for eighth grade. When we have someone to interview, a parent or someone, I'll make an announcement and people can listen to us talking. I'll prepare some questions about climate and other things too, not only disasters."

Mr. J glanced up every so often to see what students were up to. He gave them half of science class time to work on the party project.

⸻

The evening before the party, the doorbell rang. Molly and her mother stood on the landing holding trays, plastic bowls, and bags of flour and sugar. Clara reached out to take some of the stuff. "Come in. We're so happy you came."

Molly followed Clara. Her mom came behind her. She looked like an older version of Molly and wore slacks and a light jacket. Clara and Molly exchanged glances, a few awkward smiles, nothing more. Mami welcomed them and offered coffee or tea and chairs at the table. Before long, Mami and Molly's mom, who told Mami to call her Peggy, were greasing baking sheets. Molly mixed batter like it was the most important task ever. Diego waited next to her for bowls to lick, and Clara unwrapped the puff pastry. All of their hands were making baking magic for friends and for each other.

Two hours later, with sweet aromas filling the air, Molly and her mom left with containers of their chocolate chip cookies. Molly held onto her mom's arm as they walked down the steps and out into the night. Clara hoped maybe things between them would be better now.

⸻

March twentieth came fast. Overnight, actually. Molly chaired the welcoming committee in addition to working on activities and refreshments. She greeted families as they walked into the gymnasium, which didn't look like one now. Balloons bobbed in the air. Food and drinks covered tables on one side of the room, and displays hung on the walls on the other side. Small kids zoomed around, leaping up to grab long strings hanging from balloons, which were meant to be caught.

Clara watched it all. Mami was talking to Mr. J and Jamie and Diego in a corner of the gym with a soccer ball between them.

Who was teaching whom? She watched for Mrs. Thurber and Gus. They were almost family, so she had invited them. Gus and Diego would be fast friends. Maybe they could build together someday when she took Diego babysitting with her.

She had to stop herself from rushing over to the young man on crutches who came in arm-in-arm with Nurse Davis. Chills ran through her. But she would wait. Another couple, who were probably Jamie's parents, followed them in.

Jamie must have seen them too, because he pulled Diego with him and hurried over to her. "Clara. Come. Let's find your mother and introduce her to my parents." He took her hand and led her to Mami, who was talking with Rodrigo's mother.

"She'll be back," Clara said to Rodrigo's mother as she and Jamie took Mami's arms.

"Mom, Dad," Jamie said after they had they made their way through the crowd to his parents. "This is Clara, my debate opponent or . . . um . . . partner. This is Mrs. Montalvo."

Jamie's mother shook Mami's hand. "I'm so happy to meet you. How proud you must be of your daughter." Then she took Clara's hand. "I know all about you, my dear. I'm so happy to finally meet you."

Jamie's dad said he'd seen her on the news. "I was impressed. And also impressed with your research on hurricanes that Jamie told me about. I'd like to read more." He shook Mami's hand too and smiled.

Clara's face reddened. She didn't take compliments well. Just in time, she turned to the entrance. Mrs. Thurber and Gus. Behind them, Molly's mother. Molly had brought the cookies she and her mom had made and displayed them right up front. Molly smiled at her mom, then let her go. Clara ran to greet them all and thanked Molly for welcoming everyone in such a friendly way. Molly smiled but got back to welcoming others. Clara thought she understood her friend at last. Gus bear-hugged Clara's legs as he always did. She patted his head and gave Mrs. Thurber's hands a gentle squeeze, then introduced Molly's mother to Mrs. Thurber. She showed Gus the table of cookies, let him choose one, and took them all to find Mami.

When Mrs. Thurber and Mami shook hands, Clara's heart melted. They were both beautiful women, interesting, and perfect in their different ways. Molly's mom squeezed Mami's hand. They smiled warmly at each other, like good friends.

Mami knelt down to Gus.

"Are you Clara's mom?" he asked.

"I am Clara's mom and Diego's mom." She pulled Diego over to her. "Diego, this is Gus, Clara's friend."

Diego said, "Hi. You can come to our house to play. I have some cool toys. Do you like superheroes?"

"Yeah. And I have some cool trucks."

Clara smiled. Gus didn't mention the blocks. She guessed those were special, just for the two of them. She introduced Mrs. Thurber and Gus to Mr. J and finally to Jamie and Lucas.

Jamie was hanging out with Lucas and Nurse Davis, who were sitting out of the way of traffic. Introductions were short.

Diego asked about Lucas's wound and pulled up his pant leg to show Lucas his scar from the hurricane. "Yours will get better too," he assured so seriously Clara had to hold back a giggle.

Gus watched it all and, Clara could tell, took it all in. They would have so much to talk about next time they built schools and houses.

How could today be any better? Diego and Gus were following Jamie everywhere he went. Jamie kept his hands on their shoulders, like he'd take good care of them. She overheard them at one of the dessert tables.

"School's boring," Diego complained, with a mouth full of chocolate chip cookie. Gus was right next to him, crumbs covering his chin.

"Yeah. Sometimes," Jamie agreed, chowing down but on one of her crumbly guava *pastelillos*. "But it can be really cool too.

Fifth grade is okay. Sixth, better. Seventh sucks sometimes, but eighth, that's when the fun starts."

Clara escaped from being seen just in time. Ms. Dunne called her from across the room. "Clara. We need to talk."

Clara rushed over, and Ms. Dunne hugged her. "I hope you know you've more than fulfilled your community service project. Why didn't you tell me you were involved in all this?" She turned and waved her arm toward the display.

Clara's head was spinning. What to say? She'd been putting one foot in front of the other, trying to do everything she had committed to doing. "I guess I was too focused on my . . ." Suddenly it all hit her—everything she had been carrying on her shoulders this year. Tears flowed. She sobbed, tried to hide her face. She couldn't ruin the party. Ms. Dunne walked with her to the side of the gym just as they'd walked together the day she'd left school early, when Ms. Dunne had loaned her the scarf. "I'll bring your scarf back tomorrow. I'm sorry for keeping it so long."

Ms. Dunne smiled. "Good. And we can talk about the scholarship before I send the forms back."

Clara was thinking about everything she had to do the next day when her phone pinged. She looked at the caller ID. An international number.

"Hello. Papi! Oh my. I may faint, Papi. It's really you? What?" Her smile grew wider as she listened. "You're on the plane. With the governor? Thank you. Thank you." The room seemed to dance.

Ms. Dunne's eyes widened. She mouthed, "The governor?" and Clara nodded.

"Yes, Papi. We'll all be together tonight. We're at school right now. Mami and Diego are here too. Wait, Papi. I'll get Mami." Clara looked all around. She couldn't see Mami, but Diego was right beside her.

She handed her brother the phone. "Papi, it's Diego!" He shouted over all the noise, but Clara couldn't hear what he was saying. "We'll see Papi soon," she said to him and took back the phone."

"Mami's probably talking to someone, Papi. It's a big room. I can't see her. Yes, Papi. It's a celebration. The only person missing is you. And now you're not missing. I love you. Please thank the governor from the bottom of my heart for finding you. Yes, Papi. We'll be waiting at the front door. Bye, Papi. I don't want to run up the governor's phone bill. Bye. Bye. Bye. Safe journey."

Everything was perfect. And Papi didn't cough once.

Chapter Thirty-Seven

Surprise rainbow!

L ucas was out back on a lawn chair in a short-sleeved shirt when Jamie got home from the party.

"Hey. How're you doing?" Jamie called from the doorway leading onto the backyard.

"Good. Terrific party. Loved every minute, especially with my nurse escort. But what's with this summer weather in March?"

Jamie laughed. "The Year Without a Winter."

"Never saw it," Lucas said. "Is it just out?"

Jamie laughed again. "It's not a movie. It's a long story, but I'll tell you another time. So what about training today?"

"Give me about another hour. Feels great out here. Nice sun on my face. I'll get a start on a tan."

"Hey, Lucas." Jamie glanced around. He didn't see Mom, so he continued. "About taking you to class that day. I'm sorry. It was—"

"Hey, Jamie. I loved every minute. It was hard at first. I didn't know how much to say about the war, the killing, all that." His words trailed off.

271

"The kids were psyched, Lucas. You said just the right things. You could have stayed all day. Nobody would have budged. Not even Mr. J."

"Yeah, it's good talking to kids. Made me feel really useful. Like I belonged there in the classroom, even though I zonked out and panicked, probably scared the pants off everyone." He sat for a while, probably reliving it. "I think I might like to do that someday . . . help kids, maybe kids who've lost their way. Or at least point them in a good direction. Like I'm pointing you the right way with the training." Lucas grinned. "We have a lot of work ahead with you."

Jamie simply listened. Nothing could rattle him today.

"I might even take a course in psychology and see how I do. Lots of good colleges up here, you know. Probably start out online. What do you think? You'll be looking at colleges soon. You can probably give me some advice."

Jamie was thrilled to hear his brother talking so positively about his future.

Jamie's phone rang. Clara. Lucas motioned for him to take the call.

"What's up?" Jamie asked.

Clara blurted, "Jamie. I got in. The Academy. Ms. Dunne told me it's official."

He couldn't quite tell what he heard in her words . . . excitement? He wasn't sure. "Congratulations! I knew you'd get in. You can do anything you set your heart on." He was happy for Clara but sad for himself. They wouldn't be in class together anymore if she switched schools.

"You think so?" she said as if she believed him more than herself.

"Of course. You're amazing."

"I haven't accepted yet. I have time to think about it. Just a few days, though."

He smiled. A few days would be enough time. They'd talk, argue, joke, say disastrous things to each other, then make up as they had done for nearly two years. Maybe he could convince her to go. He was getting good at persuading. And Clara deserved the Academy. Or maybe Clara would change her mind and go to the public high school. Either way, they were both headed in the same direction—making their world a better place.

He listened as she repeated how great it had been meeting Lucas at the party, and how it was the best time for everybody.

"And thanks for training the guys on requesting supplies for disasters," she added. "They're ready for any answer from a store manager when we collect again."

"Thanks. I wasn't even nervous. That's progress, right? So, Clara, bring me up to date on what's happening on all these projects. I'm clueless. So many kids are coming up to me and asking how to sign up for the climate change project and how to collect supplies for kids. I don't know what to tell them."

Clara laughed into the phone. Jamie was being Jamie. Panicking. But this was good panicking. "Listen to this: Molly called and told me she googled San Juan school disasters. I think she's trying to make up with me. I might be wrong, but anyhow, she found the names of schools that were damaged. She's had the idea to send fun things to schools there—puzzles, novels, and gadgets that kids love—and she's organizing kids to collect these things. I told her about the Red Cross pickups at Lucy's house, so Molly texted Lucy and now they're working together. Mr. Morris will have to come back for a third pickup. Oh, yeah. She said we three could be partners. And maybe Katy."

"Boy am I glad that Molly's a friend, not an enemy," he said. "But watch out for selfies," he joked. "She's a stealth expert."

"Enjoy your time with your brother," Clara said finally. "Say hi for me. And tell him all the amazing things kids said about him. See you tomorrow."

He hated to click off. He could have snowboarded down Mt. Everest now.

He went back to Lucas. His eyes were closed. He seemed relaxed. Jamie sat next to him. Dad opened the back door, breaking the silence.

Jamie sat up. "Hi, Dad. Come on out."

Dad stood there, taking in the scene. He didn't have a jacket on, just a long- sleeved sweater. "Great celebration, Jamie. I don't see how you kids did all that. Mom and I were surprised." He glanced at the sky. "Wonder what happened to our winter."

Lucas raised his head and motioned Dad over. Dad pulled up another chair. He reached into his back pocket, pulled out an envelope, and handed it to Jamie.

Jamie glanced at it, then at Dad. His grades? Had Mr. J given them to Dad at school? Anything was possible. But Dad's expression didn't indicate that. Jamie didn't know that smile. "Go ahead. Open it," Dad said.

Lucas nodded with an excited but impatient expression on his face too, like, so open it already. Was his brother in on this? What *was* this?

Mom came out with soft drinks, amusement dancing in her eyes.

Jamie opened the envelope. He pulled out some papers and unfolded them. The heading said:

TIMBERLINE—ON THE PALMER GLACIER IN OREGON
Come ski with some of the world's best skiers and boarders training for national teams.

Below the headline were details for a summer camp out in the mountains of Oregon.

Jamie's eyes teared up. No way. He had no words. Then they poured out. "Dad, Mom, Lucas. How did you? What? When? This is so cool. Thanks a million. Wow!"

Mom's hands were on his shoulders.

"Well, you can't snowboard your way out to Portland," Lucas said with a big smile. "How're you going to get out there?"

Dad motioned to Jamie to keep going.

He dug further into the envelope. Airline tickets to Portland. Four. Open dated for June. "No way. We're all going?"

Lucas nodded. "Yeah, man. We're all going. The doc said my leg's looking good so far. He said he hasn't seen a burn heal like this. Has to be the efficient person taking care of it," he said. "Thank you, little brother."

"I've never been to Portland," Mom said. "I've been reading up. There's lots to see in Oregon. Maybe we'll even take a tour of Mount St. Helens. Visitors can hike there, you know. It's like Tambora now."

Jamie beamed. Tambora again, bringing something good.

"We're renting one of those big vans," Dad said. "I've never driven one, but Lucas can show me how. Of course, I'll drive, but he'll navigate. We'll drop you off and come back when your week's up."

Jamie's head was spinning but he *was* focusing—on his family. How could he ever in his wildest dreams imagine snowboarding in June? The Year Without a Summer had started it all—a science project that he'd thought he could never do.

"Mom, I want to see Mount St. Helens too," he said. "It's the most active volcano in the Cascade Range. Please wait for me."

"I think we can wait for you." She winked.

———

He stared at the Timberline Glacier paper in his hand. Clara had taught him more about glaciers in the last few weeks than he could have ever imagined. Together, in their debate and in their lives, they had discovered how really destructive natural disasters were.

He'd stuck to his guns about some good inventions and stories and art that came about because of Tambora. And Clara had convinced him of how many bad things occurred too. Their debate had been the best thing that had ever happened to him . . . as far as schoolwork went, that is. What had happened in the last few days was another best.

He and Clara had a lot of bests coming up. So, without further ado. . . . That was a favorite opening now. They were definitely on a roll. And they were almost experts on disasters. The news was spreading. Kids in class were out there, putting up posters and talking in schools. Jamie and Clara could hardly keep up with the work other kids were bringing to them. And younger kids were taking over. Jamie saw the fire in their eyes as they spoke to their peers about their planet . . . all stuff they'd learned from the eighth graders. He and Clara went to their classes to hear them. The younger students were psyched to get to Mr. J's science class. They'd keep working to make their world better.

Bigger challenges lay ahead for them next year. More homework. More projects. He might even suggest regular debates to his new teachers, and he'd definitely tell Mr. J to keep doing them. He'd even volunteer to come in and help teach the kids how to do research before a debate.

After the sun had gone down and his family was back inside, Jamie walked out on the back porch. He stretched and breathed in the air. Lucas was right. Dad was right. It should be cold at this time of the year. He looked at the thermometer hanging on the side of the house. Sixty-five degrees. It had never been sixty-five degrees in March in Albany. It was definitely a Year Without a Winter. He laughed. Nobody would believe everything that had happened just because he had googled volcanoes and found one, way back in 1815, that had caused the Year Without a Summer. When he'd read that, he'd imagined himself snowboarding in June. Now, in a few months, he actually would be snowboarding in June.

Jamie didn't consider himself sentimental but couldn't help himself. Thoughts kept flashing about the debate and arguing with Clara in front of the class. He'd never thought it possible, but researching and arguing and talking about natural disasters turned out to be amazing, almost beautiful. Like snowboarding down a powdery slope and facing moguls and dips and other obstacles. Somehow, he'd learned the skills he needed to get around them.

A new thought took hold, something he knew about snowboarding but hadn't thought about in other aspects of his life: A person had to practice what he wanted to be good at. He thought about all the times he'd reacted negatively to things he couldn't control. With practice he'd started to get better at looking for solutions. Disasters were never beautiful, but Tambora and the Year Without a Summer had brought Clara and him together.

He wondered how many kids out there might not know about Tambora and the Year Without a Summer. What a great title for a novel, or a movie. Maybe someone was already working on it. He'd have to google.

Acknowledgments

*G*ratitude. That's what I feel for my wide writing family, each fellow who encouraged me to slog through the Year Without a Summer and a Year with Plenty of Revisions. As you read the story, I hope you are reminded of your particular suggestion and remember my thank you at the time. If it didn't seem big enough then, please know, my appreciation has only grown stronger.

- My New York City Bunny Group, whose individual critiques kept me on track with their years of Bunny Gable literary wisdom.
- The Bank Street Writers Lab authors, with their in-depth knowledge of children's literature offered rigorous and focused critiques.
- Greenwich Pen Women Letters writers always nurtured me, gently prodding me ahead like thoughtful parents. I couldn't have kept seat on chair and typing without friends who listened to my thoughts about what next chapters might hold.
- Big thanks to Bridget Boland, who painstakingly kept me challenging my characters to greater heights and enduring my endless questions and doubts.
- My long-suffering husband, children, and grands offered their three-generational take on the story and their opinions on crucial details. What gifts.

- And to my teen beta readers, who offered honesty and expressed the inspiration they received as they followed the two main characters headed for greatness.
- Miguel Garcia-Colon read the entire manuscript and alerted me to cultural differences and similarities all the way through.
- I give an extra loud thank you to my husband, who always said yes to any literary request along the way.

Author Bio

*A*rlene Mark was born and grew up in steel country in western Pennsylvania before making her way to New York City to begin her career. After working in fashion, she and her husband and three children lived in London, Caracas, and Toronto before settling in Greenwich, Connecticut. Her MA in Special Education, certification in School Psychology, and internship at New York State Psychiatric Institute treating hard-to-reach children empowered her to help them communicate and grow. Her interest in writing this novel stemmed from her belief that children of all ages seek desperately to find their voices. Only then can they feel validated and develop their true potential. Her work has appeared in *Highlights for Children*, *Spider, the Magazine for Children*, *Skipping Stones*, *Adolescence*, *Their World*, and *Greenwich Magazine*. She authored *To the Tower, A Greenwich Adventure* and co-authored *Paraverbal Communication with*

Children: Not Through Words Alone. She has been a Contributing Editor to *The Greenwich Time*, offering articles about children's emotional lives. Her eight grandchildren are enthusiastic fans. Learn more about Arlene at Arlenemark.com.

Author photo © Dina D'Amelio

SELECTED TITLES FROM SPARKPRESS

SparkPress is an independent boutique publisher delivering high-quality, entertaining, and engaging content that enhances readers' lives, with a special focus on female-driven work. www.gosparkpress.com

The Forbidden Temptation of Baseball, Dori Jones Yang. $12.95, 978-1-943006-32-8. Twelve-year-old Leon is among a group of 120 boys sent to New England in the 1870s by the Emperor of China as part of a Chinese educational mission. Once there, he falls in love with baseball, even though he's expressly forbidden to play. The boy's host father, who's recently lost his own son in an accident, sees and cultivates Leon's interest, bringing joy back into his own life and teaching Leon more about America through its favorite sport than any rule-bound educational mission could possibly hope to achieve.

Colorblind: A Novel, Leah Harper Bowron. $16.95, 978-1-943006-08-3. Set in the hotbed of the segregated South, *Colorblind* explores the discrimination that an elderly African-American sixth-grade teacher and her physically challenged Caucasian student encounter at the hands of two schoolyard bullies.

Blonde Eskimo: A Novel, Kristen Hunt. $17, 978-1-940716-62-6. Neiva Ellis is caught between worlds—Alaska and the lower forty-eight, white and Eskimo, youth and adulthood, myth and tradition, good and evil, the seen and unseen. Just initiated into one side of the family's Eskimo culture, she must harness all her resources to fight an evil and ancient foe.

The Frontman: A Novel, Ron Bahar. $16.95, 978-1-943006-44-1. During his senior year of high school, Ron Bahar—a Nebraskan son of Israeli immigrants—falls for Amy Andrews, a non-Jewish girl, and struggles to make a career choice between his two other passions: medicine and music.

A Song for the Road: A Novel, Rayne Lacko. $16.95, 978-1-684630-02-8. When his house is destroyed by a tornado, fifteen-year-old Carter Danforth steals his mom's secret cash stash, buys his father's guitar back from a pawnshop, and hitchhikes old Route 66 in search of the man who left him as a child.